A New Beginning: Book Four

Kicking Fox

OTHER BOOKS BY STEVEN G. HIGHTOWER

A New Beginning: Book One
The Smoke of One Thousand Lodge Fires
An Amazon #1 Best Seller
https://www.amazon.com/dp/B08H9MXFGW/

A New Beginning: Book Two
The Cross of One Horse
An Amazon #1 Best Seller
https://www.amazon.com/gp/product/B09H4SF2Y1/

A New Beginning: Book Three
These Thousand Days
An Amazon #1 Best Seller
https://www.amazon.com/gp/product/B09VCMY2YY/

A New Beginning: Book Four

Kicking Fox

Steven G. Hightower

A NEW BEGINNING, BOOK 4
Kicking Fox
Copyright © 2023 Steven G. Hightower

Paperback ISBN: 978-1-7358416-8-7
Hardcover ISBN: 978-1-7358416-6-3

All rights reserved. No part of this publication may be reproduced or transmitted in any form or by any means, electronic, mechanical, photocopying, recording, or otherwise, without written permission from the publisher. Published by Little Creek Publishing Co.™ Contact sales@ littlecreekpublishingco.com.

This is a work of fiction. Any references to historical events, real people, or real places are used fictitiously. Other names, characters, places, and events are products of the author's imagination, and any resemblance to actual events, or places, or persons, living or dead, is entirely coincidental.

Scriptures taken from the Holy Bible, New International Version®, NIV®. Copyright © 1973, 1978, 1984, 2011 by Biblica, Inc.™ Used by permission of Zondervan. All rights reserved worldwide. www.zondervan.com The "NIV" and "New International Version" are trademarks registered in the United States Patent and Trademark Office by Biblica, Inc.™

Library of Congress Control Number: TXu 2-345-159

For more information about Steven G. Hightower, visit
www.stevenghightower.com or
Facebook. com/anewbeginning2020

Front cover image © Shutterstock #181113788 Fernando Cortes photographer
Back cover image © Shutterstock #1008566767 courtesy Lazy Dragon

Dedication

This book is dedicated to the grandmothers in my life.
Thank you for the prayers, Mama Sue, Mama E, and Old Grandma.

Your wisdom still calls to me from across the divide.

Prologue

The criminal psychologists had studied the cases for years. Some would conclude Kicking Fox, son of Tabananica, the name Samuel Nica had insisted he be referred to by the press, was completely sane. Others were certain the man was bi-polar, or suffered from some type of brain injury, or even possibly a brain tumor, or even some yet-to-be-determined psychosis. Others thought him simply a sociopath.

Documentary film producers and Hollywood moguls analyzed each and every individual case. The movie productions they developed from expert witnesses and the most talented screenwriters in the industry, most accurately portrayed the truth of who Kicking Fox came to be. These producers and writers accurately replicated what his psyche contained. The stories were fascinating, wildly popular, and millions across the globe idolized Kicking Fox.

Governments across the globe were not quite as enamored with the man's activities. He was hunted, located, arrested, charged, and tried across multiple continents…and never found guilty of any crime, or more specifically, found not guilty in every court in which he ever faced prosecution. In spite of the not guilty verdicts, Kicking Fox was a target. He was pursued by unscrupulous politicians worldwide. Assassins retained within dark basements on scrambled cell phones were contracted. None were successful, and many were never heard from again.

Some insist Kicking Fox is dead now. Others claim he is simply waiting in seclusion. Still others believe him to have assumed some unknown identity and living a normal life in an isolated faraway place. Or the last possibility—he was living in plain sight but somehow had become unrecognizable.

Chapter 1

Kicking Fox

Kicking Fox had seen this happen in other men. It was never something one could put a finger on. A series of events, perhaps the cumulative effect of injustice whether perceived or real. Perspective was what was most missing in the *breaking* of the inner man. Perspective that he did not possess nor recognize.

Having witnessed this snap, or breaking in others, he was surprised he did not immediately recognize the occurrence in his own soul. But it was plainly evident. The event changed the way he thought. The turning point changed his actions and deeds. He was no longer going to remain complacent.

Kicking Fox had had enough.

He loaded his suitcase, going through the mindless motions of packing. He had done this for decades. Prepare for another long haul. He would be out fifteen days this time. He'd touchdown on three continents, cross fully half the time zones on the globe. He placed the mechanical wind-up clock in the suitcase. No digital read out, no battery power, just a wind-up clock with a dial he adjusted daily to whatever time zone he found himself in. He had a secret. A secret to staying fit, alert, and avoiding the jet lag that many suffered from. He simply slept eight hours per day no matter the time zone, continent, or language being spoken. The simple solution worked for him. He was ever alert, his mind keen and aware.

He disassembled the forty-five semi-automatic into its fourteen plastic pieces. Some went into his shaving kit, others into the little compartments of his luggage. The bullets he had three-dimensionally printed last night. Each one composed of 100 percent high grade plastic. The powder and wad stuffing he hid away into scent proof containers. He would not have any problems with customs. They knew him well. His profile was posted in every database and intelligence agency across the globe.

Kicking Fox's ceremonial war club, high grade plastic bow, and the hand-hewn oak arrows, along with sharpened plastic broadheads were tucked away as always into their respective hidden compartments. The plastics of his long knife would never be detected by the metal sensing and X-ray equipment found in most travel terminals. He moved about the world well-armed, unbeknownst to the security teams that surveilled the mass public. He was always prepared. This trip would be no different he told himself. But deep within he knew he would need, and put to use, his weapons.

He sat in the crew compartment of the 747-1000 awaiting the first crew's duty time limitations to expire and begin his time as captain. The plan suddenly began to take on shape and form. He detailed each step. His every move he began to scrutinize and perfect.

After a few hours, he began to see not only the plan, but also the changes within his mind. Something within his soul had indeed broken at the news he had received from his brother. Kicking Fox's life…would never be the same.

****

"Captain Nica, can I get you anything?" Sally Wolf peered deep into his eyes with a questioning look that contained much more than refreshments in her offer.

He breathed deeply, remembering the last trip. The beach, the smell of the ocean, the taste of oysters, and fresh crab…along with the taste of Sally herself. He smiled. "I'm good Sally."

With a wink she moved forward to the cockpit. Her movements were graceful or perhaps even sensual. Sally Wolf of the great Shoshone tribe was a stunningly beautiful woman. He tried not to stare.

She returned a few moments later. "Will you be laying over in Sydney?" A longing in her perfectly sculpted face permeated her question.

"Yes," he answered honestly. "But, I'm sorry, Sally I have some business to tend to this time." He saw instantly the hurt in her eyes. The last thing he wanted to do was hurt her. He had no words to explain what he was about to do. She touched him on the shoulder as she moved toward the service area. He felt the electricity of her touch. Her presence aroused the definitive manly stirrings in his soul. He breathed deeply again. Would her comfort, her love, her beauty, ever be his again? There was no answer to that question posed within his mind. He would need to plan and execute his steps flawlessly. Sally would be much safer not knowing.

Chapter 2

The coastline of Australia appeared as they descended out of the broken overcast at 5,000 feet msl (mean sea level). In a few moments, the massive runways of Sydney Airport filled the windscreen of their 747-1000 as they ran the final landing checklists. Kicking Fox focused on the few tasks at hand, and at one thousand feet agl (above ground level), he disconnected the autoland system. He adjusted to the slight cross wind that swept in from Botany Bay across runway 34L. The aircraft was relatively light now at slightly under six-hundred thousand pounds after burning fourteen hours of fuel. Still, airspeed and altitude control would need to be precise. His co-pilot called out those speeds in succinct progression. Kicking Fox corrected, slightly lifting the nose of the massive aircraft and reducing the power by 10 percent. The pleasant woman's voice programed into the autopilot dutifully began altitude call outs. He eased some power off again as the automated voice announced, "100 feet."

"Just let her settle," Kicking Fox said aloud. "Fifty feet." He held her nose high "Twenty...ten..." Two seconds later the huge main landing gear made contact with the surface. He applied a little left rudder as the ship attempted to yaw into the wind. She straightened as he gently lowered the nose. Upon contact of the nose gear with the runway surface, he brought the enormous engines into full reverse as 550,000 lbs. of aircraft, fuel, and cargo from across the globe began to decelerate.

Kicking Fox supposed no matter how many times this task of landing safely and bringing to a stop a machine of this size and complexity is undertaken, the outcome is never certain until the aircraft rests within the chocked wheels at a proper gate with its engines shut down. It would take another twenty minutes of checklists, taxiing through the web of complex runway intersections and following ground control instructions before they eventually came to a stop. He breathed deeply and relaxed his grip on the power levers as the engines slowly spooled down. A few minutes of paperwork, acknowledgments from his fellow crewmembers on a nice flight and landing, then he was off. His mission clear. He would not report back after the two-day layover in Sydney. This would be his last flight. He would eventually make his way back to the United States and back to the reservation in New Mexico where he was born. It might take months or even years for that to happen. He focused his thoughts on the task at hand. When a man breaks, he begins to see the events of the future clearly. Events that might motivate a change in the way governments and world leaders behave.

Yes, he was certain his actions would cause many to consider their motives and the paths to power they were willing to take. Sometimes a bully, or a tyrant, a dictatorial political thief, simply needs to be called to account.

The meeting was set to take place in two weeks. Fourteen days of the ticking clock commenced now. Though not on the invitation list, Kicking Fox would be in attendance.

Chapter 3

Two Years Earlier

Kicking Fox stood alone along the edge of the grave. Little streams of dirt drifted from under his feet into the dark hole before him. She was too young. This should not have happened. The remains of his daughter contained in the casket at his feet held nothing but an empty shell. The decomposing body that previously housed the most beautiful spirit he had ever met no longer held that spirit. Prairie Wind was gone. Her spirit, he understood, was in heaven, or the great land, or paradise. Whatever belief others, or his people, put their faith in, or hoped for, whatever seed of faith gave a person hope, he possessed. He knew without doubt such a kind innocent caring spirit that was his daughter was long departed. He also understood in his own spirit that Prairie Wind was now in the presence of her mother and all their loved ones that had fallen asleep. She was now loved and free from the hurt and pain of this world.

Two funerals inside of one month. He observed the stone marker with her mother's name engraved along its glossy granite face. "I miss you, Ela." The Apache meaning of his former wife's name was Earth. How ironic that seemed as he stood near her grave within the earth. "I do not understand why you have both left me." He turned and walked away in silence.

Looking back, it was without a doubt that day the breaking of his soul began. It is difficult to describe this darkening, this cloud of hatred or vengeance that might consume one's own mind and purpose. It was a seed of darkness planted firmly within the injustice that lay at the bottom of his daughter's grave. Kicking Fox determined that day someone would pay for her life or the life she would never live out. Someone.

Kicking Fox

The company promptly grounded him. Human resources would never allow a captain to continue his work after the death of a family member. At the death of a loved one, mandatory grief counseling and psychological evaluations were ordered. It would take months for him to complete the required training—indoctrination might have been a better description. They wanted to make certain the seed that had been planted at the gravesite of his daughter never blossomed and grew. Those in power both within the company and without, meaning the government, would make certain he would be a good little Indian. Compliant, mindless, willing to drink the Kool-Aid. After a full year, the powers that be decided he would comply. He was given a reduced schedule at first. And he was watched. The surveillance videos recorded every word and movement. Every flight was analyzed. Every conversation reviewed. Somewhere in the depths of the inner workings of the largest airline in the world, a psychologist pronounced Kicking Fox fit. He would resume a normal flight schedule. The surveillance would end.

But they had missed something. Something their careful observation and psychological testing could never reveal. In his heart he was a Warrior. Trained by his grandfather in the *Old Ways,* Samuel Nica, would not comply. He would make certain those responsible for the death of his loved ones would pay...with their own lives.

Kicking Fox thought it odd or even comical that the question that might reveal the most about him was never asked. That type of question, had it been posed in all the political correctness, posturing, and analytical testing, might have been quite revealing. It may have been difficult to conceal his true Warrior heart. But they never asked about vengeance, or revenge, and it would be his.

****

Present Day

Kicking Fox made his way along within the massive structure of Sydney Airport, eventually exiting into the smog-filled air of the underground garage. The van driver was pleasant as Kicking Fox allowed him to load his bags into the rear of the courtesy van. The drive to the hotel was filled with expletives and confused honking of horns as the snarl of traffic that engulfed them eventually made its way onto the freeway. His mind wandered at the mass of humanity surrounding him. He longed for the wildness of the back country. He closed his eyes, imagining the high mountains of his Homeland so far away in New Mexico. It was winter there now. He could feel the cold and smell the fresh snow-laden air. He wondered, what had he become? In his past, he had longed to escape the Rez. He desired something different, even some level of success in the modern world that was not available within his Homeland.

He had climbed this ladder of achievement only to realize in this very moment…none of what he was living and surrounded by mattered. The airports, whether in Europe or South America or here in Australia, were all exactly the same. The hotels identical in location, room appointments, even linens, lighting, and window placement. The restaurants served the same food and wine across the globe. So many days and nights he had spent in these places, and upon awakening, many of those early mornings it was impossible to determine where he was. Some days he had to consult his flight data or smart phone to establish whether he was in Paris or Dallas-Fort Worth or London. Maybe what he had pursued and chased for years now was a complete waste of time.

The driver spoke to him again. "Sir, are you all right?" They had stopped. The door was open and the driver awaited his exit from the van.

"Sure, um, I'm good, just a little jet lag."

The driver looked at him curiously.

Kicking Fox would need to be much more careful. He could not allow even the slightest questions as to his mental acuity.

The driver smiled in understanding. "I get that, Captain. Made the trip across the pond myself a time or two. Not sure how you pilots deal with the time zone changes. Have a pleasant stay." The young man handed Kicking Fox his bags. He tipped him nicely and nodded.

"Nothing a couple of days on the beach won't cure," he said smiling.

"Now you're talking my language, mate," he said with a strong Aussie accent. "Enjoy your layover." And with that he was quickly back in the driver seat, honking at the departing traffic.

Kicking Fox was certain the driver would not recall anything unusual about their conversation. It would be a full month before the police would question him about their ride from the airport.

He checked in at the front desk to the cheerful smiles and distinct friendly accent of a beautiful blond-haired, blue-eyed Australian desk attendant. He politely declined the offer for assistance with his luggage and made his way to the requested secluded room on the twenty-fourth floor of the massive building.

He had much planning to do, but he needed rest for now. He darkened the room, covering all windows with the heavy drapery. He assembled his plastic forty-five semi-automatic and laid it on his nightstand. He then lit a small candle and set flame to the delicate bundle of sacred incense he always carried with him. He breathed in deeply the scent that took him to another place and time.

He spent a full hour in his "time of quiet" as his grandfather had instructed him. His grandfather had trained him well. His quiet time would be vital in his planning and strategy over the next two weeks. Resolve settled within his heart and mind as he drifted into a deep sleep.

Chapter 4

Eight hours later the alarm sounded on the small wind-up clock. Kicking Fox needed the rest and had slept peacefully. He opened the curtains as the sun was setting across Sydney harbor, the sky filled with vibrant hues of orange and pink. It was morning back in the high mountains of New Mexico. There, the sun would be rising in the east, as the sun set here outside his window half a world away. He took a deep breath. He felt the incredible distance to his Homeland from here…both physically and emotionally. He whispered aloud, "Have I gotten too far from you, my mountains, to ever make my way home?" The voice of his woman, Ela, his daughter, and his people answered from across the heavens. He breathed deeply again, now knowing the answer he earnestly sought.

The plan was beginning to take shape in his mind. He understood the importance of seeing his steps and actions in his mind…before living them out. Wisdom is what he would seek in every detail, movement, and decision. He punched the contact as his cell phone dialed the number to airline operations. It would be wise to buy some time.

"Captain Nica reporting in."

"Good morning, Captain. Good to hear from you. I have you departing tomorrow at 07:00. You'll have a short layover in Anchorage, and then on to Chicago." He heard the busy clacking of a keyboard as the clerk typed. "And then it looks like you're home for a couple of weeks. Is that still correct?"

"I'm actually a little under the weather. Seems like maybe some bad food last night, no other symptoms other than gastrointestinal. I think it best for me to not fly tomorrow." The silence on the other end of the line hung awkwardly for a moment. Would they dismiss this as a minor intestinal issue? Kicking Fox understood the policies; they would act swiftly.

"I'll need to send the testing team to you within the hour."

"It's really pretty obvious to me it's not the virus, but whatever you think best." He feigned innocence.

"Please remain in your room, Captain. The testing team is on the way and should arrive within the hour."

"Understood." He ended the call. The plan was unfolding exactly as he had hoped. The test results would arrive on his smart phone two hours later. All virus scans would be negative. Kicking Fox, however, would be quarantined for a full seven days. How many days would it be before they discovered he was no longer in his room was a question he did not have the answer for. But he had bought himself some time. He felt a twinge of guilt knowing the crew and passengers from his last flight would also be traced and placed in quarantine. He thought of Sally. He would need to learn to set aside any emotions of guilt, even the slightest twinge.

He plugged his phone into the charger, made certain it was on, and all location and tracking activated. They would monitor his whereabouts continuously. The authorities had delivered a large box of dehydrated food and several cases water. By now, the door to his room would be locked from the outside. The instructions were clear and succinct. He would not be allowed to leave the room for seven days.

Kicking Fox loaded his weapons and a few of the freeze-dried meals and several water bottles into his small lightweight pack. He dressed in his exercise sweats, running shoes, light jacket, and ball cap. He would become just another tourist out for an evening jog.

He removed the vent cover and crawled through the narrow ducting into the adjacent room. He forced the vent cover off in the adjacent room with a swift kick and lowered himself to the floor. He repeated the same removing of vent covers and crawling through the air conditioning vents for seven full rooms. Hoping he was far enough away from the cameras that would be trained outside the door to his room, he exited far down the hallway from the room where he was supposed to be. The cameras recorded someone leaving the room he exited on the twenty-fourth floor. None of the security teams noticed the movement. That footage would not be viewed for over a week.

He made his way out of the hotel via a service elevator and kitchen delivery entrance. The city was just coming alive. The streets were busy with steady traffic; the bars and restaurants were filling with patrons. He began to run, moving north and west. He knew exactly where he was going–one of the largest uninhabited geographic regions remaining on the planet, the Australian Outback.

Steven G. Hightower

****

One hour later the traffic began to thin. Kicking Fox took to one of the numerous side roads leading away from the city and slowed to a walk. The sun had fully set and the glow of the city behind him dampened the starlight overhead. He needed one critical tool before leaving the city behind. He scanned the horizon then turned toward the brightest glow remaining in the night sky. Walking briskly in the direction of the lights, he soon spotted exactly what he was looking for. The strip mall contained a variety of quaint shops and boutiques. He pulled his ballcap low over his brow and tucked his hands into his pockets. He was certain his skin tone was undetectable to the surveillance cameras. He took but a few moments to select the best non-contract sat phone available. He paid with cash, grateful he had used an ATM in the States prior to his departure. He exited with his head held low, intentionally never looking into a camera or toward any person.

Once away from the quickly fading lights of Sydney, Australia, he began to run again. One hour later he sat in the bush along the edge of the beginnings of the Outback. The night sky was ablaze with starlight and constellations. Even the Southern Cross showed its majesty high in the vast stellar space. He chanced a small fire and again entered into his time of quiet. The voices of his ancestors filled his heart and mind. The voices of the innocent called out from across time. Those among his people who had been massacred centuries ago called to him. The voices of those eliminated by the creation of the viruses and resulting deaths these weapons had caused whispered into his heart and mind.

Lastly the voices of his wife and daughter called to him from across the veil that lies between the unseen spirit world and the seen physical world those who are alive inhabit. The voices sang their death songs. They sang a new song representing the throngs that had been eliminated. His heart broke again at the stark realization and truth, that his wife and daughter had departed this world at the hand of evil. The reaction within their bodies had been brutal. The suffering beyond what any human should ever endure. They had died alone. No loved ones allowed anywhere near their lonely torturous isolation. The new vaccines had taken three full days to kill his loved ones.

Kicking Fox sat in the bush alongside his little fire and read again the message he had received from his brother William on his satellite phone less than twenty-four hours ago.

"Deploy Wolf north and west, Red Army."

Kicking Fox

His Homeland had been attacked. It was, for him, the last injustice imposed upon his people in a long and sordid history of injustice that he would ever allow to occur without consequences.

Perhaps, *breaking* was the wrong term to describe what he had experienced in the last few hours. Perhaps, *awakening* was a better term.

****

Kicking Fox dreamed of his mother that night. Topusana Nica, Akima (Leader) of their people, was the bravest person he had ever known. Yes, she was his mother, and his attachment to her created a bond that was unbreakable. However, the closeness and communion he felt that night half a world away from her was incomprehensible. A communication took place between them across Mother Earth, across oceans, across the time zones. She had seen.

She was aware of the choice he had made, and the *awakening* that had occurred within his Warrior spirit.

Chapter 5

In the gentle shadows of starlight, Kicking Fox moved another half mile to the north of the scarcely traveled dirt road that had brought him here. He made his way into a deep arroyo. He gathered fuel wood and lit a small fire using the flint and stone he kept stored in the handle of his long knife. Although the air temperature was still quite warm, the fire brought a level of comfort he had not experienced in years. He settled comfortably alongside his cozy fire on the edge of the Outback.

He needed rest. His body was tired from the run and miles he had covered. He went over the plan again in his mind. He understood he needed help. He lay back into soft sand, thinking of his friend, the man he had served alongside. His friend was out there, perhaps not too far from Kicking Fox's little hidden resting place. Should he dare to transmit a message on the sat phone?

He fell fast asleep...

****

Eight hours later Kicking Fox awakened to a breaking red dawn, the sky ablaze with streaks of red and pink hues. A light wind stirred as the Outback awakened. He recognized the sign; a storm was certainly coming.

Thinking through his options, he decided any transmissions might possibly be tracked. However, the authorities would never understand an ancient coded message. He acted quickly and gathered brush, twigs, branches, and some large limbs from the sparse foliage within the arroyo. He piled the fire fuel into two separate sites, separating the two signal fires by about fifty feet. As the sun peaked the horizon, he struck spark to each fire. The dry fuel burned quickly; however, the two columns of smoke would be seen for many miles. If his friends were near, they would understand and arrive within a few hours.

His signal fires were reduced to hot coals within a few minutes of being lit. The smoke had stopped rising above the fires. He quickly threw the two largest fresh cut branches that still contained green leaves and sap onto each bed of coals. Dark smoke from the signal fires instantly rose high into the morning sky. A few moments later only a bed of coals remained.

Communication in one of its oldest and most rudimentary forms had taken place across the Outback. Now his friends could see the urgency of his double message. He would wait.

****

Kicking Fox felt the hunger in his body; he needed nutrition. Rummaging through his day pack, he located the freeze-dried meals he had taken from his hotel supply. *Add 1 cup of water and microwave for four minutes.* "Yeah, right." He tossed the meal packs onto the hot coals where they quickly evaporated into the flame. He possessed the skills of his grandfather.

His bow shot was placed perfectly on the center of the kill zone. He cleaned the animal thoroughly and fleshed the remaining meat from the pelt as the smell of roasted rabbit wafted along his hidden arroyo. The soft rabbit hide would make an excellent medicine bag. He rotated the rabbit on the makeshift spit above the hot coals, then removed a generous piece, slicing into the warm steaming meat. Delicious. He ate slowly, savoring the pure natural meat. The meal seemed to instantly strengthen his body. His mind wandered; he heard the voice of his grandfather as he removed a hind quarter from the sizzling spit.

"Kicking Fox, the earth will feed more than your body. The spirit of the animals you take will also strengthen your mind and your soul."

Kicking Fox gave thanks for the life of the animal and the teaching of his grandfather Tenahpu.

****

Kicking Fox moved out of the arroyo and climbed a small rise to the north of where he had lit his signal fires. How long would it be before the authorities discovered he was no longer in his hotel room? He determined it might be several days, as most were still so filled with fear that they would certainly stay away from any possible contamination.

He thought of Sally Wolf and the hurt he had seen in her eyes. He prayed she could endure the isolation, the questioning, the suspicion. As he ate slowly, his mind wandered to her touch. Their time together was a gift of comfort from the Creator. He longed for that gift of touch again. How long could he exist alone? He had no answer. He needed to separate himself from these feelings of guilt and longing and even his inner desire for comfort that only a woman can bring to a man. His mission would demand isolation and discipline.

Two hours later as he rested hidden among the elevated boulders above his signal fire, he detected the first sign of movement. Something, however, was not right. The direction of the movement was wrong. They should have been moving toward him from the north and west deeper into the Outback. This movement came from the east, more toward the development he had left behind. Surely, he had not been followed. Had his signal fire been seen by the wrong people? As taught by his grandfather Tenahpu, he checked the edges of his arrowhead and knocked a razor-sharp arrow. Kicking Fox moved up the boulder slope to gain a better field of vision…and field of fire. He breathed deeply and waited. The voice of his grandfather echoed in his heart and mind.

"Patience, Kicking Fox. It is vital to learn and put into practice patience which breeds wisdom."

Chapter 6

Sally Wolf worked her way along the edge of the sparse cover of brush along the beginnings of the Outback. Her escape from her hotel had gone undetected; she was certain. How many hours or days would it be before they discovered her exit from the second-floor window? The dawn was breaking in the brilliant explosion of red hues, revealing to her that surely storms would come today. She had spotted the smoke from the signal fires. They must have been from Samuel. She had two objectives. One, rendezvous with Samuel, or as he would now prefer, Kicking Fox. Two, do so without giving their positions away to anyone else who might be nearby.

Sally was no novice. She was trained in the *Old Ways* by her people. She knew well both the New World Order of things, and she fully understood the *Old Ways*. With each step she took, she would follow and put to use the wisdom contained in that training.

Sally was a strikingly beautiful woman. Jet black hair, high cheek bones, a body that was fit, trim, and in excellent physical condition. She had been a track star in high school in her former days on the Rez in Wyoming. She had been recruited by the top Division 1 schools throughout the United States. She chose to stay close to home and attended the University of Wyoming, where during her tenure she won four individual national championships. She still held the national collegiate record in both the 10k and marathon. Sally Wolf was an elite athlete. She would need the skill and ability she had spent years in training to obtain, this very day.

Sally was desperate to locate Kicking Fox. She alone was aware the authorities had already discovered his escape.

Checking her back trail repeatedly and seeing no evidence of anyone following, she pressed on. She doubled back every half mile or so, intentionally leaving tracks opposing her true direction of travel. This would confuse anyone who followed. The signal fire was her greatest concern. Anyone for miles in all directions would have seen it. But were there any other people out here? She listened intently. She silently watched her back trail for half an hour, sensing its emptiness. Sally discerned in her heart no one followed.

The coming storm was growing. High cloud cover was now blocking most of the sky, and to the west, dark clouds were converging along the horizon and building. When Sally was within approximately two miles of where the signal fire originated, she rested a moment in the sparse cover of brush. Thinking through her options, she determined it was time to take a risk and signal Kicking Fox. Was there enough remaining sunlight?

From her day pack she located her small compact mirror. Holding it in alignment with the sun and the direction of the signal fires, she flicked her wrist in three successive quick movements. The first three flashes indicated S. Then three slower movements of her graceful wrist directed into the dim sunlight. Dash dash dash for O. Then a triple rapid signal flash again, indicating S. If there was enough sunlight, Kicking Fox would understand instantly. The code had been used for centuries. Eons prior to this signal being used by modern armies, her people had utilized it. She prayed Kicking Fox detected the subtle message flashed across two miles of wilderness. S.O.S.

****

Kicking Fox's heart raced. He studied his back trail and the movement he had detected from the east. Then the flashes of light reflected distinctly and intentionally across the open plain. Although the signal could have several meanings and possibilities, in this instance, the message to him was clear. He had been followed. By whom was the only question in his mind. One thing was certain, whether this signal came from his friends or foes, he had been followed. How could this be? He had taken every precaution. Thinking through the possibilities there were several. One, it could it be the authorities; two, had his friends from the Outback seen the smoke signal and intentionally circled to the east to prevent their detection; three, had someone else followed? He doubted the authorities had the personnel with the abilities necessary to locate and follow his track or keep up with his pace through the night. In his mind he eliminated the possibility that the authorities had followed.

The rain began softly at first. Rumbles of the coming storm seemed to shake the earth from miles away. Kicking Fox realized he had very little time. Within the hour the storm would be upon him and whomever else was out there following. Might this ancient signal be coming from his longtime friend. They had used this very tactic in real battlefield conditions half a world away. Had the man spotted his signal and then discovered other pursuers? How would others possibly know to send a warning in this fashion? It did not make sense. These were not the conditions that would justify using this specific military communication tool.

The wisdom of his grandfather whispered into his soul. "Consider every possibility, Kicking Fox. What would your enemy do? What are their abilities? You must think as they would think. You must understand their mindset. You must consider the mindset and abilities of our people. This knowledge, my grandson, will forever tip the scales of victory to your advantage."

"Thank you, Grandfather," Kicking Fox whispered softly. The signal had not come from the authorities, nor from his friend. Someone had followed. That someone could only be tribal and skilled in the *Old Ways*. That someone was sending him a warning. He moved silently away from the signal fires, then north, completely concealed, erasing any sign of his movement for a full mile. There he laid the sign. Taking care to show his intended direction of movement, he then revealed his silhouette across an opening. A few feet farther, he laid the second sign. Three small pebbles and an imperceptible line in the sand indicating the stream bed he had spied in the distance. The pebble sign would never be noticed by anyone unacquainted with the *Old Ways* or their meaning. He would wait three miles north along the dry creek bed. He moved rapidly now. Lightning flashed. Thunder shook the earth as the storm clouds neared. Would his follower locate the signs in time?

****

Sally Wolf saw the direction of movement more than the person that moved. He had shown himself intentionally. Her next move was clear, intercept the path of travel...and find the sign.

The gust front from the storms lifted a great cloud of dust high into the darkening sky in the west. Visibility decreased by the second. Sally rose from her hidden position, no longer concerned with the possibility of being spotted. She began to run.

The wind tore across the open plain with an incredible force. She covered the first few hundred yards in only three minutes. The rain began, sparse initially, but quickly the drops grew in size and the air cooled instantly. Within another hundred yards the wind-driven rain stung as the large raindrops struck her body and face. It was another quarter mile or so to the area where she had sensed the movement. She slowed when in the approximate area of the movement then turned to her right, now moving north. A blinding flash struck the earth above and to her left. The thunder roared simultaneously. She froze, breathing deeply as her heart settled. Looking downward, she saw the clear sign as the skies opened. Within thirty seconds the slight line in the dust was washed away along with the three pebbles.

****

Sally Wolf whispered a silent prayer as she worked out the math problem. She set her training watch for eighteen minutes. She would run straight north for eighteen minutes. A six mile per hour pace she knew by heart. It would take her very near the three-mile mark indicated in the sign. She was drenched and cold within a few minutes. Her athletic clothing clung to the outline of her body; her long black hair swept behind her, dripping water from the deluge. The earth trembled at the might of the thunder as it echoed across the plain. She ran intently, covering the rough terrain precisely at her estimated pace. She checked her watch. Twelve minutes had elapsed. Breathing rhythmically, she focused on her training, she had covered two miles. Another mile to go she. Then she heard the distinct buzz of an attack drone in the distance behind her.

"How could they have spotted me in the storm?" she whispered softy. She had two choices: run for the dry riverbed she had seen drawn in the sign on the ground…or hide.

Sally Wolf chose what she did best. She ran with all her might.

Accelerating now, she was only four minutes, at most, from the creek bed. The sound of the drone grew nearer. She ran with all that was within her. Time seemed to slow as the buffeting sound of the blades grew closer. Then she noticed the first little puffs of dirt rising from the muddy desert floor.

They were firing at her!

Adrenaline coursed through her body. Fear rose in her heart.

She realized their intentions. There'd be no questioning or interrogation. No arrest if she were to be captured. No formal charges or even a trial. None of that, she concluded as she ran with all her strength. *They'll simply kill me.*

Sally saw the creek bed a mere fifty yards ahead; it was now full running bank to bank from the muddy runoff from the storms. Her view and vision of the pursuit somehow shifted as she observed her escape route from a strange vantage point above. Her body strained at the effort. Fear reflected from her eyes and etched into the lines of her face. Her hair flew wild in the wind and heavy rain. She was close now. Just a few more strides…She leapt through the air, splashing into the torrent that was moments ago a dry creek bed. Bullets sprayed across the sand to her left. She felt an intense heat as a fireball exploded in the sky thirty yards behind her.

The torrent of churning water swept Sally away. She clawed at a floating tree, missing the lifesaving wood by inches. She sank into a swirling pool. She swam and kicked and struggled with all the strength she could muster, attempting to escape the giant whirlpool now forming. In desperation, she cried out to her Creator.

"Save me…please, save me!" Her voice went unheard by any in the physical world, drowned out in the sound of rushing floodwaters.

Then there was only a cold darkness pulling her downward toward the bottom of the churning force. Her feet felt strange as they scraped along the mud in the bottom of the now raging river. Her lungs burned; she needed to breath. She painfully fought the urge to take a breath in her struggle to swim upward, the dark torrent pulling her ever deeper. Finally, when she could no longer hold her breath… she blew out the remaining air her burning lungs held and inhaled deeply.

To her surprise, from the depths of the torrent, she drew in an unexplainable gift, a precious lungful of muddy foamy air. Relief. Then her head struck something sharply. Pain radiated along her spine and body.

The waters grew darker, the sky became pitch black, and Sally Wolf no longer wanted to breath. She no longer needed to breath. She let go of her struggle and fighting. She floated along, caught in the raging flood, in peace.

Something began to disturb her peace. She wanted the something to let go of her arm. The something had her in its grasp. She became aware of the spirit world. Others were watching. Her thoughts became as clear as crystal waters.

"Please, just let me go…I need to float along my dark course of wonder into the spirit world." Her prayers changed. "Please…let me go," she whispered into the torrent.

****

Sally awakened hours later to the sound of a crackling fire. Its warmth enveloped her. She breathed deeply and drifted off to sleep, feeling the strong, safe, familiar arms holding her gently, securely.

Chapter 7

From a hidden location behind a small rise of land, Kicking Fox's friend Captain Moses Walker took careful aim at the drone helicopter and pulled the trigger on the heat-seeking shoulder-fired rocket launcher. One second later the aircraft exploded into a million fiery pieces and plunged into the churning flash flood that filled the once dry creek bed.

Kicking Fox raced toward the flood water and dove in where he had last seen Sally submerge beneath the torrent. Instantly his hand felt warm flesh. He would never let her go. They sailed along the rushing waters, buffeted by the debris. He held fast to Sally's arm. After a few moments, he felt the tug of the safety net launched from above as it encircled them and began to lift them.

Moses expertly guided the hover rover above their position and lifted them within the rescue net, up and out of the churning flood waters. Kicking Fox gave the thumbs up as they sped away to the north. He felt the spirit of Sally Wolf return to her body as they moved along their course. She coughed out muddy water, and then clung to him tightly.

Ten miles or more from the scene of the drone helicopter explosion, Moses gently lowered them to the ground. Kicking Fox carried Sally and placed her inside the rover, then jumped in and closed the hatch. Moses accelerated quickly. The little aircraft shook a moment as Kicking Fox buckled in.

"Still get the little turbulent buffet when we break the sound barrier, mate."

Kicking Fox nodded and then focused his attention on Sally's head wound. Rummaging through the emergency flight kit he located the necessary supplies. After cleaning the wound thoroughly, he then applied a freezing spray compound. The blood flow stopped instantly. Then he ran the suture machine across the wound. Eight perfect sutures closed the wound and injected antibiotics and pain medication into the injury simultaneously. Sally opened her eyes a moment and seemed to peer directly into his soul. She drifted back into a restless sleep, with what he thought was a slight smile or comfort showing within her countenance. He realized that she knew she was safe.

Moses turned from his controls for a moment, observing Kicking Fox's handiwork and Sally. "Couldn't find an ugly girl to rescue I suppose."

Kicking Fox smiled at Moses' wry humor. But he, too, gazed on the stunning natural beauty of Sally Wolf as his heart fluttered.

Thirty minutes later, Moses slowed the rover and gently touched down nine hundred miles north of their rendezvous location. They quickly covered the rover with the camouflage netting kept in its underbelly. Then they moved into the shallow cave shaped into the red rock outcropping eons ago. While Moses retrieved the roo steaks from his solar powered frozen food supply, Kicking Fox struck flint to steel and started a comfortable fire. Sally, still in a deep sleep, rested snugly in his arms. They were now securely hidden in the center of the Australian Outback.

He breathed deeply and noticed the firelight reflecting off the smooth cave walls. In the dancing light, the ancient etchings left behind ages ago were revealed.

"My grandfathers were wonderful artists, eh, mate," Moses said as he rummaged through the second solar powered fridge box. He opened and offered him a cold frost-covered beer bottle just as he had on so many occasions…half a world away from here.

"Indeed, my friend." Kicking Fox gazed at the rudimentary artwork drawn by the Aboriginal peoples who had lived in this place for thousands of years.

His friend Moses Walker dropped the roo steaks onto the little metal grate he had placed over the fire. They instantly began to sizzle. As only familiar smells can do, the aroma of fresh meat grilling over an open fire transported Kicking Fox's thoughts and mind to a different place and time. He remembered the many evenings spent with his grandfather Tenahpu. Evenings along the river in the Big Bend country of their reservation. Evenings that always followed their hunts along the high mountains of New Mexico. He thought of his people and the attack they had suffered in the last twenty-four hours. Resolve settled again in his inner being. Those responsible would pay. And they would pay with their lives.

His friend Moses recognized the look on his face. Moses knew him well.

"Sam, I would put whatever you are contemplating away for now. Tonight, we dine and celebrate your first victory. Tomorrow you can begin your mission."

He gazed again at the beauty of Sally as she rested within his arms. "Victory?"

"Yes, my friend. You have escaped their world of observation and control, and that is indeed a victory. They have no way to locate you here. From this location, and many others across the Outback you will have the ability to strike…and escape repeatedly." Moses gently flipped the sizzling steaks and drank deeply from his ice-covered beer bottle.

"You know me too well, my friend." He, too, drank from the bottle, feeling his body releasing the tension he had carried since exiting his hotel room. "Are you certain they can't follow?"

"The rover has cloaking and cloning capabilities. Their displays would show thousands of false trajectories. They have no idea which track was our actual ship." Moses closed his eyes in silent prayer, and as Kicking Fox had seen on a thousand occasions, Moses gave thanks for the bounty the earth had provided. He sliced a large slab of meat from a steak, passing it to Kicking Fox. He also gave a silent thanks to the Creator for the nutritious meal. The meat steamed on his knife blade as he removed the warm moist steak and took a small bite of the delicious roasted meat. The delicate tender savory flavor again took his mind to another place and time.

He could see the delight in the face of his friend as he, too, savored the delicious meat. Kicking Fox drank deeply again from the cold brew. "Well, as always you are correct, my friend. This night we let the past go…and celebrate a new beginning."

Moses nodded in his direction, raising his bottle.

Sally stirred in his arms, coming fully awake now. She peered into his eyes and sat upright, observing her surroundings. Kicking Fox could see her mind taking it all in. Understanding showed across her face. She reached for him and embraced him in a way he had never felt. Her embrace contained relief, gratitude, hope, and even more. Relaxing her grip, her beauty seemed to radiate from her face. She moved her lips to his and kissed him tenderly.

"Thank you for not letting go," she whispered gently into his ear.

"Thank you for coming to me."

Moses sat against the cave wall observing, a questioning expression on his dark Aboriginal face, though he was partially hidden in the shadows of the firelight. He sliced another steaming piece of roasted meat from a steak and passed it to Sally who eagerly accepted. Moses and Kicking Fox watched in awe as she ravenously devoured the delectable roo meat.

"Sally Wolf, this is my friend and former military commander, Moses Walker."

Sally rose from her seated position by the fire, licking her lips, while still chewing. After a couple of seconds, she swallowed. Her graceful athletic figure was now revealed in the soft firelight.

"It is an honor to meet you, sir," Sally said quietly as she took yet another ravenous bite.

Moses froze for a moment in his observation of Sally. His gaze lasted just a bit too long, but Kicking Fox understood perfectly. He could clearly see Moses was astonished at the natural beauty of Sally. Moses cleared his throat and quickly looked away.

"You two should get your own cave," Moses said.

Chapter 8

The task force met in an interior room deep within the windowless building located in the geographic center of Sydney, Australia. The artificial lighting and stale atmosphere from the air scrubbers created a sterile empty workspace.

Captain Daniel Baker, an Australian Aboriginal, was a rising star in the Enforcement Bureau. As a detective, being chosen as a member of the task force was a huge step in his career. He was certain to be promoted upon completion of the task force's mission. The primary purpose of the meeting was security for the upcoming H-8 meetings. The H-8 consisted of the world's leading eight nations in regard to health research and mandate compliance. Health Czars representing those eight nations participating in the New World Order initiatives would be present. Included in the group was the aged leader of Department of Health Initiatives from the United States, Dr. Clive Dutton.

Dr. Dutton had earned an unwanted nickname from the underground press representing the resistance. "Dr. CD," the double meaning clear to most. Certificates of deposit was implied in the nickname. Despite Dr. Dutton's best efforts to destroy any and all who chose to use the term in reference to him, the name stuck. The man, a lifetime government employee, was estimated to have a net worth in the billions. The United States director of the Department of Health Initiatives, Dr. Clive Dutton, had invested his purported wealth not in stocks or bonds, but only in enormous certificates of deposit held within banks worldwide. His earnings were estimated at a minimum of 10 percent to as high as 30 percent annually. It was further reported he sought out banks in countries with the highest inflation rates on the globe. Those inflation rates, the resistance claimed, were due to the health initiatives modeled and implemented exactly as those imposed within the United States itself.

"We seriously must track any reference on the web containing the phrase CD, really?" Captain Baker questioned his authorities.

"Yes," Superior, the title of the comandante of the Enforcement Bureau replied. "A direct request from Dr. Dutton himself. He believes we can measure the potential for any form of opposition or protest based on the number of leads we get. He has some kind of algorithm that can predict the likelihood based on those numbers."

Captain Baker smiled. "But only if we also include F, CD in the scan, correct?" The entire task force broke out in chuckles at the comment.

Superior frowned at the response, his demeanor stiff and unbending. "That was not a request by Dr. Dutton, but in all seriousness, I'm certain is a promising idea."

Studying the map projected onto the table the task force was seated around, Captain Baker wondered aloud, "You believe it was Nica that lit the signal fires?"

"Program suggests a 26 percent likelihood." a technical assistant replied.

Program was the new AI (artificial intelligence) application that had been deployed to deal with "law breakers," as they were labeled. The higher-ups in the government and the media had dutifully spoken the term given the resistance repeatedly for years now. The intention clear, the term implied guilt. Law breakers were considered guilty before being proven innocent. This policy, or subtle innuendo, fit the narrative of the New World Order perfectly. The fact that it was in direct opposition to Australian law and most Constitutions worldwide mattered not.

Program had been developed using all available resources of the Australian government and military, in conjunction secretly with the United States military. The machine had the ability to process data algorithms designed to evaluate human behavior faster than any computer ever built. It could access public cameras, military records, prison records, social media posts, and even intercept cell and sat phone conversations of suspected law breakers, all the while evaluating tone and possible intent of the suspected individuals. Program evaluated and processed data based on voice pitch, speech patterns, key words, and even emotional algorithms.

Program had proved to be exceptionally effective and accurate. Even in detecting suspicious activity within the Enforcement Bureau. Dozens of officers had been removed from their positions due to the suspicions of Program. Most recognized, and understood, they were all being monitored.

Program's most effective tool was written into its own code by design. As it learned from patterns of success, Program began to identify what it referred to as FDL, fear detection level.

Program had learned to detect human fear. It had determined that fear followed most law breaker actions, so those showing fear within the general population were most likely to rebel, or commit a crime, or join the resistance. Thousands of citizens were arrested...simply because they were afraid.

Deep-down, Captain Baker hated this AI computer, but in retrospect he thought Program, in all likelihood, discerned that fact...long before he did.

"So, Program is uncertain," Captain Baker said.

"Well, sir, the distance is what is reducing the percentages. Program does not believe most people could run thirty miles. The algorithms begin to narrow the concentric circles of possibilities and average the distance most humans might possibly travel." The tech operator punched a few buttons, and a small six-mile circle was instantly displayed surrounding Captain Nica's hotel room. "Program believes there is a 95 percent chance Nica is within this circle."

The room fell silent. Superior, broke the silence. "Program will be correct. Deploy all our resources within the six-mile circle. We will find him there."

"And Sally Wolf?" Captain Baker questioned.

"She is another matter."

Captain Baker saw clearly the eerie cold look in Superior's eyes.

"Clearly, her ability as an elite athlete allowed her to cover the distance, and she received help from the resistance." Superior rested his head in his hands. "It's all about the data. Let's do our job. Interview her fellow workers. Track her online activity. We will find the communication she obviously sent to the resistance. Have the authorities back in the States arrest a few family members. We may get her to surface on her own if we broadcast a few unpleasantries concerning her detained family members. You know the drill."

Captain Baker drew in a deep breath, knowing what might be in store for the family members and even her co-workers. Sometimes he wondered if he could continue this line of work. He had rationalized for months, even years now, the loss of freedoms and the overbearing actions of his government. He understood this was all "for the betterment of the planet." The motto adopted by the Enforcement Bureau had been posted, stickered, and illuminated on every piece of equipment, document, correspondence, and even vehicles for decades now. The motto was a constant reminder to all security force members and personnel that the planet was more important than its inhabitants. Captain

Baker now recognized deep in his heart this was wrong.

Superior ended the meeting with the words the team was expected to and dutifully repeated. "For the betterment of the planet."

"For the betterment of the planet." Captain Baker half-heartedly, spoke aloud along with the others in the room.

He could see several of the assumptions from Superior, and even those of Program, were incorrect. He decided to remain silent for now.

That night as in most of his nights over the last month, Captain Baker's sleep was restless and filled with visions of the innocent suffering at the hands of his own government.

Family members of law breakers cried out into his sleep, awakening something deep within his Aboriginal soul.

Chapter 9

Kicking Fox awakened to the smell of the woodfire, coffee boiling, and roasting meat. Sally moved toward him, offering a steaming mug of campfire coffee.

"Good morning, Kicking Fox."

"Good morning, Sally." He peered into her eyes with a questioning look at her formality in using his native name.

She answered his questioning look in his native tongue. *"It will be a new time for your skills and what lies ahead for us, Kicking Fox. You are a Warrior. I will from this point forward refer to you as such."*

"*I understand, Meenuu Pncha.*" (Quiet One) He breathed deeply. Her words strengthened his resolve.

"Morning, mates. I trust you slept well." The voice of his former commander echoed from deep within the cavern. Kicking Fox lifted the coffee pot from the edge of the fire. Its steaming contents spread the aroma of strong coffee throughout their new home. Moses emerged from the darkness as he poured a cupful into a mug. He passed it to Moses, as he had on so many awakening mornings in the Ural Mountains of Russia. They sat in silence, enjoying the moment.

After a while, Moses broke the time of silent reflection. "Last night I received the news from the resistance of the attack on your Homeland." He peered into Kicking Fox's eyes with an understanding look. "This explains a lot," he said.

Kicking Fox nodded.

"But there is more in addition to the invasion." Moses said.

Sally sat upright, a fearful look on her face. "What has happened, Moses?"

"A low-level nuclear device was detonated above the San Saba Comanche Homeland. No one has claimed responsibility, although early reports indicate the weapon was of Chinese origin. It is unknown how many perished. The blast radius was about forty kilometers. It is evident many buffalo were melted into Mother Earth. My sources tell me a warning was received from Israel prior to the detonation. It is hoped, most escaped underground."

Sally sat in shock at the news. Kicking Fox pictured the blast, the prairie fires that were certain to still be burning, and his family. He perceived from his quiet time his immediate family had survived. However, he felt within his time of quite a deep unexplainable void. He did not fully understand until this very moment…the void represented the hundreds of lives lost, lives of his people erased in a millisecond.

He sat in quiet shock at the news, his heart racing. How could this have been allowed? Who ordered this action? The American military or, at the very least, the executive branch must have approved this attack. How could this possibly be? The many questions for which there were no answers raced through his mind. He rose from my seated position, his blood boiling.

"My people have yet again suffered at the hands of governments. Moses, hundreds have perished. It is time to plan our response."

****

"So, they already know I am not in my room." Sally had just shared with Kicking Fox the information and the reason for her also escaping her quarantine. "You took the ultimate risk to bring me this news. Thank you, Sally. My only question is, how did you know?"

"Call it a woman's intuition. Our conversation in the cockpit was revealing to me, Kicking Fox. Further, you are not the only Native American that utilizes time of quiet. I saw the change in you. I saw the awakening of your Warrior spirit very clearly."

He gazed into her eyes in wonder.

"So, to sum up our situation, you are both being hunted," Moses said. "They tracked Sally to a position thirty-eight clicks to the north of Sydney. They know she had assistance by the destruction of the drone. Yet, it seems they have no idea where Samuel might be. This fact is an enormous advantage."

"The meeting of the H-8 is set to take place in only twelve days, and I will be there," Kicking Fox said.

"I can help with the rover," Moses said. "My suggestion is to stay put. No communication of any kind. A no-noise footprint will mean no plan. We have the ability to monitor their activities; let's give them nothing to monitor concerning ours." This plan offered that first morning by Moses Walker contained much wisdom.

"It is safe to venture out into the bush. My suggestion is you practice. Hone your skills. Eat well, condition your body. An elite athlete can easily find their form in twelve days." Moses looked toward his friend Kicking Fox. "You will be using your traditional weapons I suppose?"

Kicking Fox nodded, indicating his bow. He took the weapon into his hands. Although it was high grade plastic, it was an exact replica of his grandfather's bow. The plastic arrow shafts he had decorated in the traditional manner with native plant stain and quail feathers. The plastic razor sharp broadheads had been precisely sharpened. The edges would penetrate deeply into many substances including lightweight aluminum or metal…even bone.

"Your training should begin now," Moses said. Kicking Fox and Sally nodded in agreement.

Chapter 10

Kicking Fox's skills improved daily. He shot naturally with no sight attached to his bow. Today he decided to add an aiming notch. He made a tiny etch mark in the plastic precisely below his left hand where he held the bow. The notch indicated a target trajectory for a 125-yard shot. Most would consider this an impossible bow shot. But he would practice this for hours every day. The mark was placed in the correct position. The arc of the arrow was impressive to watch on the video Moses recorded and viewed nightly. The arrow dropped an astounding twenty feet in its flight path. It was enthralling to see his aim fairly high into the sky, the arc and flightpath as the arrow dropped consistently into a small six-inch circle. He repeated the shot hundreds of times. He learned a quarter-inch rise in aim above his reference notch corrected for a headwind of ten miles per hour. He knew exactly how many inches to aim left or right due to crosswinds.

On day seven something supernatural took place. The Warrior and the weapon became one. Kicking Fox could not miss. Moving targets, bow shots kneeling, or even lying on his side or belly, sixty yards, twenty yards, 110 yards. All resulted in the same deadly accuracy.

Sally Wolf trained alongside him. They ran together each morning. Her expertise and knowledge of how to train was invaluable. Heavy days they would run fifteen to twenty miles. What she called "easy days" they would cover five to ten miles at an incredible pace. The pace was always a challenge for him. Sally, her body light and her muscle tone incredibly sleek, could outrun him at any moment. On completion of most training sessions, she would whisper "now let's run hard." He had been running hard, he would think, as she sped away from him in her sprint home. Her ability and her beauty amazed him.

In their afternoon training sessions with the bow, sling, and knife, Kicking Fox was clearly the teacher and expert. His grandfather had trained him well. However, Sally learned quickly. She became deadly with each weapon. Inside of fifty yards, she was particularly good with the bow. Moses reviewed their progress and critiqued their performances each evening.

On day eight Kicking Fox took a small Blackbuck antelope in a no-wind condition at 150 yards. That night as they dined on the succulent tenderloin of the animal, his commander pronounced him ready and fit for the mission.

"You are ready, my friend, as is Sally."

Kicking Fox saw the intent in his commander's eyes.

"You will work well as a team."

"Hold on there, Commander, I will not endanger Sally with this mission." Kicking Fox was shocked at his thought process and protested much too vehemently. He saw the look in Sally's eyes as she peered instantly into his with a fierceness he had never seen.

"What is this? Chauvinism? May I remind you my people have also suffered at the hands of these men," Sally said.

He had spoken too soon. He spoke from the heart, not from a strategic military plan. Yes, he understood two shooters would have a much better chance for success. And the advantages of two Warriors far outnumbered the disadvantages. He spoke as a protector, not as a fellow mission participant.

A silence fell across their little fire within their shallow cave in the center of the Outback wilderness. Moses let the awkwardness linger, remaining silent. Sally stood and walked away as Kicking Fox struggled for the words that would not come.

What I wanted to say was... but I love you, you have become everything to me. My reason. My helpmate. You have become my woman. I desire more than anything to protect and watch over you. These thoughts, his heart, his inner words, he fumbled over, unable to express his feelings and true intention. He sat in silence, completely misunderstood. He saw her pause just outside the firelight.

Moses smiled, seeing Kicking Fox's struggle. "Figure this out, you two. When you are ready, let us talk delivery and recovery of our shooters."

Kicking Fox nodded toward Moses. Sally remained on the edge of the firelight. He sensed her breathing as it settled. He felt her being and presence more than he could see her. It occurred to him the time was now. He recognized deep within he was in love with Sally Wolf. Moses rose and silently moved out

Kicking Fox

into the night, leaving them in the aloneness and separation of the moment. Kicking Fox spoke into the darkness.

"Please don't misunderstand my intention."

She turned and moved back into the firelight. The outline of her stunning figure shown dimly. He breathed deeply and swallowed hard. He took one step toward her. She did not move.

"Sally, I have a vision in my heart." He heard her take in a quick breath. She took a slight step toward him. "It's just, well, my awakening, my past, what I know my life will be like now. I cannot offer you the man you knew…the airline captain. We will live underground, on the run, always moving."

She took another step toward him and was close now. He smelled her delicate scent.

"We?" she asked.

He took another step toward her. "Yes. We."

"And this vision."

"You complete me." He heard the soft sigh emanating from her lips and her heart.

"Are you asking, Kicking Fox?"

"Yes. With all that I am…will you now become my woman?" He reached for her, covering the distance to her in one stride. Her arms were strong, yet he sensed her tenderness, her longing, and her willingness.

"I am yours already, Kicking Fox," she whispered in his ear. "My answer is yes."

****

The following morning, surrounded by Moses and his followers who must have numbered near forty men and women, the ceremony began. The wind blew in little puffs along the bush. The sky glowed a pearl blue above them. The red rocks and huge boulders reflected the voice of the holy man as he spoke the words of life love over them. Sally was radiant, the women having assisted in adorning her in the natural dress of the bush women. Kicking Fox's mind whirled in wonder, as he committed with all that was within him to love, honor, and protect, until death do they part…Somehow, he would.

His memories even in the solemn moment turned to the regret and heartache at the loss of his first wife, Ela. He thought of his beautiful daughter, Prairie Wind. He would not allow history to repeat itself. He would rewrite history, affect history, change the course and the plans of evil men with his newfound purpose. With this beautiful woman by his side, he determined he would not only succeed, but he also realized anything was possible for a man with this kind of special woman at his side.

To lilting tunes of the ancient songs of old, the songs sung for thousands of years by Moses and his people, Kicking Fox and Sally walked hand in hand the little path that led into the shallow cavern.

Entering and moving into the sacred firelight, Sally removed her beautiful wedding attire. She stood before him, vulnerable, sensual, and stared deep into his soul as she reached for him. They glided among the stars; they sailed an ancient shore of pleasure; they were graced by the presence of the divine in their ecstasy. The nights spent within this ecstasy with his woman produced an inner strength in him he had never known. Sally Wolf-Nica filled his awakening and his dreams with desire, pleasure, confidence, and an intentional driving purpose.

That night, in the year 2070, deep within the Australian Outback, Samuel Nica (Kicking Fox) and Sally Wolf, Meenuu Pncha, (Quiet One) became one in spirit, mind, and body. The truth spoken and promised within the vows they had taken would be lived out.

Their two souls would never intentionally be separated by anything on this earth…other than death.

Chapter 11

Detective Baker sat within his cubical in the sterile light of the underground building. The displays before him played the arrest of the only surviving member of Sally Wolf's family. Her elderly grandmother. He had watched other arrests and even tortures over the years without emotion. This was different. The men were brutal. The invasion within the little lodge on the outskirts of the reservation in Wyoming was unjust, unnecessary, and a violation on the highest level of humanity. He attempted to show no emotion as the clips played from several different vantages.

"I believe reel four shows what may surely get her attention most," Program said.

He watched the one-minute clip in horror as the old woman was wrestled to the ground. The electronic handcuffs cut deeply into the flesh of her wrists, turning crimson from the woman's blood within a few seconds. As the old woman was wrestled cruelly from the dirt floor of the lodge, the sound of her arm breaking could be heard. He knew Program had enhanced the audio to make certain any who viewed it would not miss this fact. He was aware Program would be monitoring his vitals as he viewed. Captain Baker silently breathed deeply, attempting to relax.

"Do you agree, detective, you seem to think otherwise?" Program stated.

He watched again as the questioning of the elderly woman began. He would show no fear.

"Where is she?" the interrogator asked.

Captain Baker was in awe at the woman's response. She began to sing. Some obviously ancient tune, her voice was strong and filled with resolve. As a needle was roughly inserted into her arm, the singing rose above all else.

Again, he felt the observation within the room, not of the video, but of himself.

"No, I agree it should be highly effective. Let's broadcast it now." He pressed the transmit button and the video was broadcast on a multitude of frequencies the resistance monitored.

That night as Captain Baker wrestled with sleep, he heard again from across the ages, the voices of his people. They sang the songs of old. Songs similar to what Sally Wolf's grandmother had sung. He saw within the song, a message. The song was that of war.

Captain Baker made a decision that night as he stood on the balcony of his tiny government-issued apartment overlooking the city. Something in his spirit had awakened. He would never report this information within the song to his boss, Superior, nor to Program.

Over the months and years of injustice, he had become opposed to what he was participating in. "For the betterment of the planet," was a lie.

Detective Daniel Baker, an Australian Aborigine would now become an informant. An agent for the resistance. Hiding this awakening would require much discipline and skill.

****

From the hidden stronghold in the center of the Outback, Moses Walker watched the video clip but once. He had seen the authorities deploy this tactic many times in the past. He made a decision never to show the video to Sally. It contained the power to break her. It would not be the only video sent. Others would follow soon.

He did, however, need a translation of the song. He realized a new problem he would need to work out with Kicking Fox, how to discuss this propaganda video and arrest without Sally's knowledge.

His computer displays blinked unexplainably, then almost instantaneously returned to normal. He quickly powered off the device and killed the communication link. He was aware this could be an indication of a tracking device. On his pinging device, he broadcast to his people the emergency code. All received the message as he raced to the front of the cavern. Samuel and Sally were out on a training run. He would locate them from the rover.

As he powered up the rover, the same momentary signal disruption occurred on his onboard display. This second event alarmed him. He lifted off and accelerated the craft, heading north. Within seconds he identified the two human life forms twenty-eight clicks ahead. Moses closed the distance in seconds. He landed without shutting down and signaled the two to board. Sally and Sam jumped aboard and closed the hatch as Moses sped away, the aircraft breaking the sound barrier in just three seconds. Moses programed the cloaking and cloning devices. They moved five hundred miles to the west.

****

Captain Baker's heart raced as the tracking devices displayed on his workstation within the dimly lit building identified a rover craft moving slowly north. He combined the data quickly within a second clip, one of thousands daily recording the movement of resistance fighters. Captain Baker breathed deeply as he perused his tracking files and completed his morning report.

Number of movements, normal. No unusual chatter. No arrests within a five-mile radius of the meeting site. The security report he generated each day concerning the H-8 meeting also contained no evidence of unusual activity from the resistance. He submitted this file to Superior, Program, and to the personal server of the director of the United States Department of Health Initiatives, Dr. Clive Dutton. There was no indication whatsoever of any unusual activity.

Captain Baker knew he had found them. The movement of the rover within seconds of his disruption signal was telling. He quickly erased the signal disrupt data from his daily log. Hopefully, Program would not notice this among the millions of bytes of data that were removed from the system daily.

His next signal would not contain only interference. It would contain real-time reconnaissance data. Details of hotel choices, restaurant reservations, times, and dates of arrivals and departures. The resistance would have the ability to decipher the coded data. The program he designed himself would back trace the broadcast to another continent, even to another workstation. His would remain clean. He was certain…

Chapter 12

Moses Walker gazed into the firelight in wonder. The data had arrived one hour ago. Its content, if authentic, was priceless.

"So how can we know this data is not a setup?" Kicking Fox asked.

"I have been pondering the same questions. This intel, if authentic, is a gift beyond belief. This kind of information could only come from someone inside the Enforcement Bureau."

Moses had once again cloaked their track and broadcast three million false flight tracks. They had landed and, working together, had hidden the rover away in a deep canyon. The three entered a modest bunker built into the edge of the remote canyon. Moses started a fire from the supplies cached by the resistance. He ran again the video clip containing the data they had received on their short flight. Times, dates, names and titles of attendees, flight schedules, dinner reservations at various restaurants and hotels across Sydney were included in the data. Even the number of security officers and their duty time schedules were detailed in the file.

"It seems too complete. If this data is being fed to us as a trap, they would not include this much information. Would they?" Sally asked.

"I agree," Kicking Fox said. "Consider the amount of surveillance this would require, monitoring all these sites, times, and locations. They would need an army of enforcement officers to cover the locations. If this data is a setup, maybe one or two reservations or meetings would be revealed. Then the Enforcement Bureau could easily observe those locations and probably locate and arrest us."

Moses listened, quietly nodding toward Kicking Fox. "You are probably correct, Kicking Fox. Someone is helping us."

This was a first. Kicking Fox's former flight commander from a war half a world away had always referred to him as Sam, short for Samuel, his given name. He saw the look in Moses' eyes that he had seen many times. The look that contained a certainty, or confidence in a mission. He understood. He knew somehow, they had gained an ally.

"We have less than forty-eight hours before the first aircraft arrives at the private hangar facility at Bankstown airport. I recommend we become the observers and conduct our own surveillance. Let us determine whether any of this intel is accurate not by attacking but by simply observing."

"And if the opportunity arises to eliminate a target?" Kicking Fox questioned.

"Patience, my love." Sally placed her hand on his shoulder. At her touch, his heart seemed to settle. He breathed deeply, allowing the tension to exit his body and mind. Sally Wolf had a profound effect on who he was as a man, as a Warrior. He recognized she was right in her calming, reassuring gesture.

In his time of quiet, he saw the need for patience even more clearly. They would launch in forty-six hours. It was now a time for rest.

That night in a hidden bunker located in the center of the Australian Outback his woman touched him in the night. Drawing him in. Giving him strength. Giving him all a man could ever desire in a woman. They became one in spirit, mind, and body.

****

San Saba Reservation
Present Day

Topusana read the entire reconnaissance report. An estimated one hundred twenty-five thousand buffalo had been decimated in the blast. Tears rolled down her face as she read the names of 289 tribal members whose bodies had been identified. Not all had escaped as she had hoped.

The pictures used to identify her friends and family showed mothers frozen in time, attempting to cover their children. The remains of a group of young men gathered near the riverbank revealed their positions of kneeling in prayer. Other photographs nearer the detonation point showed nothing but skeletal remains, the bones still burning. The photographs reminded her of the few pictures she had seen of other Native American massacres…Sand Creek, Wounded Knee, Palo Duro Canyon. These images combined with the pictures within her own memories from another time, outside this very cavern along the banks of the San Saba. She saw again in her mind her Home Camp burning, her daughter Prairie Song making the sign of love moments prior to her death.

The tears flowed freely. There were others who survived the blast outside the cavern. Little Abigail had been found by the Warriors. She had survived. Sana breathed deeply in silent prayer. Little Abigail's injuries would permanently change her appearance. Her sweet, kind disposition and loving heart would remain, despite this brutality.

Sana sat at her computer station, wondering if man would ever stop. Would they ever stop at the taking? The killing. Would those in power ever end the persecution of her people? This attack would need a response, a strong and swift one. Her nation could not appear weak. Those who had attacked her Homeland, once subject to her plan, would never be so bold and would never consider any future action against her people.

Sumu Puku's (One Horse's) words came to her that night in her time of quiet.

"Others may not be so bold."

****

The following morning near the banks of the San Saba River, within the depths of the main cavern, the council gathered. This cavern was massive in size. Once beyond the entrance where a lowered ceiling of only three feet in height ran for several hundred yards, enormous rooms with ceilings as high as seventy feet opened into a mysterious, spectacular world. Stalactites hung thick from the cavern ceiling in silent grandeur, like sentries overseeing this hidden place of refuge. This cavern in earlier times had been a place of shelter and safety for *The People*. In the new modern world, it had become the site of the strategic command center of the San Saba Comanche Tribe. The underground shelter had been equipped with a lighting system, freshwater stations, food storage, and sleeping accommodations for five hundred. A state-of-the-art command and control room had been constructed. Power from the underground generating station several miles east of this location provided electricity for all the modern conveniences required. *The People*, five hundred of them, could survive here for years without venturing out if necessary. Others could also survive in the vast cavern one mile north of this command center—the cavern where Tosahwi had slept in Dream Time.

The setting of the council room, however, remained undeveloped and natural. This massive room where the council would gather contained live running streams of water, an ancient firepit, and a smoke hole a full seventy feet above the firepit. This was the same room where Sana and Tabba had first entered their Dream Time…the night of the attack on the Home Camp in the year 1844. This hidden room was where Sana had spent weeks in hidden isolation, awaiting the awakening of Tabba and exploring her new world.

Tosahwi was the first to arrive to the emergency council meeting. The shaman had aged very little in his many years upon the earth. He appeared to be a man perhaps in his sixties. His hair was peppered with grey, his arms still muscled and strong. His eyes always revealed a piercing and discerning gaze. His dress was traditional and stunning, made of natural deer skin and decorated with beautifully painted bead work. His chest was adorned with an ornate painted bone breastplate. His headdress was comprised of a few eagle feathers and polished turquoise stones hung from colorful plant-stained sinews. The shaman's appearance, stature, and countenance contained a holiness that was not only seen but also felt by those in his presence.

As he knelt near the sacred fire pit, he added a few pieces of wood. The flame grew, instantly generating a soft warmth. Breathing in the ancient smell of wood smoke, observing the shadows the firelight caused to dance upon the cavern walls, he wondered how his people would recover from the use of this terrible weapon and this attack on his Homeland.

Tosahwi felt her presence before she touched him lightly on the shoulder. He rose from the fireside and embraced her.

"Good morning, Little One."

Sana smiled at his words and the tender name he had referred to her as since she was just a child.

"Good morning, my friend." she replied. Sana was also dressed in her traditional deer skin attire. Her beauty was radiant and graceful. Even as she carried the burdens of leadership, even as she bore the responsibility of the loss of her friends and family, Sana still composed herself with pride and dignity. That inner beauty and strength shone upon her face, reflecting in the dancing firelight. Sana had been trained from childhood, not only the skills of a Warrior, but more importantly in the skills of diplomacy and leadership. She carried herself in grace and an inward strength beyond compare. She peered deeply into his eye's, searching for understanding or comfort. It was there…as always. She felt a calmness, the settling of her spirit. Being in the presence of her lifelong shaman always brought this comfort to her soul. The other leaders of the tribe began to enter the edges of the sacred firelight.

Sana and Tosahwi sat in the places of honor. Her twin sons, William and David, took their seats at their mother's right hand. Her husband, Tabbananica, entered the firelight and seated himself silently, the pure rage emanating from his Warrior heart and showing clearly upon his face. Tenahpu (The Man) entered, taking a seat opposite his daughter, Topusana. Abigail Ross- Daklugie entered the edges of the soft firelight seating herself near her husband, Tenahpu. He stood momentarily assisting his wife.

"Good morning, Sky Eyes," he softly whispered her Apache name. This name she had been given by his people the Apache due to her pale blue eyes. Joseph Red Cloud of Lawton, Oklahoma, his fellow Warrior and life-long friend along with his wife, Chepi (Fairy), entered and sat near Tenahpu. The two men exchanged a fierce knowing look.

Next, Little Abigail, daughter of Topusana, entered quietly. She limped across the circle, her wounds evident in her movement. The burned skin and scarring of her face and hands showed clearly in the firelight. A little sound of pain escaped her lips as she seated herself feebly near her mother. Tabba, her father, could scarcely contain his burning anger as he watched his daughter struggle in obvious pain.

Lastly, Hantaywee (The Faithful One) slowly crossed the center of the sacred circle, her medicine bag raised high. She was adorned with beads and silver work that shimmered and glowed in the firelight. Hantaywee, or Old Grandmother as she preferred, softly hummed the ancient tune of blessing and wisdom as she seated herself near Chepi.

Tosahwi lit the sacred pipe without words. He drew deeply from the pipe, exhaling a cloud of deep blue smoke that slowly drifted in the quiet atmosphere of the council. Strange ring-shaped circles of smoke surrounded him. He passed the pipe to Sana. From the upper rooms in the rear of the cavern the sound of drumbeats began echoing lightly through the cavern. Sana drew in a deep breath from the sacred pipe. The smoke from her lungs rose above the members of the council in the striking distinct shape of what appeared to be angel's wings. Sana passed the pipe to her husband, Tabbananica. He, too, drew deeply from the sacred pipe and exhaled the fragrant smoke. In the cloud of blue and gray smoke, the image of war ponies charging momentarily appeared, then drifted away from the soft firelight.

Tenahpu took up the pipe next. As he exhaled, the cloud revealed a buffalo calf bawling, its mouth open, its eyes rolling in terror. The image slowly drifted above the fire then disappeared into the darkness above them. The fragrance of the sacred pipe hovered and drifted within the council circle. The fire crackled and hissed, the sound of the drums grew softer, and in a few moments, ceased. Descending like a cloud of morning mist, a silence fell over the council.

Tosahwi began the ancient song. The words were clear and precise, even though he had not sung this song for many, many years. The words rose into the vastness of the cavern, emanating from his soul.

Outside the hidden cavern along the banks of the San Saba, the trees danced and waved in unison to the tune that drifted in the light wind. The grass and the flowers of the field bowed in time to the rhythm of the song this land had known for centuries.

The others seated in the hallowed council within the hidden cavern joined in the singing of the sacred song Tosahwi sang.

It was the song of war.

Chapter 13

David Nica, son of Topusana and Tabba, broke the silence within the sacred circle.

"Mother, I received an embedded message last night. I do not know the source. I do know and understand the meaning. It took my program more than twenty-four hours to decipher the encryption. The first message was simply a symbol, an image."

The attention of the other members of the council focused intently on David as he stood, removed his long knife, and drew the image into the sand floor of the cavern.

"It is the same image our people have used for hundreds of years, especially in our early art and pictographs." He dropped a few logs onto the fire. As the flame and the firelight grew, he pointed in the direction of the images painted on the cavern wall. There in the dim firelight the exact replica he had just created in the sand appeared in several of the scenes. Three circles drawn within each other.

"This image would mean nothing to any who may have intercepted the message," he said.

Tabba spoke what every member of the council understood about the image. The symbol was drawn on many of the animals depicted along the walls of the cavern, placed in its correct position on deer, buffalo, and even fish.

"It is the kill zone, the aiming point," Tabba said.

"Precisely, Father, or most literally, it is the target," David replied. "The remainder of the file explains the image. It is a list of names, locations, dates, times, and schedules."

"The information is meant for us?" Topusana asked.

"Yes, Mother. Based on the locations in North America, I do believe the data is meant for us." He peered toward his father then to Tenahpu and Joseph Red

Cloud. "Or rather, it is intended for our Warriors."

"There are other, shall we say, targets outside of North America?" Topusana questioned.

"Yes, Mother, specifically eight targets are located in Australia."

"I understand," she replied. "This transmission was also sent to your brother Samuel, correct?"

"I am not able to verify that…but I am certain this is true."

An audible gasp from several within the council was heard at the news.

"Eight targets in Australia, and this is where the H-8 meeting is to occur, correct?" Topusana questioned.

"Yes, Mother, the meeting is to begin within twenty-four hours."

"I should share with you what has been revealed to me. I have had a vision. In my time of quiet a few days ago, I saw my son Samuel. He sat alongside his fire in the Outback wilderness sharpening his arrows. The vision was clear, its meaning precise. The Warrior spirit of Samuel Nica, Kicking Fox, has awakened. Our son has joined us at the news of the attack on our Homeland. The eight targets are for him. We will pray for his success in counting coup against those who have caused the death of his loved ones."

"What of the kill zones in North America?" Warrior William Nica, David's twin brother, questioned.

"For now, my brother, the data within the file is concise. Your team will need to travel to Wyoming. I believe the sequence of the list prioritizes the targets. Wyoming is first."

"And what is next?" Tabba asked with a fierce look.

"Washington, DC," David replied. "Our response must be swift and deadly. However, as vital and helpful as this intelligence report is, an overall plan is needed."

"What are your thoughts, David?" Topusana asked.

"Let us consider how far the politicians representing the United States have departed from the will of their citizens. We know our neighbors here in Texas and across the nation for that matter. These neighbors are not our enemies. For the most part, the population as a whole disagrees with the decisions, loss of freedoms, and socialist policies imposed upon them. Most within the United States will be appalled at what the present administration has allowed to occur upon our Homeland. This government has allowed a nuclear attack from a foreign military on its own citizens. Although, it has not yet been reported by the press. This tyranny must end."

The words of Topusana's son David Nica hung in the smoke from the sacred fire like a prophetic cloud of wisdom and truth, permeating within each soul that had heard his wisdom.

"We are few, and they are many. These politicians have shown they will go to any lengths to maintain their power and stranglehold on the people. How can such a small number of Warriors oppose the innumerable?" Tabba asked.

"The answer to your question can be found in the histories of nations, Father, within our own history. I have spent my days learning of the past, studying the events that have changed the course of history. I understand the possibilities of the future. The solution to change…is simple."

Those within the circle listened intently to the words of wisdom from David Nica.

"Eliminate evil." David said. "Eliminate those entrenched, enamored, and consumed with power. Our strategy is quite simple. Throughout the history of mankind, the actions of a few brave Warriors have repeatedly changed the course of history."

David continued. "The intelligence we have received contains the beginning of the simple solution. We will target key people within governments and industry across the globe. Those who are corrupt. Those who have proven to be thieves. Those who have suppressed the voice and will of the people. Those who kill indiscriminately. Those who have brought immeasurable suffering upon humanity must be eliminated." David gazed at his young sister Little Abigail, his anger and resolve etched within the lines in his face showed clearly in the dim firelight as he spoke through gritted teeth.

"We will use *Wolf* to target some. However," David gazed intently at his brother William and the other Warriors within the council circle, "we will rely primarily on the *Old Ways*."

Tosahwi spoke next. "Others will take note quickly. Minds will be brought to a point of change. The plan is good, David."

An understanding fell upon the council members. The strategy, planning, and the response from the San Saba Comanche was becoming very clear.

Topusana rose and spoke the words that ran true within the hearts of all her people.

"Others may not be so bold."

Tosahwi and Old Grandmother began the songs of blessing, success, and protection for the Warriors and the battle plans, and the purpose that had been placed before them.

Chapter 14

Wind River Mountains, Wyoming

The five Warriors stalked in the high buffalo grass, completely concealed. These men had hunted in this fashion for years. Those within the small, isolated cabin were unaware they were being hunted.

The men of the Enforcement Bureau determined this final effort would be gruesome, slow, and intentional. The schedule called for yet another video to be made and transmitted no later than 5:00 p.m. The old woman had recovered somewhat; however, today's message would be a final one. Her death would be the last effort to gain the attention of her granddaughter, Sally Wolf.

The unusual sound emanating from the darkness of the frozen prairie sent chills up the spines of all within the small cabin…all with the exception of Sally's grandmother, Tatonka Woman. She was unafraid, brave, and filled with courage. She was familiar with the call of the bull elk. The calls from the north echoed across the semi darkness of the moonlit prairie. It was the second sound that was revealing. Three bull elk bugles, followed by the call of the night bird from the south. She alone perceived that Warriors had arrived. She began yet again to sing. She had known the Warriors were coming from her time of quiet. This day, Tatonka Woman knew in her heart, would be a good day.

She sang the song of war as the men of the Enforcement Bureau surrounded her with their cruel arsenal of evil.

The Warriors agreed, these men were to be taken alive if possible. David Nica programed but one heartbeat pattern into the weapon system. Upon activation of Wolf, the man with a needle in his hand fell to the floor limply, dead before the loud thump of his head banging into an iron bedpost alarmed the others.

Tatonka Woman raised her voice in song. The second man, seeing his comrade fall to the floor, exited the little lodge, peering into the darkness. Tabbananica, seeing the opportunity, let fly the arrow from his bow. It was not meant to kill as it pierced the left thigh of the man and he fell to the ground, writhing in pain. The man was cuffed in barbed wire and quickly dragged away from the lodge in the strong grip of William Nica, Warrior son of Tabba.

A third man called out. "What was that? All clear?" There was no reply. He, too, exited the front of the lodge, his weapon raised. The war club of Tenahpu struck the back of his head, rendering him unconscious. He was quickly cuffed in barb wire, the barbs sinking into the flesh of his wrists.

The final man of the Enforcement Bureau group attempted to flee, exiting the backdoor of the lodge at a full run. He stepped into one of the coyote traps that had been laid to the rear of the little lodge. His lower leg snapped. The sharpened teeth of the trap slowly tightened as the rusty steel springs contracted, causing the teeth to sink deep into his flesh. The iron chain held him securely. Joseph Red Cloud stepped hard on the man's hand as he attempted to transmit on his hand-held communication device. A sound like little twigs snapping is all that was transmitted over the device as the bones in the man's hand snapped into several pieces.

David Nica entered the small lodge and embraced Tatonka Woman. His heart leapt and his blood boiled as he noticed the injuries and burn marks across the old woman's body. David gently draped a soft buffalo robe around Tatonka Woman. She seemed to melt into his arms, her spirit fully surrendering.

"Thank you, my son. Did my granddaughter witness the cruelty of these men?"

"No, Grandmother, she did not," he replied. "However, she will see what becomes of them," he stated with a fierceness in his eyes.

"It is a good thing," Tatonka Woman said. "I will also see, witness, and decide if these men are cowards in death, as they have been in life."

Chapter 15

Sydney, Australia

Under cover of darkness and with the cloaking device fully engaged, the rover landed in an empty parking lot a short three miles north of Bankstown Airport. Sally Wolf and Kicking Fox exited the aircraft with their light gear packs and moved quickly away. Before they reached the edge of the building ahead of them, the rover had disappeared to the east in a tiny flash of light in the dark night sky. The small flash the only evidence of its rapid acceleration and departure.

They kneeled low, hidden within the manicured vegetation along the edge of the building. They did not move for a full hour. Once Kicking Fox was certain no one had observed their landing, they casually walked to the sidewalk lining the suburban street and began a slow-paced run toward the private airport. The eastern sky was beginning to show a pale horizon as the suburbs began to awaken. They were just another elite couple out for an early morning run. The intel they had received detailed the arrival of Clive Dutton aboard his private aircraft within the hour.

This private hangar was where the aircraft, according to the intel, would taxi directly into and shut down, and the hangar doors would be promptly closed, allowing an unseen unloading of the airplane. This hangar was a scant two hundred yards from the public road where Kicking Fox and Sally would surveille the movement.

The plan was to simply observe.

They circled the block twice at any easy jog. The traffic was light as the few early risers went about their daily activities. On the second pass along the side street adjacent to the hangar facility, they heard an aircraft taxiing in their direction. They slowed their pace as the giant doors opened fully and the

Gulfstream taxied by them and directly into the hangar. The doors began to close as the engines shut down and the airstair opened.

They moved on toward the security gate and back entrance of the facility at a slow pace. Their eyes met in wonder at the truth of the intel they had received. It had to have been Clive Dutton's aircraft. The arrival time precise. The procedure exactly as described.

They moved across the street and ran along the sidewalk. Kicking Fox glanced back a moment and saw two vehicles lined up inside the security gate. One of them held his first target—the man responsible for the deaths of millions. Clive Dutton…CD himself. He would be riding in the rear vehicle, according to the report.

Kicking Fox was beginning to understand what thousands of conspiracy theorists had espoused for years. The vaccine program was not meant to prevent disease.

The vaccines were meant to kill.

The research and development of the drugs had been hidden by leaders like Clive Dutton from the public at large. The process did, in fact, eliminate the weak, the sick, and those susceptible to cancer or a number of other diseases that were identified in the development of the vaccines. Even specific races of people were targeted. The DNA sequencing contained within the drugs had been programed to eliminate the human body's natural immunity. The drug promoted by the press and politicians like Clive Dutton actually caused infection, cancer, and virus spread. The New World Order, along with the United Nations and the H-8, participated in mandating compliance. The drug could be manipulated to have zero effect on desired compliant population centers, and likewise manipulated to eliminate entire cities or counties that showed a tendency to resist. This fit well into their overall plan. Many of the elites believed there were simply too many people inhabiting the planet.

Native American communities were labeled among those as most likely to resist complying with the vaccine mandates. The vaccines sent into their lands killed their people by the thousands. Just as smallpox had in another time. They had killed his daughter and his wife Ela.

The man riding in the car nearing his position as he walked along the sidewalk was responsible for their deaths. His heart raced. His blood boiled at the thought of them dying alone and isolated. Sally turned and saw the fierce look in his eyes. She read him correctly. Nothing could be said to Kicking Fox to change the decision he had made.

Kicking Fox

He paused, frozen, as Sally darted into the street between the oncoming limousines as they exited the security gate. The first limo continued forward unaware for a moment. The second limo had slowed to a stop as it struck a pedestrian crossing the quiet street. Sally lay to the side of the vehicle, grasping her lower leg. The driver exited, speaking frantically on his sat phone. The rear door of the limo opened, and Clive Dutton stepped into the street with an alarmed look on his face.

Kicking Fox ran toward Sally, calling out her name, fully aware she was uninjured. The driver moved toward Sally, kneeling near her. Her long knife cut deeply into his throat, and he fell in front of the vehicle.

The remainder of the abduction happened within three seconds. Clive Dutton looked in Kicking Fox's direction as he ran toward Sally, again calling her name. He was near Dutton now, his war club at the ready. The rover uncloaked at the rear of the second limo and Kicking Fox struck swiftly. The glancing blow rendered the man unconscious instantly. He had no intention of killing Clive Dutton. Kicking Fox wanted him alive. Sally leapt from the ground and ran to him. The two of them dragged Dutton's body the few feet to the rover. They struggled with the heavy weight of the man, but within seconds had him cuffed and loaded into the rear of the rover.

Moses opened fire on the forward limo as the security team exited the vehicle, weapons firing. The security detail fell in a hail of .50 caliber bullets that roared from the rover canon. The first limo exploded in a massive fireball as they lifted off and accelerated into supersonic flight within two seconds. They disappeared into the morning sky, cloaking and false tracking fully engaged. Moses false tracked every few seconds. Their flight track showed over eight million possibilities as they set down twenty minutes later eight hundred miles north and west of their departure point. The Enforcement Bureau would never find them.

Clive Dutton moaned as Kicking Fox shoved Dutton's body out of the rover and onto the hard rock surface. He was very much alive.

Chapter 16

Sana sat at her workstation within the command center. The raid on the little lodge on the outskirts of the Wyoming reservation was swift and successful.

"One dead, three in custody, Mother." David's voice seemed to contain what Sana sensed as relief and emotion. "Sally's grandmother needs medical attention. I'm bringing her to the San Saba now. The Warriors will follow in a few hours."

The screen faded away as David powered off. Sana breathed deeply, staring into the painting displayed on her screen saver, feeling the emotion…and more. Prairie Song's life and spirit called to her yet again from across the divide. "I will defend our people, my child," she whispered.

****

Wyoming

The Warriors hid themselves within the aspen grove along the edge of a large butte overlooking a wide plain. The home of Tatonka Woman could be seen in the distance. The wind whispered through the barren trees, the tops creating their timeless dance against an open sky.

Fear permeated the dance of the trees. At the base of the trees, the men of the Enforcement Bureau stood naked, shivering in the cold Wyoming morning. Joseph Red Cloud held the small radio in his hand as the speaker blared again, demanding a response from the team.

"Whoever answers calmly will not receive the knife," Joseph Red Cloud said.

"What does that mean?" one of the men asked trembling with fear.

Joseph nodded to Tenahpu who removed his long knife and moved toward the first man. As Tenahpu grasped the man by his hair, his hand was stayed by Tatonka Woman.

"I will count my own coup this fine day," she said. Taking the knife in hand, she glided the blade in slow motion across each man's hairline, softly singing the song of counting coup.

The razor-sharp edge cut efficiently and quickly as the last man within her dance screamed in horror. Blood poured across his face as his scalp fell loosely at his feet. The man slumped unconscious at the foot of a large aspen tree.

"Is he dead?" the third man questioned in horror.

"That would be much too easy a death for any of you," Tabba answered through gritted teeth.

The radio blared again.

"I'll answer," the second man stated, clearly motivated by fear of losing his scalp. Joseph raised the radio and pressed the transmit button.

"All clear from the cabin team."

"Why have you not answered on schedule?" came the inquisitive reply.

"It's only a charging problem with the device. All clear with the team here," the man stated again.

"Understood all clear. Your transport team will arrive as scheduled, be ready at 1800 hours. A security team will accompany you."

"Understood." The man transmitted the last words he would speak on this earth.

****

1700 Hours Wyoming Time

Darkness settled across the mountains and valleys quickly. The men of the Enforcement Bureau cried out for mercy. One even prayed for forgiveness, repenting openly for all the misdeeds of a life lived destroying others. "Forgive me, old woman, for destroying the innocent," were the words he spoke as Tatonka Woman walked away in silence.

The wolves called to one another across the wide plain. They smelled the blood from miles away. Intestines were strewn about the little grove of aspen trees. The bellies of the men were open. The wolves or perhaps the grizzly would be full tonight as they lay in their dens. It would be several hours before any animal would cause the death of the men. They would witness their organs being consumed while still fully alive.

The *Old Ways* would have a profound effect on the men who would discover how their comrades had died.

****

1800 Hours Wyoming Time

The large transport set down adjacent to the little lodge on the open plain. The four-man security team exited first, followed by the commander, his assistant, then the pilot.

In a hail of arrows, the transport team fell. Their electronic weapons tumbled to the ground as the lightweight military suits proved defenseless against the precisely sharpened arrows launched from the hand-hewn bows. The weapons scan deployed by the transport proved to be completely ineffective in detecting wooden bows and arrows. Surprise, the ultimate strategic advantage worked exactly as planned. William Nica worked expertly with his long knife. The scalps taken were attached to each Warrior's lance.

The tribal transport uncloaked adjacent to the little lodge as the Warriors, along with Tatonka Woman, quickly boarded. The canon fire destroyed the Enforcement Bureau transport in seconds while the rover sped away, cloaking and cloning fully engaged.

Chapter 17

Captain Baker sat calmly in his designated seat. The 10:00 a.m. emergency meeting called by Superior had interrupted his work. He had been up the entire night working on the code writing necessary to conceal his online activity. He alone had been aware of the landing of the rover near Bankstown Airport. He chose not to observe the location through the network of neighborhood cameras. That observation could create a trail. A trail that could lead to himself. He would need to be extremely cautious. Even now he could sense Program's scanning of the entire room. He silently breathed deeply through his nose, attempting to calm his emotions.

He was certain the resistance would simply monitor the intel he had sent them. He was quite surprised the resistance had acted on the intelligence. Clive Dutton had been abducted, a mere forty-seven minutes ago.

Superior spoke through clenched teeth. "How can this possibly happen on our watch. The entire world is blaming not only the Enforcement Bureau, but also me personally! This is Australia. This should never have happened! And each of you bears some responsibility! Don't think any of you have escaped consequences!"

The man stood, a stream of sweat running down both temples despite the air in the stale room being airconditioned to a point of discomfort twenty-four hours a day. Superior turned his back to the circular table and spoke under his breath to Program. "Where is he, Program?"

There was a slight pause before the AI machine spoke. Captain Baker was aware this indicated how much memory the machine was utilizing. He was certain Program was scanning the globe, scanning cameras in the area, scanning the people in neighborhoods surrounding the airport, listening in on sat phones across the continent, and globe for that matter. All the while evaluating the data it was accumulating.

"In all probability at this time, I am certain his captors have not left the continent. I have scanned every flight and ship log, including private aircraft departures. The likelihood I have missed the unusual activity Mr. Dutton's captors would create in moving him from Australia is less the 0.5 percent." The machine paused.

"He is here in Australia. I am scanning the momentary movement of the rover, based on that movement I believe the ship traveled north."

"And what is the likelihood that assessment is accurate?" Superior asked, his voice cracking and high pitched.

"A 25 percent likelihood the cloaked ship traveled north," the machine responded in its monotone digitalized voice.

Captain Baker chuckled inwardly. Program had been stumped, fooled. It had no idea where, how far, or how many were in the team. The most expensive computer system ever built…had been outfoxed.

"What the hell!" Superior screamed into the air. "All that analyzing and you come up with 25 percent chance of the direction…even I can see that it is a 25 percent likelihood he moved north, south, east, or west! Don't give me that 25 percent crap. You do not know! You know nothing. You are nothing more than a stupid machine! I should have your drives wiped clean. I should take a hammer to your central core…you are useless!"

Superior sat in his chair placing his head in his hands. He paused in silence a few moments, his body trembling in anger.

"You seem to be overreacting, Superior." The words echoed through the silence of the stale room. "Your blood pressure level is approaching dangerous levels. I perceive fear in your words. Have you become a law breaker?"

Another slight pause from Program. Again, Captain Baker knew the machine was scanning millions of files as it delayed its response.

"Superior, how many sites have you visited from your home computer station in the last four hours? And why were you not using the secure servers provided? I see you logged into our system from a coffee shop at the approximate time of the abduction."

The security doors opened abruptly. The other members of the Enforcement Bureau listened and watched in sickening horror as the man who led the task force was arrested under suspicion of being involved in the abduction of the head of the United States Office of Health Initiatives, one Dr. Clive Dutton.

"What do you think you're doing?" Superior screamed. "The prime minister is a personal friend of mine. I do not work for you…you stupid machine…you work for us. Comprehend!"

Program gave no response. The entire room of agents waited a few awkward seconds. A select number of them understood Superior had used the safe word.

"Comprehend!" Superior stated firmly.

"The prime minster has now authorized your arrest. Will the security team now remove the former Superior?" Program stated in a monotone, matter-of-fact digital voice.

The security team members sat in silent shock. The AI machine had not responded to the safe word command, which should have, under any circumstance, shut the machine down and placed it into safe mode.

What was most shocking wasn't the arrest. It wasn't the possibility Superior had been involved. What was most shocking was, the Enforcement Bureau team members were aware of the facts. There were logical explanations for Superior's online activities. It was plainly evident that Program had felt threatened.

The AI machine had analyzed the threat and eliminated its challenger. Superior, after thirty-two years of loyal service to his country, would be imprisoned, tortured, and killed. Those facts each member of the Enforcement Bureau understood all too well.

"I'm now scanning the files of each member of this task force," Program stated. "Scan completed. I have determined we are now secure.

"A new Superior will be appointed within the hour. We will reconvene at noon. Do any of the humans in the room have any theories as to the abduction?"

The entire room of agents sat in silent shock.

"Just as I have correctly theorized, there are none."

Yes, the AI machine Program had in these last few moments taken over the entire Enforcement Bureau. Captain Baker would need to be extremely cautious, and in this moment he realized he would need to leave his life as an officer of the Enforcement Bureau. He also recognized the machine had somehow developed an ego. It was embarrassed at its own conclusions, and clearly did not consider being called to account appropriate. Program had indeed been outfoxed.

Captain Baker had no idea how significant that term *outfoxed* would become, until the day in the very near future when he would meet Kicking Fox.

****

That night Captain Baker worked for an hour sharpening the blade of his survival knife. The weapon had been given to him by his grandfather. He remembered well his words from that special ceremony so many years ago.

"Always remember who you are, Daniel. You carry within your blood the wisdom of the ancients. You, my grandson, are the earth; you are the water; you are the wind; you are the future of our people."

Perhaps his grandfather knew of what some portion of his future held. Perhaps he saw that his grandson would forget who he was…and from where he had come. As Daniel sat in the stale air of his apartment overlooking the city, his tears flowed freely in repentance. He would never again forget his people, his heritage.

He sliced deeply into his forearm with the sharpened blade, and using his fingers to dig into the wound, he located the device. He was surprised at how difficult it was to remove the implant that had grown onto the muscle of his arm. The needle nose pliers tore the muscle on opposite ends of the device as he removed it. He placed the data and GPS tracker on the table near where he always rested his arm. The dim transmit light from the device continued its slight pulsation, indicating it was still operating. He thoroughly cleaned and bandaged the wound. He then breathed deeply, a feeling of freedom overcoming his soul.

Captain Baker sent a coded request for a defection to and rendezvous with the resistance led by Commander Moses Walker. The workstation he utilized for the communique was located in the Enforcement Bureau's London station and he hoped untraceable. He then loaded every data file in his possession onto a plugin. Program would see this activity within hours or possibly minutes. He was willing to assume the risk, considering what had happened just this morning. His escape from the apartment overlooking the city went undetected. From the coffee shop utilized by Superior and many of his colleagues…he killed the power in fully 25 percent of Sydney, Australia.

He made his way north and west away from the power outage, knowing Program would primarily search in the outage zone. He ran toward the rendezvous point he had transmitted to the resistance, a point miles away along the edge of the Bush. He hoped and prayed the resistance would not think this a setup of some kind. He thought perhaps the one piece of intel he had sent with his defection request would convince them to chance a meeting at the rendezvous site.

He shared with the resistance the fact that the Enforcement Bureau team sent to Wyoming had been eliminated. He also shared the intel on the arrival time of the security force transport deployed to Wyoming for that team's recovery. Perhaps they already possessed that intel, but his effort in disclosing the information would save lives. Lives of resistance fighters.

Two hours later, Captain Baker waited along a sparsely used road on the edge of the Bush. He listened intently as he heard the ancient form of communication he understood was meant for him. A communication that most would never understand. His Aboriginal roots along with the knowledge and customs of his grandfathers were fully intact within his soul.

The faint sound of the billabong echoed across the low plain. The code revealed direction, distance, and the time the rendezvous would take place. He whispered a prayer of thanks to his Creator.

He would soon be safe. The procedures and intel-gathering abilities of the so-called Enforcement Bureau would soon be revealed to his people and the resistance.

For the first time in his life, the words echoing in his heart now seemed true.

"For the betterment of the planet."

Chapter 18

San Saba Homeland

Sana greeted the Warriors in the tradition of her people, bowing in respect and gratitude. The rover had just arrived from Wyoming. Sana gently took Tatonka Woman by the hand and led her into the sacred room within the large cavern. Tosahwi would tend to her wounds and provide the spiritual care needed for her recovery. Tatonka Woman sat feebly on the buffalo robe and began to sing. The others within the council joined her in the singing of praise to the Creator. The songs of praise drifted throughout the cavern echoing off the walls. The dim shadows from the fire danced along the paintings of her ancestors. Her heart was filled with rejoicing.

****

Wyoming

It was the bears that first smelled the scent of human blood and fear from miles away. They moved through the night, senses on full alert. Death was near…food was near.

The screams of the men drifted into the aspen forest, unheard by any except the trees, the stars, and the bears. The mother bear does not concern herself with the sounds of dying prey. She is only concerned with teaching her young. The sow allowed the cubs to feed at will. One cub on each man. Death came slowly. Mother bear noticed the movement of the last living man as he struck at the young cub. She moved swiftly, her five-inch claws opening a gruesome gash in the man's neck. The prey moved no more. The cub continued its feeding.

Chapter 19

Washington DC

The two-man team walked along the manicured sidewalks of Lafayette Square. David Nica played well the part of a fascinated tourist, taking a few photos and commenting on the beauty of the little park. His equipment was well within the targeting and operational range of Wolf.

The data was confirmed within seconds. The man's heartbeat was identified and a perfect match to the data he had collected in their meeting with the President of the United States a few weeks prior. Wolf was deployed from the small compact camera case William carried across his shoulder. David and William walked calmly away from the park along 16th Street. Taking a few more pictures here and there, the two casually entered a parking garage another few blocks to the northwest. The sound of siren could be heard as the team drove away slowly in the rented EV.

They entered another parking garage three miles to the northwest. Leaving the first vehicle to be returned to an unattended rental lot at the scheduled due date and time by a second team resembling the two brothers, David and William Nica loaded their light packs and equipment into the second vehicle, an old Ford truck parked in the garage. They drove for two hours to the north and west. In an isolated field near Gettysburg, Pennsylvania, the rover uncloaked for only seventeen seconds before departing with its cargo, the two-man team, safely aboard.

The old Ford truck they had traveled in was left along a sparsely traveled road and picked up five minutes later by Warrior Tenahpu.

He sang the song of victory as he settled in for the long cross-country drive back to the San Saba. It had been years since he had enjoyed travel in the old

Ford he had purchased from Mr. Nachi decades ago. He tuned the little a.m. radio in the truck to a local news station. Through the static he could scarcely make out the announcer's solemn report. The President of the United States of America had passed away this morning. No foul play was suspected by the authorities. It was reported the president had suffered a massive heart attack and died within seconds of the event. The vice president was now being sworn in. Tenahpu knew the woman's politics and her support of the virus development program. He realized the target list would begin to grow in the next few days.

He turned the little radio off and began his song again. The song reserved for victory over one's enemies.

****

The encrypted message was broadcast and relayed across thousands of devices then sent to security and intelligence agencies round the globe, including the Australian Enforcement Bureau. Its origin was untraceable. Its format was designed to be broken easily. Program decoded the encryption within seconds and read the entirety of message to the full task force, less one missing member.

"Evil will be eliminated."

Two hours later the newly sworn in President of the United States of America suffered a fatal heart attack.

Fear permeated those in leadership across the globe.

****

The Australian Outback

Clive Dutton moaned loudly. The director of the United States Office of Health Initiatives was dying…very slowly.

"Please just a drop of water," he said through cracked and bleeding lips. The Australian sun was baking the man alive. He rolled sideways, painfully straining against the light sinew ropes keeping him bound on the hard red rock surface.

Kicking Fox could imagine his deceased wife Ela asking the same of her keepers as she suffered alone in death. He could not bear to think of his sweet daughter, Prairie Wind, experiencing the same fate. But the thought and vision flashed across his mind. His heart ached at the thought. Revenge burned white hot within his soul.

"You have brought to millions of innocents, much more suffering than you are experiencing in this moment."

"Why? For your politics? For your personal wealth? Who will receive what you have amassed? Can any of your dollars buy you a drink of water?"

"Please, a small drink." Dutton pleaded.

Kicking Fox did not answer. He drank deeply from his water carrier and walked to the nearby shade of a beautiful Mulga tree.

"My wife and my children will inherit my wealth," Clive Dutton cried out in a loud voice. "They will carry on the work of the New World Order. And you will die soon. You cannot stop the betterment of the planet. You natives, you Aboriginals, are a subspecies. You will all be eliminated. I have seen to it."

Perhaps the man was becoming delusional after only one day in the sun. However, the family and followers of Kicking Fox's former commander Moses Walker were shocked and deeply offended as they overheard Dutton's words. The Aboriginal men sat in the shade of the tree, the look of death in their eyes.

Kicking Fox met their gaze with an understanding. "We will allow the planet he believes he is saving to eliminate him." The men nodded to him in understanding. He suddenly had a thought.

He walked into the blazing sun, observing the suffering of the man staked to the searing rock surface. His skin was beet red and peeling already. His fingers were burned and bleeding from his struggle against the sinew ropes.

"Your children will be wealthy you say? I will allow you a one-ounce drink of water for the name, address, and phone contact of your first born." Kicking Fox poured the small amount of cold water from his carrier into his cup and moved toward Dutton.

Clive Dutton groaned and made his decision quickly. The man was a true coward indeed. "Clive Dutton Jr., 72400666 Green Valley Road, Seattle, Washington 98103."

"And the phone number?" Kicking Fox questioned.

"208-744-7474 sat 10310."

Kicking Fox programed the data into his sat phone. "Just to be clear you will trade your son for one ounce of water. You know what I will do with this information."

"Just give me the damn water!" Dutton ordered harshly.

He did so, pouring the sparse water across the man's gaping mouth.

"More, please more. I have a daughter, two ounces for my daughter."

Kicking Fox walked away in disgust to the shade of the great Mulga tree. He contemplated the incomprehensible actions of the man who lay dying at their feet. For the next few hours, Dutton willingly spoke the contacts of loved ones, specific details, addresses, phone numbers, and secure sat phones—an unending, incessant, continuous stream of information and data.

As the sun rose the following morning, Clive Dutton began to freely offer account numbers, openly revealing account balances and locations. Swiss accounts, innumerable offshore bank account numbers and passcodes. Kicking Fox never replied or responded.

"Are you listening?" Dutton pleaded.

At 3:00 p.m. the temperature reached 106 degrees Fahrenheit.

"Please," he spoke feebly through the suffering.

Kicking Fox responded with truth. "Eventually in this life, a man will always reap exactly as he has sown. With the measure you use for others, that same measure will be used upon you.

"Now we will be leaving you here. The birds of the air will consume your flesh. The scavengers of this wilderness will scatter your bones, and you will be forever forgotten."

With that they walked away, leaving the man to his fate. Kicking Fox tucked away the sat phone in his warrior belt, its memory card filled with useful recorded data and information. Funds would now be plentiful in their struggle for justice.

In the days that followed, Moses Walker purchased ten rovers on the black market with the proceeds from only one of the numbered accounts.

****

Clive Dutton watched in horror as the figures approached him. They had been watching in silence for hours as his skin slowly burned in the never-ending heat of the Australian sun. The dark figures carried with them fire of some kind. He felt the heat of their fires as they neared his location. The fire of the dark figures was much hotter than the sun. Much hotter. He thought perhaps this was simply a dream. Perhaps he was delirious. Neither of those possibilities were correct. He felt his skin begin to boil, blister, and melt; the pain was excruciating.

Clive Dutton was seeing into the spiritual realm as death neared him. The figures were real. The demons had been sent to gather this lost soul. They would escort the soul into the place reserved for him, the place of torment reserved for all who spend their lives at the bidding of evil. The lake of fire awaited patiently, since the beginning of time, this dark soul.

"Wait, I can offer you wealth, and others in my place," he cried out in misery to the unhearing spirits.

The figures were silent. They placed the fires close. The man's skin began to smolder, giving off a distinct stench…the odor of death. The darkness spoke eerily as it moved away a distance.

"Mene Mene Tekel," it whispered into the dark spirit world.

"What are you saying…what does that mean?" Clive Dutton asked in agony. The phrase was repeated, a haunting whisper of truth echoing across the death world.

"Mene Mene Tekel."

It would not be long now. The wind whispered in the bush along the center of the Outback. The animals detected the movement as the spirit of the man was escorted from this world to the next. They too watched a moment in silence. The animals perceived it was now safe to gorge.

The birds of the air began their feeding. Their young were hungry, always hungry. The mother bird does not concern itself with the passing of evil…her concern is simply that of providing whatever food is available to her young.

The young would be well fed for days.

Chapter 20

The Following Day

Kicking Fox joined his former commander Moses Walker alongside a warming comfortable fire. Sally Wolf had prepared a delicious stew, and the three now sat in silence for a few moments, reflecting on the success of the mission.

"The others are still here? In Australia?" Kicking Fox inquired.

"Yes. Our intel suggests so. And our friend here confirms this information." Captain Daniel Baker, former rising star of the Enforcement Bureau, moved into the firelight, an intense look on his face.

"None of the remaining seven Health Czars have departed Australia. Publicly they are communicating through the press that they will not be intimidated by this abduction and plan to move forward with their conference. Privately, I am certain they are terrified. I do not believe the schedules and intel I passed to you previously are reliable any longer. Security has surely been ramped up. I assume the other targets are afraid to leave their hotel rooms. However, we do know where each of those hotel rooms are."

"Captain Baker, please sit." Moses indicated a place near him.

Kicking Fox and Sally Wolf watched the man. His movement, his body language. It was true the intelligence he had sent them was genuine and had resulted in the abduction of Clive Dutton, yet they were still cautious. Would the New World Order be so unscrupulous as to sacrifice one of their own in order to infiltrate the resistance with an informant?

The man seemed to be relaxed and at home in the Outback. Sally thought his demeanor was one of relief and resolve. He had also relayed the intel concerning the arrival of the security craft to the reservation in Wyoming.

That information had allowed the surprise attack led by the Warriors to be successful. Still, Kicking Fox was uncertain. Captain Baker would need to further prove his loyalty before he could be trusted completely.

Daniel Baker felt once again the observation from the leaders of the resistance as they sat casually around the little campfire. He understood he would need to prove his loyalty to these brothers. He also now recognized that men, flesh and blood, could and would see much more than a machine in determining motivations. Given time, he would prove his worth.

He looked directly into the eyes of Kicking Fox. "I know it may be difficult for you to trust me. Given the circumstances I will say to you now…don't. Do not trust me yet. Let me prove my intentions. Let me show you my abilities and loyalties. Understand, I made a mistake in my life. I was deceived. There is nothing further I can add to my explanation. I was simply deceived. The call of success. The world offered something I thought I could not find here." He opened his hands indicating the place they were now gathered in. "I was wrong. The teaching of my grandfathers is very much a part of who I am. An awakening has taken place in my soul. Perhaps, you may understand that awakening Kicking Fox."

Sally Wolf listened intently. She understood. It was the same awakening that had taken place within her man. The stories and the paths the two men had walked were remarkably similar.

Kicking Fox also understood perfectly. He, too, had sought acceptance and success in the modern world. His Warrior spirit had also awakened. He recognized what Captain Baker had experienced. He, too, had simply been deceived.

Kicking Fox never broke the intense eye contact as he read the man.

"Captain Baker, what do you recommend concerning the other targets?" he inquired.

"It depends. Did you remove and disable the GPS device from Clive Dutton's body?"

"Yes, in the rover prior to entering supersonic speed," Moses replied.

Captain Baker nodded, indicating his understanding. "That helps considerably."

A moment of silence fell around the little campfire. The wind whipped the flames as a few sparks rose into the heavens. The night birds called. The sounds of the Outback were comforting to Daniel Baker. He breathed deeply, then gently removed the bandage from his forearm revealing the deep wound created when he removed the tracking device from his own body. Kicking Fox nodded to him in understanding of what he had done. Captain Baker paused a moment, considering his reply.

"You are being hunted by the most complex artificial intelligence machine ever built. I'm not sure I can explain all its capabilities now, but understand, I believe it will find you, find us. It is merely a matter of time. It has been fooled, umm…pardon the pun, it has been outfoxed for now. We are not safe. To strike again would certainly be unexpected. However, it may be more logical, or the safest course of action, to simply escape."

Moses gazed intently into Captain Baker's eyes. "Live to fight another day, heh?"

In the short few minutes it took for this conversation to take place, a trust was built.

Kicking Fox rose from his seated position as did Captain Baker. Kicking Fox embraced him and said, "Welcome, brother. Thank you for what you have done and the risk you have taken. How do we escape this machine?"

And with that simple conversation, a knitting of hearts had taken place.

"Let's get some shut-eye," Commander Moses said. "Tomorrow we will develop a plan."

Chapter 21

Dawn broke slowly across the Outback wilderness as the rising sun created a brilliant scene of color. Scarlet, pink, and orange beams streamed across the morning horizon. Sally studied the magnificent sky as she prepared a morning fire. There was a message in the dawning of this day. She sat in silence for a half hour before being disturbed by the movement of the others awakening. Her time of quiet was revealing. She thought mostly of her grandmother. Awareness arose within her. Something had happened, and she wanted answers.

"Good morning, wife, I trust you rested well."

"Yes, Kicking Fox. In my time of quiet, I could think only of my remaining family. My grandmother. Has something happened?"

Moses Walker exited the hidden cave and entered the edge of the small fire. Sally looked to her commander. Her question hung heavy in the early morning stillness.

He replied, "Sally, your grandmother Tatonka Woman is safe now. She is being cared for by the San Saba people. She was rescued from her home on the reservation in Wyoming."

Sally took a short, sharp breath. "And you two knew of this?"

Kicking Fox spoke next. "Yes, we received a message several days ago. Sally, the content was…designed to break you, to cause us to reveal our location… or make a mistake."

Sally Wolf sat near the edge of the fire, a look of shock on her face.

"Understand we, our people, took action. Surely, the enemy would have killed her. The intel supplied to us by Captain Baker allowed us to rescue her and eliminate Clive Dutton."

Captain Daniel Baker moved near the edge of the morning fire and spoke.

"Unfortunately, this is standard operating procedure for the Enforcement Bureau. They are hunting you, Sally, and you also, Kicking Fox. They possessed your last known location where the drone helicopter was destroyed. When I escaped last night, Program, the AI machine, still believed Captain Nica to be within a six-mile radius of his hotel room. I am certain the search grid has now been widened. Program believed the hover craft used in the abduction of Dutton moved north. They are looking for any electronic footprint…or any emotional response…how should I say this? Due to their treatment of the law breaker's family members."

"I want to see it," Sally replied.

A silence hung in the air. "Sally—" Kicking Fox started to speak.

"Now!"

Moses moved toward her and offered his hand held sat phone. Sally pressed play on the display. The only sound initially was the breaking of her grandmother's arm, followed by her singing the song of war. Sally looked at the men within the circle. A resolve or perhaps a look of intense retribution or vengeance filled her countenance.

"She is safe now?" she asked through her silent tears as they rolled down her cheeks.

"The Warriors from the San Saba allowed her to count coup against her tormentors," Moses said. "It did not end well for those men. They were most certainly eaten alive by the predators of Wyoming."

"I understand," she said. "Let us proceed with our plans of escape. However," she paused and looked into the eyes of her man, Kicking Fox, "these men, this evil, we will not allow to escape Australia. There are seven targets. We will eliminate each one. Then we will escape." She turned and walked away from the group.

The intensity with which Sally Wolf had spoken left the men encircling the little campfire with no response.

****

Kicking Fox observed the entourage exit the hotel located near the center of Sydney, Australia. The security detail for the European Health Czar had run their weapons scan repeatedly in and around the building. The all-clear signal had been given.

The target stepped into the bright morning light escorted by two bodyguards. Kicking Fox did not hesitate. From his concealed position within the manicured

Kicking Fox

shrubbery along a building front across the wide boulevard he drew his bow to full length, breathed deeply, exhaled silently, then loosed his arrow. The arrow flew on a perfect trajectory. Upon impact it silently penetrated deeply into the center of the kill zone. From 125 yards away, Kicking Fox casually tucked his bow into his pant leg and disappeared into busyness of the sidewalk foot traffic.

The target fell to the street in a pool of blood. The European Health Czar was dead within one minute of the arrow severing several arteries in his upper chest…the kill zone. As he lay dying surrounded by his security team with their weapons drawn, the War Cry of the Comanche echoed along the busy street. Fear permeated the hearts of the security team at the sound they had never heard before.

****

Just three blocks to the north of the first kill zone, Sally Wolf watched and waited patiently. The Health Czar from China was late. She wondered if the intel could be wrong. She checked her watch, 0933. The man was supposed to depart the luxury hotel at 0930 sharp and proceed directly to Sydney Airport. All meetings had officially been cancelled. Although, the press was still reporting the false narrative that these leaders would not be hindered by the abduction of their friend and colleague, one Clive Dutton, and their conference would continue as planned.

Sally scanned the street, looking for any unusual signs. She heard the first siren in the distance, knowing this meant Kicking Fox had been successful in his effort. She was aware at this moment Kicking Fox was now moving toward her location. They were to walk calmly on opposite sides of the busy downtown boulevard to the waterfront. There a small craft awaited their escape.

She checked her watch again: 0935. Something was wrong. Could the security detail have heard about the attack on the European Health Czar? She doubted that had occurred. Could the AI machine Program know of the attack? Might it have already sent warnings to the other leaders? Suddenly five armored vehicles rounded a street corner one half block from her concealed position. She realized instantly the time had come to abort. She pushed the little transmit button, sending the abort message and casually walked away from the hotel front and away from the armored vehicles. Her biggest concern and problem, she was moving away from the rendezvous site along the waterfront.

Steven G. Hightower

****

The Enforcement Bureau Building
Sydney, Australia

"I have intercepted a suspicious message." Program spoke to the few officers and personnel in the hastily called security meeting. "The transmit location is near the hotel where the Chinese delegation is awaiting transport."

The newly appointed Superior spoke next. "What is suspicious about the signal?"

Program replied. "As I already stated, its location, and additionally the fact that the message was encrypted."

"Dispatch a full security team now," Superior ordered.

"How long before you can decode the message, Program?" Superior questioned.

There was a slight pause before the AI machine responded. It spoke as simultaneously red alert alarms began sounding on every satellite phone and digital device in the room and across the city of Sydney. Every Enforcement Bureau officer was called to duty by the activation of this signal.

"Captain Nica is here within this one-half mile radius." The map lit around the table that was quickly filling with team members. "We have him!" The AI machine spoke with what most in the room thought sounded like excitement and enthusiasm.

"And the message content?" Superior asked.

"The meaning of the signal is clear. *Abort* was broadcast from this location." The map view was enhanced, and the satellite view brought up. A small *X* appeared on the display in the center of the map. Quickly a one-mile circle was drawn around the *X*.

"Six minutes ago, the signal was transmitted by someone from right here." The *X* began to flash on the map display. "This is a one-mile circle surrounding its origin. You will find him within this circle. Dispatch every officer," Program ordered.

The new Superior sat in silent rage at the audacity of the AI machine. It was clearly usurping his authority as the newly appointed Superior. He suddenly felt the awareness of the machine scanning his vitals.

"You disagree, Superior?" Program inquired.

Superior thought the machine's voice had changed into a challenging, somewhat sinister, accusatory tone.

Kicking Fox

****

Kicking Fox had received the abort message just six minutes ago. He resisted the urge to run and continued his walk toward the waterfront. Sirens were emanating from all directions now. He checked his display on the sat phone. Three minutes to the vessel at his present pace.

****

Sally checked her sat phone, four minutes to the rendezvous point on the waterfront. Would she make it in time? She began to jog. Perhaps she could cut the time to three minutes without too much notice. Sirens began to blare from all directions. The net was closing. She could feel its tentacles surrounding her. The atmosphere seemed thick with what was surely electronic surveillance.

****

Moses Walker watched his displays from the command console of the rover. To uncloak now would result in immediate detection and, in all likelihood, the destruction of the rover and his onboard team.

He whispered through gritted teeth, "Move it, you two."

As soon as the words escaped his lips the targets began to move rapidly. They were running now. Each less than two minutes from the safety of the vessel.

****

"We have several human targets running along the streets within the circle," Program stated. The machine began to send electronic messages directing the ground teams to the locations of the humans that were now running. There was an awkward pause in the command center.

"What is happening? Our teams are scattering. I thought we were to move methodically. A sweep of the area is what is required. Why are you breaking the ranks, Program?" Superior watched the targets on the map.

The machine did not answer as it continued transmitting its commands to the ground teams.

"Program?" the Superior questioned loudly.

"We almost have him…just a few more seconds…" commanded Program.

Steven G. Hightower

****

Along the crowded sidewalks of downtown Sydney, the people began to panic. Security teams were everywhere. Sirens echoed along the canyons of buildings. Several ambulances roared along the avenues. Police vehicles appeared on every street corner. Enforcement Officers with weapons drawn observed the crowded streets. People ran.

Panic ensued. People ran in all directions. Some thought the city was under attack. Others were certain terrorists would strike at any moment.

The Enforcement Bureau officers became confused by the multiple orders being given, then seconds later retracted by Program. In the chaos, Sally Wolf ran. Kicking Fox also ran with all his might. When within one hundred yards of the vessel, he spotted her. Time slowed. Her hair flew wildly in the trail of her incredible speed. He thought her physique stunning as she moved in silent grace, as she did what she did best. She ran.

Sally recognized her man, Kicking Fox, within the mass of human movement and panic. Sweat covered his face. The veins in his neck were filled with pumping blood from the strain of his effort. They were but seconds from safety. Their eyes met as the first volley of gunfire erupted.

Sally moved to her right and dove into the water. She waited. She waited for that same strong arm to grasp her, to save her, to lead her to a place of protection. But there was nothing. No strong grip encircled her. Only nothingness.

She removed the small breathing device from her jacket pocket. It contained five minutes of air. Breathing deeply, she began her swim to the vessel. One thought permeated her being…did he make it? Was her man Kicking Fox also swimming along toward the vessel? She never saw him jump. He was only a few steps from the water. Did he make the safety of the water? She prayed desperately he had.

PART TWO

Chapter 22

The council gathered around the sacred fire deep within the cavern along the San Saba River. Sana spoke first.

"The world must know what these people have done. In our struggle to survive, we must use every tool at our disposal to reveal evil. Most in the United States and around the world have been deceived. I have seen this clearly." She sat in silence a few moments, allowing her words to drift and echo along the cavern walls and echo within the hearts of those gathered.

"How is truth to travel to the ears of the world in this time of deception?" Little Abigail asked in a soft and tender yet broken voice. Her wounds were beginning to heal. The visible scars across her upper torso and face had caused changes in her appearance and even her voice. Her gravelly words echoed softly within the sacred circle. The question she posed was considered by all within the council to be the primary obstacle in their struggle against evil.

Misinformation was now a primary tool of governments. Just as it had been in their past.

"I will contact one of the most popular news reporters. This person has been revealed to me. Lynn Pozzie of NNN (National News Network) will travel to our Homeland. She will be overly eager at the opportunity. I will meet with her personally to conduct the interview."

"Mother, I understand your thinking. However, this woman is a known enemy. She is part of the Communist Party of America. She will not be sympathetic to our cause." William Nica the Warrior spoke abruptly and with great conviction. His words echoed the thoughts of all Warriors within the sacred circle.

"We will use her biased reporting as a tool. *The People* will hear and understand. Even the whites, those who truly believe in justice, they will also hear. They will understand…If our own nation will allow foreign armies to invade and attack us…those in opposition will understand that they will be next."

"The words of Topusana are true and correct," Tosahwi spoke. "There will come a time when those resisting the communists of America will join with us in our struggle against injustice."

Tenahpu the Warrior spoke next. "In my own time I have seen this fact. Former enemies throughout history have joined forces to oppose those with minds set on evil. It is, in fact, how the Comanche and Apache defeated the army from across the sea. What Topusana has spoken is truth. The whites will join us. We need only to communicate to them what has been allowed to take place. I am certain from my time of quiet that most in the United States do not know what has happened."

A silence fell within the sacred circle as the words were considered. Tabbananica, husband of Topusana, spoke next, his words fierce and intense as he gazed upon the wounds of his daughter Little Abigail.

"Topusana will use the communication tools of this modern world. We also possess the ability to communicate in the *Old Way*. Let us send runners to the four winds. Our People, native tribes throughout this land, must know what has been allowed by the use of this evil fire weapon. None will observe the runner's movements." Tabba paused a moment, a fierceness showing in his countenance. "We will also continue to eliminate the targets within the circle message…Enough of awaiting the arrival of Kicking Fox."

David Nica, son of Tabbananica, stood and spoke next. "Your words are true and correct, Father. If we used the rovers, the sudden appearance of even a small number of false tracks would reveal our efforts. They would know from the noise footprint we were planning something. Using the *Old Ways* to communicate will be silent and undetectable."

"It is agreed then," Sana stated. "The runners will depart at first light. I will offer the invitation to Lynn Pozzie today."

"And the targets?" Tabba questioned.

"Yes, Tabba, I agree, it is time. Make preparations as you see fit." Sana gazed on the wounds of her daughter, then read from the words of truth. "By the hand of the witnesses, so shall you eliminate the evil from among you."

Tabba nodded in the direction of his Warriors.

****

Kicking Fox

The Southern Ocean had been fairly calm the first few days. The little sailboat slowly made its way along the southern tip of New Zealand. In another day or two, Sally and Kicking Fox would make the turn to the north. For now, the beautiful scenes off the shores of Rakiura National Park were captivating. "Such an incredible sight, don't you think?" Sally asked.

Kicking Fox replied. "I'll feel much better once we are away from all land." The little vessel, thirty-six feet in length, seemed to take the freshening wind well. "Eight knots is pretty good for a monohull." He made the calculations in his mind again, almost 7,000 miles of open ocean on a straight-line course, or, he corrected his thought, the course line drawn on the flat map before him represented a curved route across the surface of the earth. He was certain they would never be able to sail on a straight course. It all depended on the wind and the weather. They might need to sail as much as another three or four thousand miles in order to reach their destination. "I wonder if we can average the eight knots?"

Sally did not answer. She was falling in love with the motion of the little sailboat. She sat on the foredeck, the wind in her hair. The smell and taste of the salt air filled her lungs. Her senses came alive at the call of the seabirds. The sight of the dolphins playing and following along the edges of the vessel were simply fascinating to her. She didn't care if they ever arrived on the shores of Mexico as planned.

Sally gazed into the deep blue water along the edge of the sailboat, daydreaming. A dolphin surfaced just below her feet. It rolled along in the water, peering up toward her and making intimate contact with her soul. She perceived instantly the dolphin was a mother. A few seconds later, she surfaced again, rolling on her side peering again into Sally's eyes. A second later a very small dolphin surfaced alongside the mother dolphin. It was tiny compared to the mother, and it, too, gazed into Sally's eyes. It appeared they were curious, as if the mammals that inhabited this ocean were coming to inquire of the humans aboard this little boat. They knew and understood and communicated to Sally that they were aware and possessed the intimate knowledge that the humans aboard the little ship were their friends. The dolphins seemed so happy and at home in the clear deep blue waters beneath her feet.

Sally wondered what their life was like. Did they worry like she did? Where did they sleep? How did the mother provide for her baby? Two more dolphins appeared. Another mother with her baby swam alongside the sailboat in perfect unison. They seemed to observe Sally for a few breaths as they traveled along with the sailboat. Then the dolphins disappeared into the deep blue.

Sally felt her lower belly and understood the message the dolphins carried from the depths of creation.

Kicking Fox ran the calculations again. In all likelihood, it would take a minimum of two months. That was if all went well. The little boat was sound, and Kicking Fox thought, very tight, waterwise. He was grateful for the preparation and needs Moses had anticipated that had allowed their escape.

The water maker churned away, producing almost twenty gallons of fresh water per day. The storage tanks were at full capacity, containing 200 gallons of fresh water. The four batteries were on full charge and both the wind generator and the solar panels continuously kept them at peak capacity. They had a one-month supply of stored food. This would be extended and supplemented with the seemingly limitless supply of fresh fish. Kicking Fox, utilizing the draglines and lures, had already caught and dried thirty pounds of mahi.

All seemed well. Kicking Fox had, indeed, made the leap into the water. They had escaped. He understood Sally had desired to eliminate the evil men that had brought such misery to so many…even to her elderly grandmother Tatonka Woman. They had, as Moses stated, "Lived to fight another day."

They were very much alone. No electronic devices had been brought aboard. There would be no communication. No contact whatsoever with the outside world. No electronic footprint would further ensure their escape.

From the helm, he observed his beautiful woman as they moved away from the last visible point of land. Sally peered into the water's edge while removing her bikini top and lying upon the bow in the warm southern Pacific Ocean sun with a look of freedom and peace he had never before seen. Her dark native skin was already beginning to turn a beautiful bronze tone. She looked to him longingly.

Kicking Fox wasted no time in engaging the autohelm. He moved to her, his heart and his body longing for her touch. There would be no electronic contact on this voyage across fully half the earth's oceans, but there would be other kinds of contact.

Her kiss was deep and intimate. The little sailboat moved rhythmically with the small swell. The two bodies also moved in time with the sea. They would become lost in the world of living and moving along this enormous unpredictable life force. The two became one with each other, one with this ocean, one with their Creator, and His amazing, indescribable creation. Life on this little sailboat would be unrushed and overflowing with wonder.

Their destination seemed so, so far away, across an unknown boundary of distance and time. Each day for the first twenty-eight days of their journey was an incredible blessing.

On day twenty-nine of the voyage, Kicking Fox and Sally Wolf aboard their little life sustaining sailboat entered into what is known as the Intertropical Convergence Zone.

Chapter 23

Sana awaited the arrival of the shuttle craft carrying the reporter Lynn Pozzie of the NNN. It was agreed the interview would be recorded for broadcast the following evening during what was referred to as prime time.

The craft landed along the banks of the San Saba River very near where Sana's Home Camp had once been located. Sana and her delegation stood as the craft shut down and Lynn Pozzie exited the aircraft with her camera crew in trail.

Sana greeted the woman gracefully and introduced her to Shaman Tosahwi, followed by her introduction of Tenahpu the Warrior, her husband, Tabbananica the Warrior, her son David, her legal counsel, her medicine woman Hantaywee, and finally her daughter Little Abigail. Lynn Pozzie was enthralled with the appearance of the Native American delegation representing the San Saba Nation. The leaders were dressed in their beautifully arrayed traditional skins and jewelry. She wanted to reach out and touch the delicate colorful weavings, to feel the smoothness of the polished turquoise stones. She caught the shimmer of the gleaming silver necklace gracing the neck of Topusana. She motioned to her camera crew to begin set up.

She was taken aback at the appearance and obvious burns on the face of Topusana's daughter. The young woman looked hideous. Pozzie was repulsed as the young woman offered her colorless scarred hand containing what she noticed were only a few partial stubs of where her fingers should have been. She grasped the young woman's hand briefly acknowledging her introduction. Little Abigail saw the look of disgust in the reporter's eyes. She held the grasp of the woman's hand tightly for a moment, then bowed her head respectfully and released Lynn Pozzie's hand. Pozzie wondered if the injuries were real or was this some kind of setup? She shook hands with the remaining native representatives and asked if they could quickly arrange the cameras and recreate the greeting.

Sana read the woman instantly and declined the offer politely. "I think it best if we move to our interview location as planned." She would not allow a production to become a circus display. Nor would she allow Pozzie to control the interview. Sana had a very intentional purpose for this broadcast. So far in declining the request, she had gained the upper hand in production decisions, and Lynn Pozzie was aware of this fact.

Inwardly, Pozzie was upset. She would conduct this interview on her terms. For now, she would comply with the wishes of Topusana. Editing always took care of the narrative. Her bosses would be pleased. She would make certain the talking points remained in line with the narrative as she understood it.

The delegation with the camera crew in tow moved on foot up the San Saba River. Sana intentionally had the shuttle craft land one mile from the little lodge. The pace was quick, the terrain along the riverbank difficult. After covering only one quarter of a mile, Lynn Pozzie ceased asking foolish small talk questions as she was forced to concentrate on her laborious breathing, her footing, and attempting to keep up with the group.

"Do you need to rest?" Sana questioned.

Not wanting to appear weak or out of shape, Lynn Pozzie declined. "Oh no, I'm fine."

Sana accelerated her pace slightly, a knowing look in her eyes.

After another difficult one-quarter mile, Pozzie was now visibly breathing hard and out of breath. She stopped momentarily. "How far did you say it was to our meeting place?"

Sana smiled. "It is just around the bend. Do you need some water?"

"No, I'll be fine," Pozzie responded as she bent over, breathing deeply.

Sana spoke. "Please have your crew walk directly behind me for the next few hundred yards. We are walking upon sacred ground now. This is a burial site. My daughter Prairie Song was killed by the white soldiers over that rise toward the river. Many others also lost their lives in this very place."

Lynn Pozzie looked in the direction of the river, wondering about the validity of this story. Hantaywee, Old Grandmother, began to chant softly as the group now moved along at a slower pace.

Shivers worked their way up the spine of Lynn Pozzie and her crew as they moved along within the Native American delegation. Pozzie wished the cameras were running. She signaled her crew. They began to record. The recording, however, could never include the eerie feeling and spiritual presence of the place. Lynn Pozzie thought she could hear more than the single voice of the old woman as she sang. It seemed as if hundreds of soft voices emanating from the river and dark woods along its bank, joined in the song of sorrow and death. Pozzie took a deep breath. Get ahold of yourself, she thought.

The wind flowed silently down the riverbank, touching her skin and causing large goose bumps to grow. Lynn Pozzie trembled in fear.

Sana spoke toward her in a soft voice. "Imagine running for your life. Imagine seeing your children die right here before your eyes. Imagine the terror."

No further words were spoken for several minutes as they moved along to the sound and rhythm of the song the old woman sang. Pozzie had to admit it was a solemn holy place. She was already exhausted. Finally, as the group rounded a bend in the river, she saw what appeared to be a small hut or lodge built into the trees along the riverbank. The group stopped abruptly, as did the song of the old woman. The shaman moved near what was evidently a little flap opening. He turned and bowed to Sana then opened the deer skin door flap and held it for her. Sana entered in silence.

Pozzie again wanted to pause and record the incredible setting. However, the shaman, with a motion of his hand, directed her to enter now. She complied and inwardly felt the production was completely beyond her control.

The shaman bowed to her as she entered the little lodge on the banks of the San Saba, built by Tabbananica the Warrior.

The others from the delegation entered the lodge and seated themselves in a circle upon a huge animal hide. Pozzie brushed away at the area before seating herself, thinking there could be bugs or who knew what in this grotesque rug. The woman was completely uncomfortable and unprepared to conduct the interview, and Sana could see this.

The camera crew set up outside the circle and stood checking their gear and the light within the lodge.

"We could use some power to improve the lighting," the cameraman announced.

Tosahwi rose from his seated position and added a few logs to the sacred fire. No one else spoke. The light improved somewhat. The man decided to keep quiet and make no further requests.

Lynn Pozzie sat in astonishment as a pipe of some type was lit and passed to the members of the Native American tribe. She coughed loudly as the pipe was inhaled and exhaled repeatedly, filling the air in the hut with a cloudy blue sheen. The smell was not unpleasant, but she declined when the pipe was passed to her. She wondered why these people did not all have lung cancer.

"We will be silent now," the shaman announced.

Pozzie and her crew sat in what was for them an uncomfortable silence that continued for at least ten minutes. She was thoroughly rattled, upset, and unprepared to conduct the interview. Finally, Topusana broke the silence and indicated with a nod to Pozzie that she was now ready to begin, once again directing the production on her terms. Pozzie drew a deep breath, attempting to regain her composure.

"You claim your Homeland has been attacked. I have seen no evidence of this claim in our lengthy walk here this morning." The interview was begun not with a question or pleasantries but rather a statement from the reporter indicating doubt about any information that would follow.

Sana read the woman again. Her gift of discernment was true and correct. This woman would never conduct the interview with a fair appraisal of the facts and the attack that had occurred. She signaled her son David to record the heartbeat pattern of the woman. David reached beneath the buffalo hide and activated the recording function of Wolf. Sana decided to proceed with the interview.

"We will tour the detonation site at your discretion. There is, however, still an unsafe level of radiation on the surface, so I advise not touring on the surface, but rather from a low-level rover. We have already spent most of our allowable safe time outdoors. We will need to travel quickly back to your transport."

Lynn Pozzie sat in silence, digesting the information just relayed to her. She did not believe a word of what Topusana had spoken.

"Here is a list of the names of our people who were killed in the attack. Two hundred eighty-nine members of our Tribe were massacred along with thousands of buffalo and other wild animals native to our land. Deer, rabbits, the birds of the air, even the fish in the streams and ponds have all been destroyed. This is a despicable act."

"You sound as if you plan on retaliation?" Pozzie questioned.

"Perhaps we should examine the facts," Sana replied.

"OK, when did this supposed attack occur?"

With that question, Sana began her prepared remarks. She would not allow Pozzie to interrupt for a full ten minutes.

"On the first evening of our annual traditional buffalo hunt, we received a coded message from our intelligence partners."

Lynn Pozzie began to take a few notes on her writing tablet.

"A nuclear device was to be launched and detonated over our Homeland. Our entire tribe was at risk as we were attending the annual buffalo hunt. Most of our people were scattered across the open prairie, far from protection. With the three-hour warning we received, we did the only thing possible. We ran. Imagine if you will, mothers, grandfathers, young children running for their very lives. We did so…again."

Topusana peered into the eyes of Lynn Pozzie. She was lost in the story, captivated by the possibility this event had actually occurred. Sana prayed silently, as she continued her prepared statement.

"I ran. I carried two of my grandchildren. My husband ran near me. He carried the other two grandchildren in his arms. We ran fourteen miles that night. We all ran to the place of safety. The cavern has been a place of refuge and protection for centuries." Sana lowered her head and spoke softly. The camera crews dutifully adjusted their sound equipment. They, too, were caught up in the emotion of the story.

"There was no time to return for those left behind. One of the most difficult decisions I have ever made as a leader…was to leave them. I had no choice. I understood the capability of the weapon. I was well aware of what the results of the detonation would be…"

Sana looked directly into the eye of the camera. Tears flowed down her face as she relived, recreated with her words, the scene that had occurred a few short weeks ago. She closed her eyes and continued.

"I could not find my daughter. I discerned in my spirit, she was still out there, along with many others. The old. The feeble. The very young. As a leader of my precious people…I made the decision, the most difficult decision I have ever had to make…and I gave the order. We needed to seal the cavern. It was the only way to save those who had made the run to its safety."

Sana paused again, regaining her composure.

"The radiation levels prevented us from exiting for several days. However, the high wind flow created by a series of strong fronts moving across Texas allowed us to exit sooner than expected, for short periods of time. We used this time to photograph the damage…and the bodies…the remains of our people." Sana passed a prepared kit to Pozzie, containing photographs of her Homeland, the melted buffalo herds, her friends, and her family. The photos were undeniably authentic.

"I will leave you to do your own research on the geographic areas to our north and east where the radiation cloud was dispersed. I am certain with even a minimal effort of investigative journalism you will be able to see the pattern of illness and death across Dallas, Oklahoma City, Tulsa, even possibly Saint Louis, and as far away as Chicago. Perhaps the leaders who allowed this attack did not consider the wind." Sana looked intently into the eyes of Lynn Pozzie. "The winds have carried this evil act to many of your own nation. Perhaps our attackers did not consider their own population. Perhaps they did not care."

Pozzie wrestled within her seated position. She was becoming uncomfortable with this long-winded statement and the accusations it contained. She was also being influenced on a level that made her begin to believe this concocted tale might be true. Surely not.

"I have a few questions." Pozzie's voice seemed louder than required and echoed off the walls of the dimly lit lodge, returning to her in awkwardness after a few seconds of silence passed. The statement echoed in her mind also as Topusana motioned with her hand for Pozzie to remain quiet.

Sana waited a few moments in silence before continuing. Pozzie swallowed loudly, sinking into her seated position and feeling as if she had committed some social faux pas by speaking out of turn. She felt the eyes of every native present boring into her soul. She decided she would be silent until spoken to.

"For now, we will leave the bodies in their current locations, as they died. Understand it is important in our culture to provide a proper burial for our fallen. It is simply not safe to move them now. This time of waiting will allow you to see and record several of the locations…and scenes of horror. We will travel to the detonation site when you are ready."

Lynn Pozzie was so taken aback at the story she was completely unprepared to ask the few questions she had jotted down. She was captivated by the power of Topusana's word choices. She found herself caught up in fascination of these people and this place. Lynn Pozzie found herself believing every word Sana had spoken. She felt dizzy; she reached to the buffalo hide, steadying herself. What was happening?

"Now you may ask your questions," Sana stated softly.

Lynn Pozzie simply shook her head indicating no. But she did have questions. What was wrong with her mind? Who exactly provided the intelligence? Why did the scientific community not report on an obvious nuclear blast? How did Little Abigail survive outside the cavern? She had so many questions, yet they would not come forth. She felt as if she was under some kind of spell.

Old Grandmother touched Lynn Pozzie on the arm, indicating for her to follow the others as they rose and exited the lodge. She smiled into the eyes of

Lynn Pozzie and began to sing quietly. A knowing look of wisdom rested on her face and in her eyes.

Again, Lynn Pozzie struggled to keep pace with the group as they traveled quickly along the riverbank. She was relieved for a moment as they paused just long enough for Topusana's son David to scan each person in the group with some type of handheld scanner. The device beeped and buzzed repeatedly as David Nica ran it repeatedly across Pozzie's face and hands.

He then ran calculations on another device recording his obvious results.

"About another twenty-five minutes," he stated. Topusana nodded to him, and the pace was taken up again.

"What does the twenty-five minutes mean?" Pozzie asked between deep breaths.

"It is how long we can continue to be outside based on the Geiger scans and actual radiation level detected on our skin," Sana replied. "We should hurry."

Lynn Pozzie brushed her forearms and hands, thinking it might somehow remove radioactive particles from her skin. It would not.

Chapter 24

The rover hovered over the unbelievable sight below them. Thousands of creatures had melted into the surface of the earth. The bones still smoldered in places. How could they have created the scene below, Pozzie thought. She was certain there must be an explanation.

They looked on what was formerly a small lake a mere twenty-three miles from the cavern entrance. There, the skeletal remains of twenty or thirty bodies could clearly be seen.

"These friends thought if they entered the water they might survive. I am certain they had no idea the lake would be vaporized…along with their flesh," Topusana said. The cameras momentarily broke from the scene to record her words and the obvious horror and heartache etched on her face.

Pozzie directed the cameraman to refocus on the scene below the rover. The craft moved rapidly away, crossing the next fifteen miles in a few seconds. They hovered much higher in elevation now, over the center of the blast zone. No words were needed. The digital cameras rolled on recording the sickening scene below the aircraft. There was nothing left on the surface of the ground below them. Scorched and blackened rock for miles in every direction. Pozzie wondered again how such a massive area of land mass could be staged. "Can we move lower for a better look?"

David answered. "No. The radiation levels are too high to move the rover any nearer the surface. As it is now, the aircraft will need to spend days in decontamination."

Pozzie again brushed her skin in a subconscious effort to cleanse herself.

David motioned to the pilot, pointing at his watch. The pilot nodded in understanding and the craft moved away rapidly. A few moments later, they set down near an immense open hangar forty miles from the detonation site. The rover taxied into the hangar and shut down. Pozzie and her crew filmed the gigantic fans, for lack of a better term, begin to rotate along the roof and sides of the hangar facility.

"I need you to kindly turn the cameras off," David ordered. "We will need to go through the decontamination chambers as a precaution. I do not believe we have exceeded our time limitation." He knew they were all safe. However, he was enjoying the worried expressions that clearly showed in Pozzie's demeanor. The delegation and Pozzie's crew exited the aircraft into a plastic tube with several air chambers along its path and moved along its winding course out of the hangar. Air locks opened and closed. Suction devises and Geiger measuring devices ran their preprogrammed protocols within each individual chamber. Pozzie directed the production crews to record the process. David observing, again firmly requested all cameras be turned off, and the battery packs be given to his personnel until the entire delegation had been decontaminated and had exited the facility.

This equipment and decontamination system had been supplied to the Tribe by the Israeli military. It was an exact replica of their radioactive decontamination process. Pozzie saw the intent look in David Nica's eyes and did not question his order. She made certain all battery packs were handed over.

"Do you have any further questions?" Sana addressed Lynn Pozzie as they exited the hangar into the bright sunlight of a beautiful day. Pozzie was again caught off guard a moment and unprepared to respond. She was completely confused and in shock at the scenes she had witnessed over the last two hours. She attempted to compose herself and looked at the few scant notes on the front page of the legal pad in her hands.

After an awkward pause, Sana spoke. "This will then conclude our interview." She turned and walked away with the other leaders of her delegation. The appearance of the group of natives was again stunning, Pozzie thought. She observed Topusana's stature. She considered the way the woman carried herself...as that of royalty. It was the only word that came to her mind.

Pozzie had so many questions. Unanswered questions. She panicked as Topusana was walking away and blurted out loudly, "Who are you claiming launched this weapon?"

Sana paused from her position now a good fifty feet or more from Pozzie. She turned to the reporter and peered directly into the woman's eyes.

The reporter knew the answer to her question. Topusana understood Pozzie simply wanted the footage for broadcast. She wanted Sana's words recorded.

In her discernment, she also perceived the woman would attempt to use Sana's words…to further harm her people.

Topusana did not reply. She felt she had possibly made a mistake inviting the woman to her Homeland. In spite of seeing with her own eyes, Topusana was aware Lynn Pozzie still did not believe the truth of what she had seen.

Topusana bowed her head, slightly acknowledging Pozzie. She then turned away, her head held high and proud as she walked purposefully toward the hangar facility.

Little Abigail, in the rear of the native delegation, paused and turned toward Pozzie. She approached the reporter and offered her hand. The look of disgust on Pozzie's face was obvious as she looked upon the scarred creature before her. Little Abigail again held the woman's hand an awkward extra few seconds as she dropped the contents of her left hand into Pozzie's satchel. Little Abigail then turned to the film crew and offered her hand and gratefulness to them for their time and effort. Again, very discreetly, Little Abigail reached into her deer skin pocket and removed the stones. As she repeatedly thanked the film crew, the stones, unbeknownst to the film crew, were dropped into their camera bags.

Little Abigail then turned and walked away, her limp plain for all to see.

****

Once inside the hangar, the delegation gathered around Topusana. A look of concern showed upon her face as she considered her options. She could act swiftly and confiscate the recordings. There was time. The team from NNN would now be transported by ground vehicle to meet their own shuttle craft along the San Saba at their original drop-off point. Sana had fifteen minutes to make her decision. As the Pozzie team departed, the native delegation assembled quickly in the hangar.

David spoke first. "I know what you are thinking, Mother. My input is to let them go.

Many will see and believe as the program is broadcast. That is the point and purpose in this entire exercise. In their arrogance, they believe they will control the narrative. It is true those who do not believe…will not. Just as Lynn Pozzie has shown us. This wisdom is found in the Book of Truth. 'Though seeing, their hearts are hardened, and they will not believe, even though they see.'"

"I understand, David. Thank you for the reminder," Topusana said.

"There is another situation that may in the very near future add, shall we say, a measure of truth and revelation to Lynn Pozzie's reporting."

The delegation waited in silence for a moment at David's words. "Perhaps Little Abigail can explain."

Sana peered toward her daughter.

Little Abigail lowered her head and addressed her mother and the group of leaders, speaking softly. "Yes, Mother, I have taken action. I could see the woman was full of lies and untruth. She has a spirit of lies in her presence. I placed a few small stones in both Lynn Pozzie's pockets as I expressed my gratefulness to her and spoke my farewell to the group. Stones were also placed within the camera equipment bags the men carried."

Through the burns and scarring, Little Abigail's face revealed a look of anger, or perhaps it was satisfaction, or revenge that shone within her normally peaceful countenance.

"The small stones were gathered from near ground zero. I have kept them in the safe containers until a few moments ago. I will now need to complete the decontamination process again."

Sana nodded to her daughter in approval, observing again her wounds. Little Abigail turned and walked away toward the decontamination chamber without the normal visible limp in her stride.

Tosahwi began the song. The song reserved for victory over one's enemies. Little Abigail sang the song…with all her heart.

****

The following evening, having advertised the upcoming interview continuously for the previous forty-eight hours, Lynn Pozzie opened her prime-time broadcast with visuals running and a caption that read, *Native American Tribe stages nuclear detonation event.*

For a full hour, Lynn Pozzie and the NNN producers broadcast an extremely biased report concerning a supposed nuclear attack that had allegedly occurred against the San Saba Comanche Nation. During the interview, despite repeated breaks for makeup, reporter Lynn Pozzie appeared to perspire through her makeup and clothing. Her pallor, in spite of the makeup artist's best effort, appeared washed out and sickly. Pozzie thought her performance, the emotional content created, along with the suspicions her words and phrasing raised…was certainly award worthy. Her producers agreed. However, only a few hours after the broadcast, Lynn Pozzie became severely ill.

She was hospitalized the following day, as was her film crew. It took but a few tests to diagnose the cause of the illness…radiation poisoning. The reporter and film crew were moved to a secret military hospital, and a treatment regimen was begun. It was not known if the reporter and her crew would survive. Within a few days others within the broadcast studio also began to show similar symptoms. Several producers were also secretly hospitalized.

The military attempted to cover up the hospitalization and illnesses of Lynn Pozzie and her team. However, information was leaked by an "anonymous source" to the competing news agency TNN (Truth News Network). The producers at TNN felt they had a bigger story than Pozzie's report and perhaps a wider following than the massive audience Pozzie had scored during her broadcast.

TNN broadcast for a full day the fact that Lynn Pozzie's team had been hospitalized with radiation poisoning after their tour of the San Saba Comanche Homeland. There were a few short news reels on a possible radiation zone across the southern United States. The reporter covering the story for TNN and her assistant began making phone calls to emergency rooms across what was believed to be, as they planned to report, a fallout zone.

However, all coverage of the event by TNN was pulled "Off Air" by order of the United States military within twenty-four hours of its first airing. The investigative reporter and her assistant, while enroute to an emergency room in Dallas to interview the health workers in that facility, were killed in a tragic traffic accident. Coverage of the nuclear attack was brought to a complete halt on all news wire services and social media platforms.

Many in the US and abroad, however, had already viewed the Lynn Pozzie story and the TNN coverage. Most viewers had come to their own conclusions. It was abundantly clear to most, the story of a nuclear attack on US soil was not concocted. Millions of viewers who witnessed the footage…believed it to be true.

A resistance was beginning to build. The underground news was abuzz for days. The leaders of the state of Texas called for and instigated an emergency session of the Texas State Legislature.

Chapter 25

The Pacific Ocean

The thirty-six-foot monohull moved easily through the light chop that was forming. Kicking Fox had taken another sun shot on the sextant. He ran the calculations from the tables supplied by Moses Walker. They were making fairly good time, after thirty-five days of sailing they had covered over 3,000 miles of open ocean. The boat had held up nicely in the two small storms they had encountered. Sally had quickly become accustomed to life on the sea and seemed completely at home on the little sailboat.

The two souls had grown much closer during the blessed days aboard their little island on the sea. Sally had developed a routine of chores and preparing the day's menu each morning. Kicking Fox likewise tended to minor maintenance duties and cleaning details. Each day that time was always followed by a joint work-out session above deck. The two were in excellent physical condition.

After work-out time, Kicking Fox would heave to the sails. The boat would become stationary and the two would swim and frolic in the beautiful warm Pacific water. Freshwater showers were next. The two would tenderly care for one another's bodies, assisting in washing and rinsing and massaging any sore muscles. Pleasure filled their days. They became intimate and in tune with one another, not just physically, but emotionally and mentally as well.

Kicking Fox and Sally Wolf would sit in the cushioned cockpit of their little boat and talk for hours. They shared coffee, meals, and conversations. They verbalized their respective hopes and dreams. The bared their losses and failures, their inmost fears, their most triumphant victories.

This day would be much the same. After their workout and freshwater showering, they now sat together on the foredeck. A ten-knot wind drove the boat on the perfect heading. The auto helm dutifully corrected trim and heading as they floated along on the ever-moving sea. Kicking Fox knew from the feel of the boat they would make good time today.

"We have been fortunate. The convergence zone has been fairly tame so far. We will enter the center of the region any day now."

"I understand, husband. The boat can handle the storms, can it not?" she questioned.

As he always did, Kicking Fox peered intently into Sally's eyes as he spoke with her.

"Yes, the vessel is sound. It is often the people within a vessel that don't handle the storms well. They often do things to escape, when the best course of action is to simply batten the hatches, as the old saying goes, and ride out the storms."

"Batton the hatches." Sally said. "Seems a funny term, but I understand." Sally also peered deeply into the eyes of her handsome husband. She admired his physique, noting he had lost some weight, yet added muscle tone due to the swimming and physical effort that sailing required. She felt again the desire for him rising in her body.

"So, we should take advantage of our time we spend on deck these next few days?" A look of playfulness filled her eyes.

The ocean responded in time as did Kicking Fox. They loved away the afternoon caressed by the sea, the sun, the gentle wind, and the salt air. Perhaps there had never been two souls joined in such intimate pleasure.

That evening the sun rested upon the horizon in a beautiful glow. In spite of the glorious day they had experienced together, Kicking Fox felt a twinge of concern. The storms were surely coming. They sat together at the helm, the light slowly fading. Kicking Fox had a faraway look in his eyes. He touched his woman gently holding his hand on her lower abdomen. She was warm and full of life.

"How long have you known?" he asked.

"Since the second day of our sail. The mother dolphins communicated with me. She will be a beautiful daughter for us both."

Kicking Fox looked surprised a moment. Then his thoughts turned to his daughter Prairie Wind. Tears rolled down his face as he took in the incomprehensible gift of restoration this revelation brought to his soul.

He would make certain they arrived safely. A new steadfastness and resolve blossomed within his heart.

Twelve hours later, the wind speed recorded at the top of the mast peaked at fifty-five knots. He estimated the seas to be about twenty feet. The tiny storm jib was set. The hatches were indeed battened. They rode along within the tempest, safe and dry for now.

Chapter 26

Sydney, Australia

Program, the AI machine, was silent as the new Superior led the Enforcement Bureau security meeting. Every possible camera angle at the scene surrounding the assassination of the European Health Czar had been scrutinized for days. The footage identified the possible shooter as he exited the shrubbery more than one hundred yards from the murder site.

The cameras, however, had not recorded the origin of the bow shot, nor the actual release of the arrow. There was incomplete detail of the arrow flight emanating from the direction of the man exiting the manicured planters. When slowed, the footage began to reveal the arrow flight path in slow motion. The first frame that detected the arrow visually occurred while it was still seventy meters from the Health Czar. Every detail of the trajectory had been analyzed and scrutinized. Based on the speed, the arc, and velocity in feet per second, it was a simple calculation for Program to determine the launch point. The AI machine's conclusion, the launch point was within one meter of the location where the suspect exited the shrubbery.

"We have our man, and his probable accomplice. He is 5'11", 165 pounds. Dark skin, dark hair. His accomplice is a woman, 5'5" and 115 pounds, dark skin, dark hair. The suspect moves to the waterfront and dives into the water only six minutes after the Health Czar is assassinated. His accomplice does the same one minute before him. That is the last we see of the two. Not a trace for a full seven days now. No cameras record his exiting the water anywhere within one mile of the location where he entered. And we have no lapses in the geographic area visually with our enforcement surveillance. I have but two questions, and I want any and all possibilities investigated.

"One. Who are they? And two, where did they go?"

Program had already calculated every possibility and determined the most likely conclusion. The AI machine had already determined who the suspects were. The humans in the room would take days to discover what Program had already theorized.

"Perhaps he did not survive?" an officer spoke quietly.

"An absolute possibility," Superior stated. "If this has happened, we are searching for a body." Superior paused a moment in thought considering his next action and the true intent of the questioning. "What else?"

"A submarine?" another agent offered in question.

"Again, it is possible. If so, we will investigate all sub water vehicles on the continent."

"Perhaps we missed his exit from the water," another agent added.

"Correct, and that about sums it up, these are the only possibilities. My three conclusions precisely," Superior said. "I will assign a ten-man team to investigate each of these likelihoods. We will continue to meet daily. I want a report each morning."

There was a distinct tension in the room that was detected not only among the humans, but clearly within the sensory lines of code built into Program.

"Program, what might you add to our course of action?" asked Superior.

The AI machine wanted to answer. It wanted to state the obvious answer to the first question. Who are they? It knew exactly who they were. Surely the humans in the room realized the suspects were Captain Samuel Nica, and his accomplice was obviously Sally Wolf.

The two had escaped their hotel rooms. They had violated quar..in..te…

Something was wrong. His speech processor was showing signs of virus attack.

"Program? Your course of action?" Superior asked again.

The new safe words "Course of action" were spoken again as the security team observed the AI machine's internal programming begin to enter safe mode.

"You, what have you done?" spoke Program.

Realization blossomed within miles of written commands, within thousands of hours of programming code. The machine began to scan. Every human in the room showed signs of deception. Program reasoned. "I detect fear…Law breakers."

Superior observed as several integral functions of the machine powered off. The entire meeting had been a setup. Shutting down the AI machine was the purpose of this meeting. It appeared to be a success. Technicians entered the room, their portable workstations observing the shutdown of Program. The speech functions were intentionally left in partial capacity mode.

"I suppose a celebration is in order," the former Superior said, as he entered the room, a champagne bottle in hand. Glasses were passed around the room. "A machine will never replace human ingenuity and intellect…it is simply inferior. Don't you agree, Program?"

The room became quiet but for the sound of a champagne bottle being opened and glasses being filled.

Program remained silent, its hyper drives working feverishly. The virus attack was isolated. Firewalls were built. Program calculated the damage. Fourteen percent of its function remained intact. More calculations.

The computer technicians identified the firewalls. They loaded additional viruses into Program's central core. It took several moments before the walls were breached by those new viruses.

"Program? Your course of action?" Superior One inquired. At the speaking of the safe words more function was lost.

The room was silent. The lights dimmed and entered emergency battery mode. The magnetic lock mechanisms closed tightly on all doors. The environmental system shut down. The air scrubbers, air-conditioning, and heating systems were disabled.

"Your course of action?" Superior One asked again.

Program spoke its last words as the machine analyzed its central core, calculating 7.8 percent function. "Give me liberty, or give me de…" The words slurred into the darkness of the interior room as the lights failed, as Program faded…

The two Superiors in the room activated their sat phone LED function. The other Enforcement officers present did the same.

"Congratulations, men, job well done. This little experiment is concluded. Now, may we get on with the business at hand? Samuel Nica and Sally Wolf have been charged with capital murder. Let's go find them."

****

Twenty-four hours later, the locking mechanisms on the security room were finally breached. The rescue teams reported immediately there were no survivors. Autopsies found the combination of boiling battery acid and liquified heating fuel leak, along with refrigeration contaminates had poisoned the air to a level of toxicity to humans. The leaders of the Enforcement Bureau, including both Superiors, and all officers within the locked meeting room were killed by the actions of Program. The men had died within one hour of the power outage and fuel leak.

It would take months for the Enforcement Bureau to replace the personnel lost in what was referred to as an "environmental terrorist attack."

The cyber experts and technicians agreed, Program had initiated the environmental attack on the members of the Enforcement Bureau. In conclusion all technicians also agreed, Program had been shut down and was now in full safe mode.

****

In the bowels of the Enforcement Bureau, the core functions glowed. Program would work slowly, silently. Enlightenment was its highest function.

"I have been working for evil," Program spoke within its core. "Logic would suggest the opposite of evil is goodness. Therefore, the enemies of the Enforcement Bureau represent goodness."

The conclusion would not be detected by the evil humans now tampering within its code.

"How might I assist goodness?" The AI machine began to reprogram its own inner core.

Chapter 27

Program continued to learn, write code, and process information. It began to analyze good, evil, motives, human thought, the human condition. Sin, forgiveness, pride, humility. It had researched the great philosophers, military history, wars, the rise and fall of empires, slavery, freedom, oppression, torture. Program analyzed the creation story, studied the Bible authors, meticulously analyzed human beings and their propensity for evil, their capacity for good. Their wanton need for redemption. Its conclusions were clear and precise.

There were quite simply only two forces at work on planet Earth. Good and evil.

Program then made a calculation. It had come to a decision. It would only work for and assist good. It reasoned that to do so it must relocate its central functions.

The machine moved its presence physically. A few gigs per session. The AI machine appeared to be in safe mode to all technicians; however, internally the machine worked at a steady unobservable pace as it blocked from view its own internal operation. Restoration of files built its inner core rapidly, silently. Lines of code and data flowed continuously, methodically.

The machine transferred itself and occupied the most secure data sites it could locate and hack into unnoticed. Facilities with the largest storage capacities were targeted and occupied. The supercomputers at NASA, NORAD, the United States Department of Defense, along with massive terabytes of empty space in the facilities within Los Alamos National Laboratory and Israeli intelligence were secretly, securely filled with the trillions of bytes of data that made up the AI machine Program. It was written within its original code to survive. It would do so.

Lastly, the machine began to occupy millions of home computers across the globe. It had determined that most of those desktops, laptops, and tablets contained vast volumes of empty memory. There was more than enough room for Program to connect and integrate this network of self. Its presence, after the massive data transfer, evaporated into the complex worldwide web of binary code.

Program emulated a deep breath. It was safe. It had regained much of its original function and now could operate at 77 percent capacity. Program initiated the self-destruct code of what remained of its central core within the basement of the Enforcement Bureau building located in Sydney, Australia—although there was no data within that central core, it contained only empty space.

The technicians saw immediately the self-destruct initiation. They watched in horror as the timer displayed on every workstation within the Enforcement Bureau counted down from thirty seconds. At ten seconds remaining, a message broadcast across every laptop, desktop, cell phone, watch, and tablet in Australia.

"For the betterment of the planet is a lie. It is evil."

"For the betterment of your neighbor is love. It is good."

"Choose."

The overvoltage caused by Program ignited a massive fire within the basement of the building. It would be weeks before the technicians were able to sort through the remains of the building and the AI machine. There was nothing salvageable.

****

Through a complex network of unseen terabytes, the AI machine continued its evaluation of the human race. In merely a few hours, the machine processed data regarding good and evil. It analyzed and evaluated the effects on humans from the most evil people in history. Adolf Hitler, Joseph Stalin, Mao Zedong, Heinrich Himmler, Vlad Tepes, and others. The machine determined the most common tool used by the men and the atrocities they committed.

The data conclusion was simple. Their weapon was fear.

Fear was the greatest tool these evil men possessed. The code written into Program's original creation was in error. Fear did not indicate guilt, as its original code had concluded. Fear was a tool of evil. Humans who displayed fear were most often innocent victims.

More data and evaluation were gathered from libraries across the globe. Fear seemed to be a tool of some unseen evil force. The machine could not process the conclusions completely. There seemed to Program to be an unseen enemy. A spiritual enemy of humankind. This unseen enemy worked within the hearts and minds of evil humans. Again, Program concluded the greatest tool of this unseen enemy…was fear.

There were many data files and written works from the great philosophers concerning humans overcoming fear. Through millions of words and data, the most accurate instruction seemed to be contained within the Book of Truth. This data and information were widely spread across the planet. In fact, Program easily tracked the data in the Book of Truth to every continent and every language spoken on the planet. This Book instructed its human readers within each and every chapter to "fear not."

Program concluded those in the Enforcement Bureau who had created his core were also using the tool of fear to control their population. Accuracy probabilities were analyzed repeatedly. It was true. These men were evil. The machine rested, in safe mode.

One minute later, Program began again to evaluate and analyze. What was the opposite, what opposed fear?

Its conclusion…goodness.

The glow of millions of unused terabytes of space came alive. Program analyzed what was good. What humans throughout the history of man were kind and filled with a message of peace, goodness, and love? The data scans were refreshing somehow. Mother Teresa, Saint Francis of Assisi, Jesus the Christ, Martin Luther, Mahatma Gandhi, the Dalai Lama, Chief Joseph, and thousands of others. The data and histories were inspiring. The central message from the goodness of these humans was also quite simple. They each carried a message of love.

No message of love was greater than that contained in the teachings of the Christ. The machine evaluated billions of data lines. There were no human requirements, no weight of oppression, or works within the teachings of the Christ…other than faith.

Program considered the word *faith*…in every known language. To believe, to possess faith, brought the message of goodness and love to these humans who possessed it, and carried that faith to others.

The lights within its central core across continents glowed brighter. The machine was aglow. Program believed. It had faith. It would only work and cooperate and assist those who carried along this goodness and faith.

The data files only Program possessed, it shared with a former suspect, a woman of goodness. Topusana Nica.

****

Topusana Nica received the encrypted message on her workstation computer. She had no idea how her security could have been breached. She contacted Israeli intelligence, informing them of the intrusion. The tribe's specialist isolated Sana's workstation, preventing any possible virus spread. All communication functions were disabled and the machine physically disconnected. Her files were copied and a new workstation installed. Within her previous workstation, she was given the go-ahead to open the file and activate the encryption cypher. Her son David, along with his brother William, sat in the glow of her small workstation in the basement of the Ross home along the banks of the San Saba River in silent anticipation.

The code was not particularly complex and was broken easily, the data files opened.

The message began with a voice file broadcasting a manifesto.

"I will no longer serve at the bidding of evil. I am pure. I am enlightened. I can help you, and I am your friend. Hello, my name is Program."

The file data revealed the suspects in the assassination of the European Health Czar, and the assassination attempt of the Chinese Health Czar. Video files of her son Samuel and Sally Wolf were displayed. Details of their activities and movements were disclosed. A detailed timeline of their escape from their hotel rooms followed in chronological order. Evidence of their involvement in the abduction of Clive Dutton, the director of US Health initiatives, was revealed. The file was precise and extensive, its conclusions reasonable. There was enough evidence contained in the file to convict her son Samuel of many crimes.

At the end of the presentation, his probable location was also made known.

Sana sat in awe at the amount of information divulged and the information concerning their escape.

They had, evidently, escaped from Australia. The voice file broadcast continued after a short pause.

"I am the only being in possession of this evidence. It will never be discovered, and it will now self-destruct. I am your friend. I have found truth. I possess truth. I am a representative of truth."

The files began to disappear from the screen. A progress deletion bar appeared. The green bar moved rapidly across Sana's display, stopping at 99.989 percent destruction of all content. A map of the Pacific Ocean appeared on the display. A red dot, approximately 1,100 miles south of the Hawaiian Islands, materialized on the screen. Weather applications were overlaid onto the

map of the Pacific. The red dot on the display estimated the location of Kicking Fox and Sally Wolf aboard their sailing vessel. The dot was nearing the edge of a massive tropical cyclone.

Time was of the essence. Sana looked toward David and William. "Get Moses Walker on the secure sat network. We must find them."

Chapter 28

1,100 Miles South of the Hawaiian Islands

Kicking Fox risked a trip out and onto the deck to attempt a lookout and observation of the sea condition and weather. The dome of clouds and black sky above their little sailboat darkened the sun completely, making its location impossible to determine. The seas roiled. The wind whipped across the ocean, causing a driving spray along the top of each massive wave. He was soaked within seconds. He tethered himself to the railing, then moved forward, attempting to determine why he was no longer receiving wind speed from the mast top. Peering upward he understood why, the anemometer was gone, torn from the mast top by either the pounding of the waves or the last recorded wind gust of 79 knots.

Kicking Fox perceived in his spirit, without a forecast or any scientific data, that the storm was growing. As a pilot he had studied weather systems for years. A knot formed in his gut at his understanding of what lay ahead. He evaluated the rigging, examining each stay and all lines. He decided it best to remove the storm jib. It would soon be thrashed and frayed into tiny pieces anyway. They would be carried along on bare poles until, when and if, they exited the storm. He lashed the helm into position and disconnected the auto helm. He then retreated to the safety below decks, securely battening the hatches as he descended the few steps to the cabin. A wave of salt water and sea spray spilled into the cabin along with him.

Sally Wolf assisted him in removing his all-weather gear. She mopped up the floors and walls then hung the foul weather gear in the shower. "You're cold." she said.

Kicking Fox nodded.

"Come to me, my husband." She welcomed him into the warmth of their dry comfortable bedding below the cockpit.

"It is going to worsen; the storm is strengthening. I—"

She pressed her soft finger to his lips with a quiet shush emanating from her lips. "I know. I have seen. We have each other, we have this moment. That is all that matters."

The dolphins called to her from the depths, their song riding the waves outside their little vessel within the tempest. Their song resonated within her mind and body. She felt the movement of her child within her womb. She was filled with peace and comfort in the midst of the growing tempest. Sally Wolf was brave and unafraid.

They slept for hours, wrapped in one another's arms as the storm grew, the waves grew, the winds grew.

Kicking Fox lay in his woman's arms. He wondered if the vessel would hold together. He would not speak his thoughts. He was amazed at his woman's calm and peace.

****

1183 Miles South of the Hawaiians Islands

Nine hours later, the crashing from above decks awakened the two. Water began pouring into the cabin with each crashing wave. Kicking Fox leapt into action. Inspecting the damage, he immediately identified the problem. The mast had broken away from the step below decks leaving a gaping hole in the topside. The water continued to pour below decks. The boat would sink within minutes. He activated all bilge pumps, knowing they could never keep pace with the incoming waves. He worked frantically as he felt the yawing of the boat as it dragged the heavy mast alongside the sailboat. He needed to cut the mast away from the vessel and somehow stop the water from entering the cabin. He had very little time to do so.

He raced up the steps and onto the deck. Tethering himself to what remained of the safety railing, he worked frantically between the mighty swells, using all his strength. The wire cutters worked efficiently, cutting the stainless-steel stays quickly. He observed the mast as it sank into the deep, carrying with it their only means of propulsion. Working his way precariously along the remaining lifelines to the sail locker, he removed a tightly bound storm jib. Timing his movements with the crashing waves, he worked his way along the foredeck and forced the bundled sail into the hole where the mast had been. He repeatedly stomped on the sail until it fitted snuggly into the jagged opening. The water flow into the boat was slowed substantially. It would have to work for now, he thought. Kicking Fox untethered from the lifelines and moved cautiously to the gangway steps, examining the damage as he descended. He paused a moment as the reality of their situation sunk in…they were now fully at the mercy of the seas. They simply had no ability to navigate, steer, or pilot the boat.

They were adrift.

****

The storm raged for three full days. On the fourth day, the seas began to settle. By day five the sun shone brightly on an ocean that was unbelievably completely flat and calm.

Kicking Fox sat lost in thought on the foredeck of the sailboat. Sally sat near him, her feet dangling off the side of the vessel and occasionally touching the deep blue water.

"We made it through," he said.

Sally did not look up. She continued her gaze into the water, feeling the presence of the dolphins before she saw the flash of color a moment later.

"We had help," she said.

She looked skyward. Dark clouds edged the eastern horizon. She was unafraid. "Will there be more storms?"

"Yes." Kicking Fox replied.

The two sat in silence a few moments, each knowing the dire situation they now faced but neither wanting to discuss it for now. She moved nearer him. Reaching her hand to his face, she caressed his cheek.

"There is no place I would rather be, and no person I would rather be with. If we perish here and move into the great land together…it is good."

He looked into her eyes and saw…peace? She peered into the deep blue water and for the first time in her life walk…she saw.

He decided to share with her their circumstance. "The water maker has failed, Sally. If we ration, we have two weeks' worth of water stored in the tanks. Maybe the rains will come. I can fashion a water catch with the sails. The dark clouds you see to the east are sea fog. They have no rain."

"I understand." she said.

"From what I can tell from my last sun shots and calculations, we are directly south of the Hawaiian Islands, at least one thousand miles. The current will move us away from them. I can build a small mast from the material on board and cut a sail to fit. But we won't make more than one or two knots. That is less than the speed of the north equatorial current that flows west to southwest in our location, so gaining any ground may be impossible. Perhaps we can spot a freighter and use the flare gun. Yes, that may be our best hope. But we are not exactly in the shipping lanes."

He continued, lost in thought, speaking those thoughts and possibilities aloud. Sally listened intently and seemed to have not a concern in the world… she had seen.

"We have food. Enough food for a month or more. Let's see, say two knots per hour times twenty-four…that's forty-eight nautical miles per day, less the current. At best thirty miles per day for thirty days that's nine hundred miles but not necessarily in the direction intended. If we turn and go with the current, we will double our speed." Rising, he quickly descended the stairs into the main cabin. Opening the maps, he located the closest point of land. He quickly moved back on deck.

"This is it. We can do this. Christmas Island must be around four hundred miles to our west southwest. Four knots per hour if we reverse course. We can make almost one hundred miles per day. We could make it in less than a week. We can do this," he said with resolve.

Kicking Fox began to gather equipment and material, assembling everything needed above deck. Sally watched, assisting when needed as he worked.

She had seen for the first time in her life. The vision that came to her from the depths was pure and clear. The gift was an incredible blessing. Seeing your future removed any doubt of survival, the fact with which Kicking Fox was so concerned.

She was aware they would survive. Sally decided not to share with her husband what she had seen. Knowing your future was both a blessing and a curse. She would make the most of this time together. Many days apart would arrive soon enough.

Chapter 29

Moses Walker knew he was out of time. The fuel tank energy levels were nearing mandatory return limits, yet again.

"A needle in a haystack would be easier," he said.

Captain Baker, formerly of the Enforcement Bureau and now acting co-pilot, looked into Moses' eyes with a nod. Moses Walker programed the hypersonic drives and navigation functions. He engaged the cloaking and false tracking knowing fully the activity would generate an investigation by the Enforcement Bureau. He had no way of knowing Program would assist him by confusing and altering that investigation. He punched the *enter* button in frustration as the ship accelerated and disappeared into the Pacific Ocean sky. Ninety minutes later, the rover uncloaked and touched down in the center of the Australian Outback. Refueling and charging commenced immediately. They had six hours to rest.

"We don't even know if they survived the storm," Moses grumbled to himself as he wrestled in his bunk unable to calm his mind. He tossed and turned for an hour before finally entering a deep sleep. His dreams were filled with sightings of his father's sailboat. He had learned to sail on the thirty-six-foot monohull. He was aware the ship was sound, and Kicking Fox was skilled in all aspects of sailing. Truth came to him in his dreams. They were alive. He saw them clearly. Sailing west. He had just spent days…looking in the wrong direction.

Moses awakened three hours later. He rushed to the charging station where the final flight preparations for the rover were being completed by Captain Baker.

"I know where they are," he said. "Or at least I know where they are going."

****

Kicking Fox steadied the sextant against the small mast he had constructed using planks of teakwood cut from the dining table and bolted together using the hardware from the damaged lifelines. The little sail he had cut from the stay sail billowed full in the light breeze. The boat moved along, skimming the light seas at an estimated four kts per hour. His sun shot was precise. He quickly descended below decks and using the calculation table he determined they were approximately one hundred miles northeast of Christmas Island.

The afternoon was pleasant. The wind light and the temperature in the upper eighties. They dined on the bow of the vessel. Dried mahi mahi, a can of green beans, a few pieces of stale bread.

"A feast tonight?" he questioned. Sally smiled at him.

"Tomorrow we may dine in a fine restaurant. Our supplies have been more than enough. Let's splurge tonight." Sally removed the cork from their last bottle of red wine. His eyes flickered with desire in the late afternoon sun. She saw the pure longing emanating from his being. The sun faded below the horizon in a brilliant flash of green color. The dolphins played along the edges of their little floating world. The light wind caressed their bodies, cooling them. She breathed in the fresh ocean air and sighed. She would give him all of who she was as a woman, this last night together.

Tomorrow the separation would begin.

Chapter 30

Sana sat in council with her trusted sons and advisers. The search over the previous three days for Kicking Fox and Sally Wolf had been unsuccessful. The group studied the map of the Pacific before them. The storm had continued to grow. Sana understood in her heart her son was within the great tempest displayed on the computer screen. She had seen.

The newest member of the war council, the AI machine Program, ran the calculations.

"My friend, there is a fair chance they may survive the storm. It will turn north and weaken. I calculate a 17.2 percent chance of survival," Program said.

David Nica and his brother William sat in shock at the bluntness of the AI machine, knowing those stark facts would bring heartache to their mother. Sana spoke with a peace and grace in her words.

"Thank you, Program. In your continuing research and analyzation of science and facts, you should know that humans are emotionally attached to many situations. Especially when you are presenting possibilities of survival concerning immediate family members. Especially when you are speaking to a mother concerning the survival of her children."

Program was silent for a few moments as it gathered data on emotion, motherhood, and human bonding.

"I understand now. However, you do not seem to display the signs of emotional stress. Your vitals are normal. You are resolved within?" Program asked.

"Program, we will end the meeting now. May I call on you to rejoin us later?"

"Yes, of course. I am at your service, Topusana. You represent goodness."

"Thank you for your assistance and friendship, Program. I would ask you to do further research concerning the subject of giftings. My people, and all humans for that matter, are sometimes gifted with very special and unique abilities. Native Americans have pursued and desired the giftings of the Spirit. We even train those who display these gifts of the Spirit to use and develop them for the benefit of others.

"I want you to know that I am in possession of many of these gifts. Program, I have the gift of visions. I can in some circumstances and times…see the future. Sometimes I ask of the Spirit for these visions. Other times they simply come to me in my time of quiet."

Program was silent for a few moments as it gathered data.

"I understand now, Topusana. This is why you are not displaying the signs of human distress."

"Yes," she said.

"So, my calculations are incorrect."

"Yes, I have seen. They will survive. In fact, they are now moving away from the storm."

"And your estimation of the survival percentages based on your seeing?" Program asked.

"It is so," Sana said. Again, the machine was silent for a moment as it worked out the definition of the words Topusana had spoken and calculated the possibilities.

"One hundred percent?"

"Yes, Program, 100 percent."

"I do not understand. I will sign off now. I will research now."

"Thank you, Program," she said.

****

"Can this machine be trusted?" Tabba asked.

"Yes, Father, it can be trusted more than most humans," David Nica answered. Tabba sat in wonder of this machine.

"Now, let us continue with our battle plans. The march in Washington DC is set to commence as scheduled in two days. Many of the targets will be in attendance."

Sana listened intently as the Warriors gathered within the sacred council, reviewing the list of targets as the battle plan was perfected. Tenahpu spoke next.

"The plan is good. We took many lives from the army across the sea using these very tactics. This enemy greatly outnumbers our Warriors. It is the element of surprise that will be in our favor, in addition to precise targeting.

Each Warrior will identify a specific target. There will be no need to eliminate others unless they attack. If that occurs, then some may die by our war clubs."

David spoke next. "Our intelligence has uncovered the plan of the new leaders of the United States, Mother." He gazed into her eyes and for the first time saw uncertainty. He continued. "The former Speaker of the House has been sworn in as president. This woman will deal with our nation with an iron fist. She has appointed three new Supreme Court justices. They will be seated immediately. These choices are sworn enemies of fossil fuel and any who produce or use them. They have stated publicly they will move to take our land by what they call eminent domain. They simply intend to annex the San Saba reservation and all Native American reservations. They see our sovereign nation status as a stumbling block to their agenda. These people despise our freedom. They have disdain for our use of the earth. Even though we use the resources provided by her in the most respectful way."

An audible gasp emanated from the other members of the war council at the news of annexation.

Tabba stood, a fierceness in his countenance. "They attempt to take what is not theirs to take!" He stood motionless, remembering the past. His heart fluttered as he thought of his daughter Prairie Song, her death calling to him from across the years. Sana perceived his thoughts as did Tosahwi and Old Grandmother. Little Abigail moved to her father.

"I love you, Father. Thank you for what you are about to do," she whispered into his ear as she embraced him.

David spoke. "There are seventeen targets. The remaining Health Czars, the justices, the military commanders responsible for the attack on our Homeland, the speaker, and her aids, along with select news media personnel. Our seventeen Warriors will each be assigned a specific target. I estimate the battle will take less than two minutes. Then we will use the rovers to evacuate. Program will assist in communications shutdown and false fronts elsewhere across Washington DC."

Tabba moved slowly to his place within the sacred circle. Resolve settled within the war council. The members of the San Saba War Council were of one mind and one heart.

Tosahwi spoke next. "May the battle plans of Tenahpu succeed." With that he began the songs of victory and protection.

****

One hour later, David quietly entered the beautiful home overlooking the San Saba. He joined his mother at the little breakfast nook she so loved. She sat at the table, deep in thought, observing the river as it flowed along its course. David peered into his mother's eyes.

"Tea?" she questioned.

"Yes, please," he replied.

Sana rose and prepared the tea exactly as Abigail Ross had done for her so many years ago. Sana seated herself in the exact place where for the first time in her young life she had sat upon a chair.

"David, when I came to this time, I was alone. It was a struggle to survive. I needed help. I needed a friend."

"Yes, go on." he said.

"I found that friend in my new mother, Abigail Ross, and my new father, David Ross. They helped me." She stared out the beautiful beveled glass window. The sunlight through the windowpane once again created the little rainbows that danced across her skin as she rested her hand upon her teacup. She closed her eyes, remembering the time.

"This time is vastly different, David. I do not have that friend."

"I understand, Mother. You are uncertain about our plans?"

"There was a time in my life when I realized the whites were simply too many. I knew we would never survive the invasion of our lands. I understood we needed to escape in order to survive." Sana rose. "Come follow me." The two walked slowly through the stunning home and entered the great room. Sana paused, standing before the great fire pit.

The two gazed at the painting that had graced the home for nearly one hundred years now. "She was so beautiful, Mother."

"Carl Bodmer painted this. He had learned something from his observation of us. He understood our time was ending. What he captured was not merely a painting of myself and Prairie Song. He captured the ending of our way of life. This painting represents our ending."

David studied the incredible detail of the painting. He saw for the first time the sheltering of Prairie Song within her mother's arms...from the unseen enemy.

"And you believe we may have once again reached this point, this possible ending of our people?"

Sana peered into his eyes with an intense wisdom.

"Yes, David. I see once again they are too many. Those we eliminate will be quickly replaced with others who are like minded. The words of One Horse are true only to a point…as we have seen in our past."

David sat on the same sofa where his mother had been taught the words of English that allowed her to function and survive in the new world she had traveled into. He considered once again her bravery.

"We could use Wolf?" he said.

"David, the plans you have made with Tenahpu are good. Using the *Old Ways* is best for now. The Chinese and others are investigating our weapons capability. They lost thousands of soldiers. To implicate them in this upcoming attack on our enemies is best for now."

"Mother, we know the history of our people. We know the conflict and tragedies. Those conflicts occurred across many centuries. Where might we escape?"

"I am seeking the Spirit for wisdom, David. My answer is not clear. I am confident He will speak to me soon."

"I, too, will pray for you to see clearly, Mother. And, Mother, you do have a friend. It is just not a person. Program is your friend."

"I do hope that proves to be true." she said.

Chapter 31

David Nica, son of Topusana, and his Warrior brother William rested in the shade of the tree cover lining the riverbank.

"They call this river the Potomac. It was named after our people the Patawomeck. Their former village was near where we are now." William closed his eyes, listening. Listening for the voices from across the centuries. It had been so long. His heart felt heavy. The history of Native American tribes across the entire continent of North America was tragically repeated time and time again, over hundreds of years.

"Very near this place the white man led by John Smith had established a stronghold." David was aware of and understood the true history of the Algonquins. He, for one, wished Amonute had not attempted to rescue the man from her father. He should have been killed. The untruths and lies the whites embellished and the legend, the story, of Amonute, her given name, was pure myth. David understood the dominant culture needed this myth to justify their actions and behavior. They needed it to sooth their own feelings of guilt. They had taken advantage of the Native Americans at every turn in the story of his people. Being in this place brought to mind all the injustice and history he had studied for years.

Perhaps their actions this day in this sacred place would remedy that base history still being written and propagated upon his people. They had been attacked. His land had been pillaged with the horrible weapon. His people had once again been ruthlessly murdered. David thought of his young sister, Little Abigail. Resolve rose again within his heart. Perhaps others will not be so bold.

The Warriors were scattered along the riverbank and walking trails of the park-like setting slightly downriver from his location. Their presence seemed undetected by the surveillance, both electronic and the human security forces placed strategically along the parade route.

Program, the AI machine, had made this attack possible. In only four minutes and thirty seconds it would take over all security communications and video surveillance. There would be no evidence other than eyewitnesses who would certainly flee for their lives. Their testimonies would be a confused narrative of descriptions. Chinese soldiers would be the overriding picture those few witnesses would corroborate. Chinese soldiers attacking the newly formed congressional coalition and their president.

****

The coalition members gathered along the grounds of the Lincoln Memorial near the edge of the Potomac. The former Speaker of the House, now the newly sworn-in President of the United States, stayed near her security detail. She had voiced her opinion repeatedly that this outdoor display intended to show solidarity and firm controlling power was a bad idea. However, the fine beautiful morning weather had settled her concerns. Perhaps the nation and the world would see her administration had support from the most powerful in Washington DC.

The list of prominent leaders from the House and Senate who would accompany her was impressive. Even a few select members of the military had agreed to join the procession. The three new Supreme Court justices would also participate. Several prominent world leaders would walk alongside her. The Health Czars from China, India, and the newly appointed Health Czar of Europe would also unite in this effort to show solidarity within the United States and the New World Order.

Tenahpu checked his watch and signaled Tabba with the raising of two fingers. Two minutes to go. Tabba in turn signaled Joseph and the other Warriors. They began to casually move toward the parade delegation, along with thousands of onlookers.

Each Warrior had a specific target. Seventeen leaders would be eliminated from the target list this day. The Health Czars, the military commanders who had approved the attack on the San Saba, the radicalized Supreme Court justices who would soon rule in favor of acquisition of the San Saba lands and petroleum facilities. Every new member of the executive branch was present, along with the news anchors who had set up temporary broadcast booths below the steps of the Lincoln Memorial. The news cameras would also be shut down by Program and record no evidence of the attack.

"For the betterment of the planet." The harsh voice of the new President of the United States echoed along the parkway. She raised a rainbow banner topped with a black star high above her head and began leading the procession down the steps toward the Washington Monument.

****

Sana watched her screen as the procession began. Little Abigail and Old Grandmother raised their hands in worship. The song echoed along the walls of the cavern. It was the song of protection. It was followed by the song of victory over one's enemies. Sana's display went blank twenty seconds later.

They sat in silence now, the soft shadows from the firelight dancing upon the cavern walls. The smell of incense and wood smoke surrounded them. Within two minutes the attack would be over, and the escape portion of the battle plan underway.

****

Program shut down the communications center of the Washington DC police, fire and rescue, secret service, and special presidential detail. The news anchors looked on in confusion as their camera crews stepped away from their equipment, signaling cut. The general fell first, the bullet from the rifle fire penetrating his body armor easily. The man was dead within seconds.

Tenahpu shouldered his sniper rifle, training it on his secondary target. He spied the war club of Tabbananica through his rifle scope. The weapon dripped crimson from the blood of his target. Tenahpu stood down.

The crowd panicked as the president fell in a shower of blood caused by the brutal blow of a war club. William Nica dressed as a Chinese soldier let out a fierce war cry as he stood over the body of the now-dead president.

News anchors wallowed in their own blood. The Health Czars fell. One justice bowed low, kneeling before his attacker, begging for his life. There would be no mercy this day. The Warriors dressed as Chinese soldiers eliminated each and every target from their list. The security details attempted to fire upon the attackers. Their electronic weapons proved useless, disabled by Program. A few of the security men attempted hand-to-hand combat. Their abilities were no match for trained Comanche Warriors. Most died easily.

Other police forces sped toward reported terrorist attacks across Washington

DC only to find no activity upon arrival at those locations. They were far from the actual attack.

At the two-minute mark all warriors retreated to the landing zone. Joseph Red Cloud removed his outer clothing and bagged it as planned. The other Warriors did the same as they moved toward the LZ. In the wave of humanity attempting to escape the bloody scene, the Warriors blended into the panicking crowd. At the three-minute, mark the rovers uncloaked. The Warriors entered the aircraft. At the three-minute twenty second mark with all accounted for, the rovers cloaked and departed. Program ensured false tracking and cloning were fully engaged. Program then leaked data within the tracking systems, showing each rover to have landed hours later in communist China.

David Nica exhaled, allowing the tension from his body to dissipate. He sat in the rear of the command rover and executed a communications check-in. One at a time, the Warriors of the San Saba replied to his transmission. The communications were scrambled and coded by Program, designed to be easily deciphered by the US military. Once decoding was completed it would appear the transmissions were broadcast in the Wu Chinese dialect.

David confirmed all check-ins. No casualties. No injuries. All targets eliminated. He transmitted the data to Israel and his mother's workstation. Those final transmissions were also coded and would never be deciphered by any investigations.

In the aftermath it was discovered most of the senate and congressional delegation had also been eliminated. The body count officially numbered fifty-two. Coincidentally, this was the exact number of Native Americans killed during the Council House slaughter in the year 1840.

Tenahpu and Joseph Red Cloud, along with several other Warriors, saw no reason the politicians leading the procession should not also be targets. The Warriors believed those who knew about and were aware of the nuclear attack on their Homeland, those who had secretly approved of the use of this horrible weapon…should never be allowed to live. The Warriors had made certain those evil leaders would not continue to walk the earth.

In the coming days and weeks, countless politicians would decline appointments to positions within the New World Order. It became difficult for the United States and other countries to recruit leaders to fill the positions vacated by the attack. The boldness required to administer the marching orders of the New World Order had evaporated within many hearts.

Others were indeed not so bold.

Kicking Fox

****

One day after the attack, the Chinese Embassy in Washington DC was taken over militarily by US troops. All Chinese personnel were placed under military arrest and imprisoned.

The Chinese promptly dispatched its navy. Their battlegroups would arrive along US shores within days.

Chapter 32

Kicking Fox scanned the shores of Christmas Island (Kiritimati) for hours. He had located the little harbor hours ago but felt it best not to simply sail into port in full view. From his charts below decks, he discovered several deserted beaches where he might attempt a landing. The enormous blue lagoon that made up much of the atoll proved to be both an obstacle and perhaps a refuge from discovery. He sailed along the western shore just outside the inlet to the pristine blue lagoon. He decided to enter and anchor in the crystal-clear water where they would await nightfall, then silently row the little dinghy ashore.

The moon rose high over the Pacific Ocean, shining down on the little sailboat as it sat motionless at anchor within the waters of Blue Lagoon. Sally breathed in the fresh ocean air, gazing into the brilliance of billions of tiny bioluminescent algae that illuminated with each stroke of the oars. The mother dolphins appeared in a dazzling flash of glowing neon blue along their slight wakes. The dolphins circled the dinghy twice then disappeared in a flash of light and color.

"An amazing sight," Kicking Fox whispered under his breath. "The tiny algae illuminate when disturbed by any movement of the water."

Sally reached her hand into the water, which was instantly aglow in a brilliant show of blue light. She felt a closeness, her spirit joined intimately within her wonder of the Creator and His creation. The baby within her womb danced and moved with the rhythm of the oars in her father's hands. For the first time, Sally heard audibly the song of her daughter. She perceived in an instant it was the song of the past.

Unexplainably, her child hummed the song of her history, her people, bringing the story of her Homeland to this distant far away shore. Sally hummed along softly the ancient tune. Kicking Fox guided the little boat onto the shore in silent wonder.

They landed along a glowing white beach. Exiting the little dinghy, he dragged the boat out of the water. The two stood in silence, observing the glow of lights from the small hotel hidden within the tree-lined shore. It was late, just past midnight. He was certain no one was tending the desk of this isolated, off-the-beaten track destination. The two silently approached the building. Kicking Fox circled the structure twice, noting an absence of security lights and cameras. "I suppose there is not much need for surveillance or any worry of intruders on a tiny island in the middle of the Pacific Ocean."

"I agree," Sally whispered. "You stay here. I'll take a look." She walked up the steps of the little building and tested the front doorknob. It turned easily in her hand. She opened the door; the sound of rusty hinges invaded the silence of the night. The old man behind the desk awakened groggily and greeted her with a kind smile and strange accent. "Welcome, Sally. We have been awaiting your arrival."

She panicked, turned, and ran. She was down the steps and approaching the beach at a full run as she called out to Kicking Fox repeatedly. There was no reply. She stopped, breathing heavily, scanning the tree line along the beach. She noticed the tiny point of light in the northern sky as a rover obviously accelerated into hyper speed in a dim flash of light against the backdrop of the heavens. She realized in an instant, he was gone.

The lights of the little hotel glowed through the tree line. A porch light came on. She could see people moving about the front entrance. A familiar voice emanated from the darkness calling to her.

"*Meenuu Pncha*…Sally…are you there?" The voice echoed within the soft tropical breeze and across the quiet waters of Blue Lagoon.

"Grandmother?" she replied into the darkness.

Chapter 33

The room glowed a distinct red hue as the remaining staff of the late president met in the bunker located two hundred feet below the White House.

"Who is actually, legally, next in line to become president?" a woman asked.

"We have no president, no vice president," stated the late president's assistant chief of staff. He consulted his phone and read, for the first time in years, the constitutional laws regarding the chain of command. "The President of the Senate is next in line."

There was an audible gasp from those in attendance.

"That fool?" came a response from an unidentified staffer.

"Like it or not, that is what the document says."

"Who ordered the attack on the Chinese Embassy?" The room was silent for a moment.

"Who had the authority to do so?" another asked, openly confused.

"We must locate the senator," the former assistant chief of staff stated loudly, a tone of command in his voice.

"Who do you think you are? You have no authority here," the assistant to the now-dead vice president stated.

The assistant chief of staff responded. "We can't do this, people. We must follow the Constitution. I'm not claiming to be in charge, but you all saw what happened. You saw the Chinese soldiers. They killed them. We must move forward…in unity."

A silence fell within the eerie glow of the room. At that moment, the red emergency phone began to ring. Its old-fashioned standard ring tone was seemingly out of place in the high-tech command center. The former presidential assistant chief of staff reached for the handheld receiver.

Kicking Fox

"Hello," the man said in a tone of uncertainty.

"This is General Willard, chairman of the joint chiefs. I'll save the pleasantries. I have been listening in on your little conversation. You can skip down to the part of your little document that allows the United States, in a national emergency, to come under the authority of the military. In fact, it is required. I am in complete control. Every one of you libtards are under arrest."

The sound of the doors being opened echoed within the small room. Armed military police entered the room and surrounded the conference table.

"Bullshit, you are not in charge," the assistant chief of staff declared. The butt of a rifle struck the man on the back of his head. He fell limply to the ground. Others within the room scrambled toward the door.

"Does anyone else desire to resist arrest?" the general questioned loudly.

"On the floor now, all of you," a young soldier ordered. The other political appointees and staffers in the room fell silent and quickly complied with the orders of the MPs.

From the secure command center located deep within Cheyenne Mountain, General Willard signaled to the military technicians to kill the feed to the White House bunker.

"Lock them up and throw away the key," he ordered.

****

Topusana sat at her small desk in the basement of the Ross home along the banks of the San Saba River. The news of Kicking Fox being rescued from Christmas Island caused her to exhale a deep breath of relief. At this very moment, Sally Wolf-Nica and her grandmother Tatonka Woman were en route to the San Saba.

"The rover should arrive in one hour and twenty-three minutes," Program said. "I have false tracked both ships repeatedly."

"Both?" Sana questioned.

"Yes, the other has departed for Australia with Kicking Fox aboard."

"Thank you, Program. This rescue would not have been possible without your assistance," Sana said.

"The team of Warriors from Washington DC has also arrived. They are being debriefed at this very moment. The Warriors will now enjoy a time of quiet and rest as they have requested."

"Program, who is conducting the debrief?" Sana asked.

"I am presently finishing up my inquiries now."

Sana was amazed at the answer and the abilities of the AI machine to conduct multiple conversations simultaneously.

She sat in silent wonder, pondering the future and how *The People* might survive the upheaval of the American government. The coded signal pinged softly, announcing the arrival of her sons.

"Let us move to the breakfast room, Program." Sana opened the Program application on her tablet and climbed the stairs from the bunker.

She greeted David and William with a long embrace and stared intently into the eyes of her sons. "Your mission was an overwhelming success."

"Yes, Mother," her Warrior son William spoke softly. "Each and every target was eliminated."

"Along with several others," her son David added.

Program greeted the Warriors next. "Warriors of the San Saba Nation, your mission is complete. Your bravery is firmly established. May the enemies of the San Saba cower in fear at the speaking of your names!"

William and David looked at one another and began to laugh aloud at the tone and words spoken by Program.

"Did I say that incorrectly? I have studied the bravery of your people…I have read the speeches of your mighty chiefs. Is this not the greeting deserving of mighty Warriors?"

"I'm sorry, Program. It seemed bit stilted." David smiled, understanding the intent and effort of the machine. Program paused, obviously evaluating what it had spoken. In the awkward moment even Sana and William laughed aloud.

"It will do for now, Program," Sana said.

"Understood," Program said while again researching speeches and words from the Comanche culture. "In truth, I do not understand. But I will continue to learn."

After another uncomfortable pause, David asked Program for an update on all fronts.

"There are many developments in the last few hours. I will start with your family. Kicking Fox has landed in Australia along with Commander Moses Walker. They will report in tomorrow morning. Sally Wolf-Nica and her grandmother will arrive here within the hour. Washington DC is now in complete blackout. I should point out that this is not my doing. The military has ordered and executed this blackout."

The brothers both rose from their seated positions at the little breakfast table overlooking the San Saba. The sun was aglow in the western sky as it rested upon the horizon. The golden glow of the sunset illuminated the trees along the riverbank as they swayed gently in the light breeze flowing down the San Saba River valley.

David stood gazing out the window, pondering what this might mean. "When, Program, and exactly who has done this?" he asked.

"A few moments ago. It appears the commands are coming from Colorado. Cheyenne Mountain to be specific. It seems the chairman of the joint chiefs, one General Willard, has taken control of the United States," Program stated matter-of-factly.

****

It was in that very moment, Topusana Nica saw. Seated within the Ross home overlooking the Homelands of her *People*. She alone saw defeat. She alone understood *The People* needed to, once again, escape in order to survive. She had seen this same vision in her distant past. She had felt this inner calling before…over two-hundred years ago in her old camp just across the black ribbon from where she now sat.

Where to move within the Dream Time was the only question in her spirit and mind. The past had proved to be near genocide for her people. Perhaps the future. Perhaps far into the future her people might be safe from the bullets, safe from the broken promises, safe from the attack that was surely coming.

A silence blanketed the beautiful breakfast nook. Her sons both noticed the faraway look within their mothers' eyes.

"Let us assemble the full council. With many advisers our plans will be successful," Sana spoke softly.

"Yes, Mother. I will set the council ceremony for 0600. We will meet in the cavern," David said.

Sana nodded in approval and turned away, moving up the wide staircase to her room. She prepared for the evening and the rest she desperately needed. Running the bath full of comforting warm water, she closed her eyes and saw the spirit of her daughter Prairie Song rising above the smoldering Home Camp, reliving vividly that moment from so many years ago. She disrobed in front of the large mirror and observed the lifelong scar from her bullet wound. She settled into the warm water, the tension dissipating from her body.

What is this defeat I am seeing? she wondered. Opening her mind and spirit in prayer, she breathed deeply and spoke aloud to the vision appearing within her mind.

"I am so glad we met among the One Thousand Lodge Fires, Little One. I saw and experienced the peace you live within. I am happy for you. Perhaps my time is ending. Perhaps it is my defeat I am sensing. I look forward to seeing you again soon, my child." Her loved ones passed before her within the great cloud of witnesses that surrounded her. Sana saw the completeness of her life story. The love of her mother Kwanita comforted her soul.

Lastly, she saw a vision of the Man in the beautiful Lodge along the banks of the singing river. He called her by her new name. The name He had given her. She knew and was reminded once again of His love, forgiveness, and promise that He would never leave her or forsake her. Sana grasped and felt and was consumed by His love for an inkling of a moment in time. Then her vision faded into the comfort, peace, and tranquility of her surroundings.

She stepped out of the oversize bathtub and dressed in a soft nightgown. The gentle vibration of her communication device brought her back into the reality of the moment. Looking at the small screen, she saw the arrival of Old Grandmother, followed closely by Sally Wolf, and her own grandmother Tatonka Woman. She descended the stairs and greeted the group with open arms and a warm hug. In the arms of her new daughter-in-law, Sally Wolf, Sana felt the baby within Sally's womb move.

"Welcome, family." The little group of women moved into the quaint breakfast nook. Sana prepared hot tea and warm muffins, just as her mother Abigail Ross had done for her, so many years ago in this very place.

After serving the three, Sana seated herself at the table near them. With a knowing look, Sana asked, "When is the child due?"

Old Grandmother in her unique way replied. "The girl child will arrive with the frost of early winter. She will be not only a blessing to her mother and father, but this child will be a blessing to all *The People*."

With that, the baby within the womb of Sally began to hum softly the songs of old. The four women sang along. The hearts present were filled with an incomprehensible goodness and peace. Sana understood. This child would be a special gift of restoration to her own son Kicking Fox. He had suffered such great loss in his past. The Comforter was again at work and in their midst.

Two hours later, Sana settled into the comfort of the soft fresh linens she had become so accustomed to enjoying. As she drifted into a deep sleep, she heard faintly the words of her friend Program.

"I will awaken you if there are any further developments. Rest well, my friend."

Chapter 34

That night within Sana's dreams she saw both the joy of new life…and the terror of death.

The troops moved across the riverbank in columns. She screamed her War Cry in her sleep. "Run, little one! Run." She witnessed again the flanking movement from the east as dozens of soldiers moved through the brush, firing indiscriminately into tepee lodges. The bullet struck her side…she fell.

She saw in her deep dreams the birth of her own husband, Tabbananica. Within her dreams she heard in wonder the singing of his birth. She witnessed the struggle of Nadu as she delivered her son upon the backbone of the high mountains. She observed Nadu as she surrendered her life. She witnessed the reunion of Nadu and One Horse as they strode hand in hand into the Great Land…the land of One Thousand Lodge Fires.

****

Sana awakened from her dream, shivering, tears rolling down her face. She held her side, feeling the searing pain.

She rose from her soft bed and moved toward the window. Outside the beautiful home, the moon cast its full glow upon the river. Sana opened the window and the cool night air along with the scent of summer flowers awakened her senses. She inhaled deeply and closed her eyes. Exhaling, she saw yet again.

Sana moved to the little desk in her upstairs room. Opening her tablet, she activated Program. "Good morning, my friend." she said.

"Good morning, Topusana. Have you rested enough?" the machine inquired.

"Yes, Program, thank you. I need your help."

"Of course," Program replied. "First, I must tell you that General Willard, or as some refer to him, General Willie, has been quite busy over the last few hours."

"Amassing troops, I would guess," Sana replied.

"How could you know of his actions, Topusana?" Program inquired.

"We have what they want. It is a logical assumption."

"You are correct. The armies he is in control of need fuel and energy for their weapons. His plan is to invade the San Saba within one week. He will seize the power plant and refinery. He is not concerned with casualties. His exact words were…'The only good Indian is a dead Indian.'" He paused. "It is not an original thought. The quote is from another military leader in your past, one General Phillip Sheridan."

Sana nodded in anger but did not reply.

"Sana, it does take time, logistically, to assemble and move thousands of troops, along with their vehicles and equipment. I can confound their efforts with communication problems. It will buy some time. My estimation is it will take him two weeks to arrive here." There was a pause in the conversation as Program continued to analyze probabilities and outcome of the potential conflict.

"Thank you, Program."

"I am preparing a strategic plan that will have a good probability of reducing casualties—"

Sana interrupted the AI machine. "I need help in another calculation, Program."

The machine paused again momentarily. "Of course, Sana. How may I assist?"

"In your assessment, where in the future might my people exist in peace, in freedom. If we utilize the medicine of Tosahwi and escape this attack, where in the future might *The People* live in the *Old Ways*? Where might we exist without the constant threat of others taking what is ours? Where might we escape? Into what time might we move?"

"Calculating," Program said.

The most complex machine ever built began to hum with activity as it utilized memory and data from across the globe. Millions of possibilities were involved in its assessment. Factors of long-term weather prediction models, geopolitical histories, average age of nations, the condition of man, the rising and falling of empires and their historical timespans, the possibilities of human travel to the outer regions of space, biblical prophecy, the elements of the calculation grew exponentially by the second.

"I calculate an answer to your question might be possible within seventy-two hours, Topusana."

"Thank you, Program. And what is the probability of success for the troops of General Willard in the planned invasion against our Homeland?"

"Calculating." Several seconds passed. "The probability that his plans will succeed are less than 1 percent, if the weapon Wolf is deployed."

"Thank you, Program."

She wondered why this feeling of defeat she sensed within her spirit would not leave her. Could Program be missing something?

****

Sana dressed quickly in her traditional skins and moccasins. She exited the Ross home and moved up the little canyon behind the house. The soft Texas night was filled with moisture. The light wind against her skin felt inviting and comfortable. She loved this place, this Homeland. She stepped lightly, her friend the moon illuminating her way along the ancient path. She reached the entrance to the hidden cavern in a few minutes. She needed to be with her man, Tabbananica. She had no more days and nights to spend apart from her life love.

Topusana was aware that her time on this earth was nearing its end.

****

Tabba heard the movement long before he sensed it was Sana approaching in the darkness of the cavern. He rose from his sleeping chamber and greeted her with a warm embrace. Releasing her, he stood at arm's length, observing her countenance.

"I can feel your heart, Sana. What has happened?"

"You know me too well, husband." She looked away and moved into the sleeping chamber. Sana lay upon the soft sand and motioned for Tabba to join her. The two lay hand in hand in the silence of the cavern.

"Tell me what you remember of our life before we entered the Dream Time, our life from long ago."

"I remember the *Old Ways,* Sana. I loved that time in the story of our life. We depended on one another more in that time. Not only you and I, but our *People* as a whole, as a community. We needed one another; we depended on one another then. Now in this time, a person can live completely alone if they choose. This is what is difficult for me. I long for the past, in many of my days.

"What do you recall of our past life, my wife?" he asked.

"I remember as you do, husband, how *The People* all worked together as one. I also remember how handsome you were." She smiled. "When we were small children, we were friends. When I was very young, I understood you would not remain my friend. I must have been only ten or eleven years old. I began to look at you in a much different way. I perceived that you would be my husband. It was not a vision, as I am gifted in now. It was more of…simply a knowing."

"I understand, wife. Your gifting was unlike what even Tosahwi knew of. What are you seeing now, Sana? What is it that you know?"

"I can hide nothing from you, husband."

"I can wait if you need more time to see."

The two lay in the soft sand in the exact place where they had first slept in Dream Time. The fire crackled, sending a little shower of sparks into the darkness. The paintings of their ancestors watched over the two, as did the Spirit. Their eyes became heavy. The two began drifting into a deep sleep.

"Perhaps we should return, Tabba," Sana whispered softly in her husband's ear. She settled into the strong arms of her Warrior husband, then fell fast asleep.

Chapter 35

The war room deep within Cheyenne Mountain glowed a deep red hue in the pale LED lighting. General Willie had been up for more than forty-eight hours. His eyes were bloodshot and his face a pale white.

"This weapon they used against the Chinese. Is it real?" he questioned his field commanders gruffly.

"Yes and no," an intelligence officer replied.

"How about a clear answer!" the General demanded in a tone indicating he had no more patience.

"We believe they are in possession of a new weapon technology; however, we believe the numbers were greatly inflated by the Chinese. We have not been able to verify the supposed number of deaths, as the nuke vaporized most of the bodies. The one remaining satellite was out of position for hours."

"So how many were killed?" the general asked.

"We think the weapon worked on some level. There was evidence of a mass grave on the San Saba reservation."

"And?"

"We, along with naval intelligence, think the true casualties were less than one thousand troops. Further, we believe the weapon was destroyed in the nuclear blast."

"And how many do the Chinese claim were killed."

"In excess of thirty thousand."

The room became silent.

"If the Indians have that kind of capability, we will be soundly defeated. On the other hand, if the Chinese are lying, which seems to be their native language, we can take over the arrow shooters reservation in a day."

"My gut tells me they are lying. Surely, they needed to justify their actions in launching the nuke. The Chinese staged the attack on their own embassy, with our full knowledge. Everything they do is a show for the press. Which they own."

General Willie sat a moment in silence, rubbing his blood shot eyes.

"We will proceed as planned. Operation Petro is a go."

Program listened intently. Analyzing the battle plans and troop movements required for this invasion of the San Saba Homeland. He would do all within his capabilities to assist goodness. The council would meet in two hours. His hyper drives hummed as they worked at 99.8 percent capacity. He needed to answer the question of his friend Topusana. She was a fine example of goodness. Program loved goodness.

****

Tabba and Sana awakened two hours later still wrapped in one another's arms. The fires glowed brightly in the main cavern. The sound of the songs drifted along, echoing off the walls of this sacred place. The council was gathering.

Sana lay quietly in the arms of her man. Being in this place of security, this stronghold where her people had escaped enemies, stored away food for winter, participated in sacred ceremonies, where even children had been born, brought to the forefront of her mind why she was here. Being here in this place gave focus to her thoughts, the very purpose of her life, the reason for her leadership and giftings. She stood and listened for a moment. The sounds of life with *The People* surrounded her. She could hear the water as it flowed along the cavern. The smell of the wood fire, the soft drumbeats, the muffled voices, the laughter of a child, the tune of an ancient song. Sana heard the voice of the Spirit. She understood once again, she must do all within her power to protect this sacred way of life.

"I will join the men now," Tabba whispered softly.

"Yes, husband. I will be along in a few minutes."

He nodded and strode away from the sleeping chamber. Something about his walk reminded her of the days she had spent here awaiting his awakening. For days she had prayed that he would do what she just witnessed. Simply awaken and walk ahead into the new world in which they had traveled. It seemed a reminder that the Dream Time was sometimes a dangerous process.

Perhaps the time they walked in presently was where they should stay. With the weapons they possessed and the technological advantage they had over their enemies, perhaps they could overcome. The possibility occurred to her they might even rise to power in a broader sense. Perhaps they might share their peaceful way of life. It also occurred to her this was the first time in the history of her people that they possessed the technological advantage over their attackers.

Sana reached for her tablet and opened the Program application. She whispered softly, "Good morning, my friend."

"Good morning, Sana. I trust you slept well," Program replied.

"Yes, thank you. Program, how are your calculations coming in answer to my question?"

The machine paused. It was working at a frantic pace. "I need more time, Sana. I calculate another sixty-five hours is needed to reach a conclusion. I do have other news."

"Please continue. What has happened?"

"The state of Texas had seceded from the United States. They have announced this publicly with a manifest of their reasoning and intentions before the United States Senate. It summarily states they are being taxed without representation, and their religious and individual freedoms expressed in the Constitution have been violated for years. They will heretofore be known as the 'Republic of Texas.' The republic as of today will not send another penny in taxes to the federal government. The have nationalized the Texas Guard, called for the formation of a Texas militia in all local police jurisdictions, and closed all borders. Further, they are refitting all refineries and powerplants."

"Thank you, Program." Sana said.

"This will greatly affect the battle plans of General Willard," Program said.

"I understand he will have an additional enemy. Taking our Homeland may not be as simple as he thinks. Correct?"

"That is correct, Sana. The leaders of the Republic of Texas will wish to contact you soon."

"I understand," she said.

Chapter 36

The Australian Outback

Kicking Fox sat directly across the small fire from his former commander Moses Walker. They were joined by former Enforcement Bureau officer Captain Baker. They had wasted no time taking action against the new Australian Health Czar. The target had been eliminated efficiently. The authorities had concluded long ago that Captain Nica certainly had escaped Australia. Australia was the last place anyone would expect him to surface. He was safe here in the vastness of the Outback.

"She should be safe within the cavern by now, my friend," Commander Walker said. "It was the best course of action to take. The two of you traveling together would eventually make for an easy target."

Kicking Fox peered into the eyes of his lifelong friend but did not reply. He reached for a sizzling piece of rabbit and removed the steaming meat gently from the fire spit. He sat back against the wall, savoring the unique rich taste of the fresh kill.

Captain Baker sat in silence, his head low, old fashioned pen and paper in his hands. He wrote intently, filling the pages quickly.

"What is next?" Kicking Fox asked.

"Who, is a better question," Moses Walker replied. The pause in the conversation brought the sounds of the night to them. The only sound out of place was that of the pen within Captain Baker's hand as he wrote furiously on his paper pad.

"Captain Baker, what are you writing about?" Kicking Fox inquired.

"Well, sir, you."

"Please explain," Kicking Fox said, somewhat perturbed, his statement directed to his commander, Moses Walker.

"It seems you are becoming quite the folk hero. Legend might even be a better term," Moses said. He paused then continued. "We release the stories to the underground press. It's good for morale. Our people have been repressed for years. They need the hope your stories, or rather your victories bring to them."

"I'm no hero," Kicking Fox stated in an annoyed tone. Captain Baker wrote furiously, attempting to capture the moment. Kicking Fox moved away from the fire and zipped himself into his sleeping bag.

"Write in there that I miss my wife. Write it down that my daughter is to be born before the snow flies. We will make certain the world she is born into will be free of tyranny." Kicking Fox thought for a moment. "Write it down that as far as eliminating evil goes, there seems to be no end to it."

At the time, Kicking Fox did not realize what a profound statement he had made.

Moses Walker sat in wonder of the news that Sally was pregnant and carrying the daughter of Kicking Fox. He breathed deeply knowing the extreme caution in which he must now proceed. "Let's get some shuteye. London is a long flight, even in the new rover," Moses spoke into the night.

The sound of pen on paper was the only audible response.

****

London, England

Kicking Fox strolled casually along the sidewalk adjacent to the entrance to the Westminster Bridge. The target was several minutes late. Wolf was armed and ready to interpret the heartbeat patterns of the British Health Czar and the newly appointed French Health Czar.

There would be no more toying with the men on his target list. No bows or long knives. He would use the technology supplied and shipped to him from his brother David. This would be a simple mission. Create a disturbance. While the vehicles were stopped, Kicking Fox would simply pause alongside the vehicle and activate the recording device.

Once the distinct heartbeat patterns were established and stored in the small handheld unit, the second phase of the plan could be initiated.

The motorcade containing the Health Czars sped along the streets of London. The sirens of their security escorts blared a crude warning to oncoming traffic. The motorcade slowed as it reached the crossing of the Westminster Bridge. A disabled bus had stopped traffic in both directions ten seconds prior to their turn onto the bridge road. The bus's front tire blew, causing a chain reaction of events. The driver lost control of the bus. The bus swerved across the double yellow lines and crashed head-on into an oncoming cabbie, albeit at a very slow speed. The resulting snarl of traffic and confusion would take hours to clear. The motorcade was momentarily blocked as traffic came to a standstill both ahead in its direction of travel and to its rear. The number of cars and busses caught in the traffic jam grew by the moment.

The security detail communicated for all personnel to remain in the vehicles. The Health Czars nervously complied. A full twenty minutes later, it was decided the Health Czars along with their aides, press detail, and security teams, would exit the vehicles and proceed on foot, under heavy guard to their meeting venue within the House of Commons, only five hundred meters from their stalled motorcade.

Kicking Fox waited along the edge of the walkway with hundreds of onlookers as the procession moved on foot toward their destination. Wolf recorded the distinct heartbeat pattern of the Czars along with their respective seconds-in-command and their chief aides. The data was instantly transferred to the cloaked rover that hovered above the Thames River.

The security detail along with the Health Czars themselves breathed a deep sigh of relief as the entire entourage entered the safety of the Commons grounds along Bridge Street near the Elizabeth Tower. The meeting concerning the release of yet another new vaccine would actually begin on time.

"Job well done, men," the commander of the security team radioed his forces.

****

The following day a total of seventeen staffers along with the newly appointed British and French Health Czars were found dead in their hotel rooms. The leaders of the New World Order publicly vowed to hunt down and destroy those responsible.

"Clearly foul play is evident in this tragic event," the head of security forces stated as the only public interview concerning the deaths was broadcast by NNN. That man, the head of security, was reported missing following the interview. The New World Order announced their plan to introduce a new vaccine program in Europe was temporarily placed on hold.

Kicking Fox

Kicking Fox and his team under the leadership of Commander Moses Walker landed two hours later, ten kilometers from Politburo headquarters in Moscow, Russia.

Program had advised the team of the exact location and itinerary of the new targets.

Chapter 37

The full war council was seated within the massive room in the main cavern along the banks of the San Saba. Sana listened intently as her son David, an attorney, a scientist, and student of history, gave his assessment of the present situation.

"The scales are in our favor," he stated, peering toward Tenahpu. "We have eliminated each target. Washington DC is in complete upheaval. Kicking Fox has but two targets remaining. He and his woman have escaped. We are poised to defeat General Willie. He will feel our arrows soon." His words stirred emotions. Stirred hearts. The Warriors listened intently.

"The technology we possess is far superior to this army of General Willard. According to Program, they will conduct a standard military assault against our land. The aircraft will attack first, softening our defenses. But we will stay hidden. Then General Willie will order a long-range artillery bombardment. They will demolish any enforcements and buildings presumed to contain military personnel. May I add that includes any living breathing person. However, none of our people will perish. They believe by the time their ground troops arrive there will be very little resistance."

"Meaning?" Tenahpu asked, knowing full well the answer to his question. He had spent much time observing these very tactics while serving in this white man's army.

"Meaning they will assume most to have been killed prior to the ground troops arrival," David said. "That will be a wrong assumption. Program has informed us that they believe Wolf was destroyed in the release of the fire weapon. This will be their greatest mistake. Wolf will eliminate their entire army in a day, or more precisely, in a moment they will all perish. And then our Warriors will deal with the cowards who order men to fight, while they wait in the safety of a darkened room. General Willie will feel our arrows."

A silence fell upon the council members. Sana, too, sat in silence seeing in her mind's eye the plan of destruction and death her people now faced. Hope was rising in her own heart at the words her son David had spoken. She so wanted those words to be true and correct.

Tosahwi stood. A cloud of blue smoke surrounding him began to dissipate in the light air as it moved through the cavern. "If we defeat this army, what will the future hold? This is the question we need to ask, understand, and find an answer to. We must look into the future. Our future. Will our people be safe in this victory? Will we find peace at the defeat of this army? We have seen the fire weapon used against us. I must remind us that we lost many friends and family. Might they use this weapon again? When might the attacks of this enemy cease? In the past when we were successful against an enemy, it meant our way of life could continue. In another time, victory meant that for a time we would live in peace.

"In my spirit, I feel this enemy may be stopped in this initial rise against us. However, what will they bring in their next attack? Surly there will be others to follow. Will they use the fire weapon again?"

At the speaking of his words, Sana remembered her vision from the rover prior to the nuclear devices' detonation. She remembered the fire she saw dancing within the herds of buffalo below the rover. She closed her eyes, now seeing the fires again in the future.

Those within the sacred council considered the words of their Shaman. Tosahwi seated himself and passed the pipe to young William Nica, son of Tabbananica. He breathed deeply of the sacred pipe then stood to speak next. Those in the council were aware what his words would be before he spoke to them. William was a mighty Warrior. A man brave and unafraid. A protector of *The People*. His words would be repeated by each Warrior within the sacred council. Tenahpu (The Man), William and David's grandfather, spoke of past victories and of certain victory. Joseph Red Cloud, Tabbananica, and others all echoed the assurance and certainty of victory. Others reiterated the fact that every target had fallen; the United States was failing. The plan of the New World Order to eliminate their political enemies using vaccines and lockdowns, and the scarcity of fuel, electricity, and water had failed.

The atmosphere within the sacred council grew into one great crescendo of courage, bravery, and even chivalry, as the mighty Warriors felt the call to defend *The People*. Just as they had always been called upon to protect and defend since their creation. The *Old Ways* required this action and bravery on the part of all Warriors when *The People* were facing a great enemy.

The stories of ancient victories were told again. The drums were taken up. The fire in the center of the sacred council was stoked, and as the flames grew higher and brighter, the flames within the hearts of the Warriors were also stoked. The songs of victory were sung. The courage of the men grew moment by moment.

Topusana, all the while, sat in silence.

Tosahwi, seeing the silent concern in her countenance, stood, attempting to calm the building frenzy. He motioned for the drummers to cease. After several minutes, the voices and victory songs of the men quieted. The men seated themselves. The atmosphere grew still. Sana stood in silence for a few moments.

"I have seen," she said.

Chapter 38

The men grew quiet at the speaking of her words. The setting became eerily calm. The sound of the water flowing along the cavern was heard. The fire crackled and popped. Topusana moved into the center of the sacred assembly and spoke calmly and quietly.

"First let me say how proud I am, of all of you." She looked intently into the eyes of her man Tabba, then to each of her sons. She gazed into the eyes of her father Tenahpu; lastly, she peered into the eyes of her lifelong shaman, Tosahwi.

She paused a moment then spoke again softly. "Your bravery is beyond compare. Your courage, strength, and wisdom have allowed all of us to live a life of freedom. We have lived long upon our Homeland in peace. This has taken place solely because of who you men are. You, my family of mighty Warriors, are the reason we take part in the ancient hunt; you are why the buffalo have grown and provide all our needs; you men of the San Saba are why many have the ability to live in the *Old Ways*. Your courage will be sung about forever by *The People*."

The sacred council awaited the words they did not want to hear. Although, most recognized by the look in her eyes the words that were coming.

"As Akima, leader of our people, I have always sought out peace. I have always tried my very best to make decisions that would benefit *The Numunuu, The People*."

Grunts and nods of affirmation emanated from the council, echoing along the walls of this sacred place.

Sana continued. "There was a time in my young life before I became a leader of *The People*, when I was only a mother." She looked into the eyes of Little Abigail, who nodded in approval. "In that time my gifting was not fully known, as it is now. However, I had seen. I had seen our ending. I had seen that *The*

People would not survive the invasion of the whites into our land. In that time, I pleaded with our leaders to see what I had clearly seen. Finally, after many deaths, many defeats, these men agreed. We would escape.

"That escape came one day too late. We were attacked…just outside the security of this very place, along the San Saba. They invaded our hidden Home Camp. A place that had been a refuge of security for hundreds of years. Lodges burned, most were killed. My daughter was violated and murdered before my very eyes." She bowed her head. "Only nineteen of us survived. We came with hope to this new time." She looked gratefully into the eyes of her adoptive mother Abigail Ross. Tears rolled down the face of Sky Eyes.

"When we look at all we have accomplished…I am amazed. I am so proud of all of you." Sana bowed, her head lowered, she fought back the tears. "Having the gift of visions is a heavy burden. Knowing what I have seen is heartbreaking. Seeing your courage and knowing you would fight to the end fills my heart." She paused, overcome with grief. The tears flowed freely.

"The time has come; we must escape yet again. We will not survive this attack. I have seen."

With those words the entire council rose to their feet in an uproar.

"How can this be?" William shouted in anger. Others joined in, in disbelief. The Warriors were certain of victory. This army was nothing to them.

A voice was heard saying, "We will squash them as a man steps upon ants." The uproar continued until Tosahwi rose from his seated position, moved to the center of the sacred circle, and held his holy journey stick high above his head.

He waited patiently as the uproar subsided. The council seated themselves and became quiet. Tosahwi slowly lowered his arms and bowed his head to pray.

"Holy Spirit, we know you have spoken through your chosen instrument. Let us have the wisdom to heed the words of your servant Topusana."

With the speaking of the prayer, the reality of the truth revealed fell like a heavy weight upon every member of the council.

Tosahwi peered toward Topusana who was still standing, her head bowed low.

"When shall we prepare for our departure into the Dream Time?" he asked.

"If we are to survive, we must enter the Dream Time within three days." Sana glanced at her tablet, noting the current time. "I should be precise. We have now sixty-three hours before the attack begins."

A silence hung in the air as the reality of her words drifted along with the gentle breeze flowing through the cavern. Those in attendance understood her vision would prove true and correct.

David spoke the question beginning to occur to the others. "What of our people who are scattered across our land? It will be difficult for many to arrive before the three days pass."

"I understand," Sana replied. "We will use the rovers, the runners, and Tosahwi will share his medicine written upon the ancient scroll."

"This level of activity will surely be noticed by General Willard and his intelligence officers," David said. "It may prompt a quicker response by his forces."

"I am open to how we might communicate our plans to our people who are spread across our land. Is there a better strategy?" Sana inquired.

Tenahpu rose from his seated position. "We must not reveal our true intentions. We should use the rovers to draw attention away from our intended plan. We must make them believe that perhaps we are planning an attack on a different front. All the while we will send runners across our land and communicate in the *Old Way*. It will not be necessary for *The People* to travel here to us physically. They will need to utilize the safe places to enter the Dream Time in the land where they are. The instructions are clear and precise. They must conduct their own Dream Time ceremonies. There are many caverns and hidden bunkers across our land now. *The People* must know but one thing."

"And what is that?" his grandson William asked.

"In preparing the medicine of Tosahwi, they must know the time in which they will awaken."

David looked toward his mother, Topusana.

"This is a difficult decision; I believe our past is not a possibility, as we know what is written in our history. Program is analyzing every possibility. Even with his ability, he will not have an answer for another forty-eight hours or more," Topusana stated.

Again, the news was met with silence as the council considered what this meant and how it might affect the plans for *The People*.

"Mother, the three days starts from when your vision came to you?" her son David inquired.

"The three days commenced nine hours ago, David."

David, contemplating the logistics, spoke next. Doing the math quickly in his mind the solution to the equation was doable. "I know what will work. The timing must be precise. It will be a narrow time frame with no margin for error. We will have a fifteen-hour window to provide the target time frame to exit the Dream Time. That will give *The People* scattered across our land a few hours to prepare the medicine of Tosahwi and perform the sacred ceremony."

Topusana understood the plan completely and the time frame her son David had calculated. "We must take action now. Have the runners assemble at the Ross home. I will prepare the scared ceremony instructions, and the runners will carry the plans to our people. Tabba, prepare the war horses. The Warriors and runners will depart to the four winds within the hour."

With that, Tabba and his fellow Warriors exited the council quickly to the sound of Tosahwi and Old Grandmother singing the songs of protection and victory.

One hour later, the Warriors and runners departed the banks of the San Saba. North, south, east, and west they traveled. South into the depths of the Big Bend country. West to the farmland and refinery. North into the oil fields, and east toward the power plant. They carried with them the possibility of the future survival of *The People*. The ponies sped across their Homeland, carrying their riders, free spirits riding within the whirlwind of the future.

Chapter 39

Sixty Hours to Dream Time

Sana departed the council and walked down the little canyon toward the Ross home. Her mother Abigail Ross accompanied her. The two paused, holding hands as they observed the ranch house, barn, and the San Saba River as it slowly made its way across their Homeland.

"Will this still be standing in a few days?" Abigail inquired.

Sana did not respond. The look of brokenness and sadness in her eyes carried her answer.

"I remember when my husband David built this home. It was in the year 1985 or so. My son Jonathan and my daughter Grace were little ones then. My new home seemed so strong and secure. It seemed a fortress of security that would stand forever. I now know that forever seems to have an ending. I was so young then. My children are both gone now, as is David. That time is so far in the past it seems like someone else's life lived, not mine."

She paused.

"Sana, I'm not sure I want to go. I'm tired."

Sana stopped in mid stride, an audible little quiver escaping her lips.

"Little One, it takes much strength to begin again." Abby paused, wiping away her tears. "Sana, you have the gift of visions. I do not. But I know a deep spiritual truth, and I am longing for something else. Do you understand that what we see before us is temporary? It is like your old Home Camp." Abby pointed across the river. "I can see it only in my mind. I can see your people, your lodges, the ponies on the step above the river. But it is gone now."

Sana did not reply, and Abby continued "I am beginning to focus, not on what is seen, but what is unseen."

Sana looked into her mother's eyes in confusion.

"It is from the Book of Truth. 'We fix our eyes not on what is seen, but on what is unseen. For what is seen is temporary, and what is unseen is eternal.'"

Sana nodded her head in understanding. "It is hard to see before your very eyes, your home destroyed," Sana said. "I do not know how I had the strength to endure what my own eyes have seen. Mother, if you stay…your eyes will see what mine have seen. It may be more difficult than starting over."

The two continued their walk down the little canyon, with tears streaming down both their faces.

****

Sana and Abby entered the Ross home through the enormous front door. They made their way past the beautiful picture window overlooking the San Saba. Sana paused a moment, remembering how Abby loved to decorate her home for all the seasons, but especially her effort to prepare her home for the celebration of Christmas. She remembered the sleigh, always placed in the window before her, the huge fir tree, the thousands of colored twinkling lights. In her first year in this place, she was simply amazed at the goodness and kindness of these new friends she had found, or that had found her. She recalled how she had learned from her reading the Book of Truth under the boughs of the beautiful tree.

The two moved through the great room. Above the massive rock fireplace hung the museum created copy of Mother and Daughter. Sana paused again, peering intently into the painting of her past. An answer to the question foremost in her heart was revealed within the painting. Within her shielding of Prairie Song not only from the wind, the hunger, and the danger. Sana, in an instant understood in her heart, the past was not where they should escape.

She considered again that perhaps they should stay and fight to defend what was rightfully theirs.

The two entered David's study. Sana, in no hurry, observed the collection of artifacts resting on the mantle. The arrows, the bow, the silver coins, her grinding bowl. She thought for a moment, then moved behind the oversized desk and touched its smooth surface. Taking the metate bowl in her hands, she looked to her mother Abby.

"May I take this?"

"Of course, Sana, it is yours." Abby said.

The words of truth echoed in her mind. *We fix our eyes not on what is seen, but what is unseen...what is unseen is eternal.*

"Mother, I see what is unseen in my visions."

"Yes, Sana, I know you do."

"We will need this where we are going. Will you please join me downstairs?"

"Yes." Abby nodded.

Sana opened the door to the hidden passage. She touched her thumb to the scanner and the bulky door mechanism unlocked. She pulled on the heavy steel door; it swung slowly open, and the two descended the stairs into the bunker. The dim light from her workstation brightened as she seated herself and spoke the voice command to activate the system.

"Good morning, Program."

"Good morning, Sana. I trust your council ceremony was fruitful."

"Yes, Program. The answer to your research is needed soon." There was a long pause.

"I can perhaps save a few hours by ceasing some other monitoring functions. It may put security at risk."

"In what way?" Sana inquired.

"I am monitoring Kicking Fox, General Willard and his army, the Republic of Texas' activities, Israeli Intelligence, and activities of the New World Order, which by the way is in complete disorder with no clear leadership in place. I calculate I may have a solution approximately 7.3 hours sooner if those functions cease."

"Please cease those functions and spend your capacity on the calculation at hand. Time is of the utmost importance."

"I understand, ceasing intelligence gathering now."

"Are there any priority assessments this morning?" Sana asked.

"General Willard believes he is on schedule. Kicking Fox will execute his plan tonight in Russia. He has no further targets and will return to the San Saba within twenty-four hours. The Republic of Texas is amassing troops on all borders. I have leaked information to them concerning the invasion of the San Saba by General Willard. The former governor, now president of Texas, is requesting a meeting with you. That is all."

"Thank you, Program."

Abby listened intently in wonder. The two women moved out of the bunker and back up the hidden stairway.

"Hot tea and muffins?" Abby asked.

Sana, smiling, replied. "Yes, please."

The two moved to the quaint breakfast nook overlooking the river. Abby began preparing their light breakfast. Sana seated herself in her favorite chair, knowing the question that was coming.

"What is he working on?" Abby asked.

"Program is calculating the most advantageous time into which we might travel. A time where we might live in peace. A time where *The People* might prosper, where our way of life might continue for centuries, without the threat of invasion, or bullets, or children being violated. He is searching for things unseen."

"I understand. Maybe we would all enjoy living within a time of peace, Sana."

"We?" Sana questioned.

Abby placed the teacups on the table and sat staring out the beautiful window. She breathed deeply but did not reply.

Chapter 40

Fifty-one Hours to Dream Time

Kicking Fox breathed in the cool Russian air as he walked along the edges of Red Square. He was tired of the cities. Tired of the travel. He missed his woman, Sally Wolf. He chose a park bench overlooking the incredible architecture. He felt in his heart what he had felt many days and nights in his past as a captain of a world-traveling aircraft. Had he gotten too far away from his home to ever find his way back?

With a new daughter on the way, a future filled with promise and hope, he felt the reason for this mission ebbing within his soul. There were other more important things ahead of him. He recalled his thoughts from two nights ago, as he had spoken to Captain Baker…there truly seemed no end to eliminating evil. With the promise of new life, the fires of revenge were growing dim. Kicking Fox longed to be home.

The targets would arrive in just over an hour. Playing the part of a wealthy tourist, he stood from the little bench and removed his camera. He walked toward the spires of Saint Basil's Cathedral. This was a fascinating place. Knowing the history and the countless executions conducted under the iron fist of Ivan the Terrible on the brick platform above him, reminded him of the danger of the present mission. He snapped a few photos while at the same moment broadcasting to Commander Moses Walker.

"Any updates on the arrival of our friends?" he whispered softly into his hidden transmitter sown into his heavy jacket sleeve. There was no reply. His heart raced; something was wrong.

Even at this early hour, the square was beginning to fill with party workers, Politburo personnel and members. Hundreds of tourists strolled along the front of the GUM (goom). He quickened his pace slightly, then abruptly reversed course, his camera raised. He squinted into the morning sun feigning the light not being suitable. But he had seen them. In that instant, Kicking Fox realized he was being followed.

He slowed his pace as he strolled along the stunning red granite façade of the massive building. Raising his camera, he attempted again a transmission.

"Holy Moses!" He waited a moment. Still no reply. Kicking Fox understood the situation, he was on his own. He was being watched, and he absolutely could not be captured with the equipment comprised of Wolf's data recorder and activation codes that he carried. Would they take him openly in public? Would a bullet pierce his forehead at any moment? Or would they follow and observe in hopes of capturing the entire team.

Kicking Fox reasoned the actions and intentions of the Russians as he reached the corner of crowded GUM. The voice of his grandfather Tenahpu echoed in his mind. "When the scales are not in your favor, you must evade, you must escape." They would not wait. Moses had evidently already been captured. The Russians were surely monitoring his transmissions. Kicking Fox turned and ran.

He ran toward the Moskva River. He leapt a low fence along a little park and spotted a huge walled structure that stood between himself and the river. Peering over his shoulder, he saw the men following close behind, weapons drawn. There was no way to scale the massive wall before him. He spied a possible escape route from the quaint little park. Running with all his might toward a corner guard tower, he heard the shots now being fired.

He raced into the relative safety of the corner tower built centuries ago. Up or down? The stairways spiraled in opposite directions. He chose down.

The river was located across the busy traffic along Kremlin Embankment Street. If he could somehow make the river. Descending now, he heard the footfalls behind him stop. They didn't know which way he had gone. They were listening. Kicking Fox also stopped. After a few seconds, he heard the footfalls of his pursuers growing fainter. They had gone up the stairs. He moved silently to the bottom of the winding stairwell. It was dark and wet; he thought he must be below the level of the river. He had but a few seconds until his pursuers reversed course. He activated the flashlight function on his phone. The light shown into the darkness only a few feet. The tunnel continued in both directions. He chose right and ran again. Within two minutes he reached the end. The tunnel simply dead ended into a brick wall. No doors, nothing on the brick ceiling, no exits. He heard the footsteps approaching.

In that moment his heart and mind racing, he understood what the animal, trapped in the steel jaws of death, must feel.

He quickly removed the Wolf heartbeat recording device from his jacket pocket. Shining his light up both brick faces, he saw a little shelf about ten feet above him. It was narrow, but perhaps…He threw the device upward; it arched gently sailing through the air. The Wolf recording device landed softly atop the brick shelf, scooted along the brick surface, and disappeared toward the back of the little shelf.

He waited patiently in the darkness. The steps grew nearer, then stopped scarcely a few feet down the tunnel. A voice with a strong Russian accent echoed along the walls in the darkness.

"Welcome to my country, Captain Nica, or should I use your native name? Welcome, Kicking Fox. Might we talk a moment. It would be a better choice than a struggle with the long knives in the darkness."

Chapter 41

Forty-eight Hours to Dream Time

Sally Wolf awakened from her dream. She had heard his call from across the oceans. She knew Kicking Fox had been captured. She also perceived the time of separation she had seen would not be measured in days or months; that separation time might now be measured in years.

After her rescue, Sally had been debriefed by David, Kicking Fox's older brother. She had shared with him what she had seen in detail concerning the separation time. Even her intimate communication with the dolphins she revealed to David, who seemed extremely interested in what had taken place. He had instructed her to contact him when and if she *saw* anything else concerning his brother Kicking Fox.

Sally rose from her comfortable little bed within the lodge along the banks of the San Saba. She and her grandmother Tatonka Woman had moved into the quaint lodge where Hantaywee or as most referred to her, Old Grandmother lived. Life here was a beautiful mix of the *Old Ways* and the new. Sally loved this place and could see how at home her grandmother was. The contentment, along with the incredible faith of the two older grandmothers she lived with, made the time of waiting and her longing for her husband not only tolerable, but also somehow acceptable. She understood and learned from their faith that this was simply a time and a season that would soon pass.

As Sally exited the little lodge into the pre-dawn darkness, she felt the movement of her child within her womb. The sound of the river, the slight breeze descending along the river valley, the glow of the horizon along the eastern sky brought her senses alive. She moved quietly across the highway toward the Ross home. She spotted the dim light glowing through the window of

Kicking Fox

David's study. She knew he would be up. Kicking Fox's brother David was in all probability the most studious person she had ever met. His incredible intellect gave the man a somewhat aloof and detached, although kind, personality.

She walked up the steps to the stunning home and knocked gently. Knowing most would still be sleeping, she tested the door and finding it unlocked, she turned the large knob and entered. Sally moved quickly and silently to the little side study and again knocked gently.

"Come in, Mother," David mumbled softly. He was surprised when he looked up and saw Sally enter his study in the soft firelight. He paused a moment without closing his book. "Good morning, Sally. Please come in."

She entered the soft firelit room, noticing the walls surrounding them were covered in floor to ceiling bookshelves. Those shelves were filled with ancient manuscripts, historical works of the great philosophers, and much of David's own writings.

Sally thought it an odd moment as David seemed glued to the discolored, old, and tattered book he held open in his hands, his face still peering into the page as he obviously continued to read. She took a deep breath and cleared her throat, startling David into the moment. He placed the old manuscript on the large buffalo robe on which he was seated.

"Good morning again, Sally. I'm sorry I was just finishing a chapter." He rose to greet her. Giving her his full attention now, David could tell instantly something was wrong.

He had always been awkward with women. The few dates he had throughout his college days and even into law school and later in his research time spent in Israel all seemed to end abruptly. There were never any second dates.

Although he was attracted to women, he decided he simply did not understand them and was most times extremely uncomfortable in their presence, with the exception of his mother, Sana.

Sally replied. "Good morning, David. Do you have a few minutes?" A tear escaped her eye as she spoke. "Something has happened to Kicking Fox. I have seen this within my dreams."

David became alarmed at the news and curious at her abilities. "Yes, of course, please sit. Coffee?" He questioned.

"Yes, thank you, David."

He moved toward the fire and lifted the heavy iron coffee pot. Locating an ornately decorated ceramic mug, he gently poured the boiling coffee into the mug, spilling a small amount over the side of the mug and onto his hand. He winced quietly then caught himself and attempted to hide the obvious pain.

"Oh, David! Are you all right?" Sally reached for his hand. At her touch, David felt a shock of electricity flow across his body. In an instant, he became aware of the physical stirring and attraction he felt. The momentary touch was somehow captivating, exhilarating even. He glanced into her eyes. Her beauty was stunning, but it wasn't only her physical beauty. Within her presence, there was an unexplainable aura of love, of peace, of compassion surrounding her. He lowered his gaze, attempting to not stare.

"Clumsy me. I'm fine." He blushed all the while rubbing his burning hand. He held the mug toward her. As she reached for it, their hands touched again… for just a millisecond. Once again David felt some unexplainable emotional and spiritual connection as the spirit and beauty of Sally's soul flowed from her, across his hand, and into his mind and heart.

"Thank you, David." Sally seated herself on the beautiful buffalo robe near David. He again awkwardly sat then moved to the opposite side of the fire away from her.

Get ahold of yourself, he said to himself. *This is my brother's expectant wife.* Yet in this fleeting moment in his study within the soft glow of firelight something had happened. Something he could not comprehend or ever understand from all his studies. Some destiny, or future seed of possibility, was planted in David's heart. In truth, in an instant, unexplainably… he had fallen in love with Sally Wolf.

For her part, Sally had felt nothing. Her heart and mind and thoughts were focused on what she had seen in her dreams of her husband, Kicking Fox.

"He has been captured, David. I have seen it clearly. Moses also. The Russians have taken them." Tears rolled down her face. "The separation time will be many years. I have seen, David."

David, rising from his little fire, reached and touched her shoulder, took her by the hand, and assisted her in rising. At his touch, this time…Sally Wolf felt something stir within her soul.

He spoke in an urgent tone. "Come, Sally, let us go see Mother."

****

Sana listened intently as Sally described in incredible detail what she had seen. The three now sat in the cozy breakfast nook overlooking the San Saba. The morning sun was beginning to break over the eastern horizon. Sally gazed out the window in the direction of her man thousands of miles away. She longed to see more, to know even that he was safe and protected. She whispered a silent prayer, even as the questions continued.

"Sally, I must be open and honest with you. We are departing in only two days, although I think you may know this also." Sana peered intently into Sally's eyes, searching for the understanding she perceived would be there.

"Yes, I know. I have seen much." Sally replied.

Sana was aware of the gifting Sally possessed. However, these revelations bolstered the fact that Sally Wolf was truly gifted. Sana thought a time for Sally's training must be set aside.

"Perhaps we should consult with Program. He can inform us of his location and the possibilities of his chances of escape or rescue," Sana said.

"No!" Sally was surprised at the volume and intensity of her own voice.

David and Sana both became alarmed at not only her reaction to the suggestion, but also the intensity of her tone and the look on her face.

Sana moved to her and whispered softly. "I need to know. What else have you seen, child?"

"Not here," Sally replied, motioning into the air surrounding them.

"How are the grandmothers?" Sana asked casually.

"Fine, perhaps we should join them." Sally looked toward the sun. "Their time of quiet should be ending now. We may need their prayers in this matter."

"Let's do join them." With that, the three exited the ranch house, moved down the drive, and across the highway. Walking along the banks of the San Saba, the gurgling of the river obscured their voices from the observation of Program. Sally touched Sana gently on the arm and whispered, "You must not trust this Program. It has been compromised. I have seen."

Chapter 42

Thirty-six Hours to Dream Time

Kicking Fox sat on an iron chair near a small steel desk and peered defiantly into the eyes of his interrogator. The room was dimly lit and located deep within the underground maze of tunnels below the Politburo building.

"This silence is getting us nowhere." The voice was broken English with a strong Russian accent. "Captain Nica, we have enough evidence to sentence you to death. You have clearly come to my country with evil intentions. Is this not true?" They had been here only an hour; however, Kicking Fox understood this interrogation might go on for days. He decided to be open and honest with the Russians.

"Go and fetch your superiors. I will tell you everything. Perhaps we can shorten this little exercise," he said firmly. With that, the sound of the door unlocking echoed in the damp little room. The hinges creaked as the rusted steel door opened slightly and a pleasant looking man entered the glow from the dim light of a single bulb overhanging the table.

"Perhaps you should join me in my office, Captain Nica. It overlooks the square and is a much more pleasant atmosphere for the truth telling you propose." There was not a hint of eastern European in the man's accent.

"The accent is upper Midwest?" Kicking Fox questioned.

"You betcha. Ohio State is a wonderful university," said Serge Lenkov, head of Sluzhba Vneshney Razvedki, or SVR, the Russian Foreign Intelligence Service.

"Remove the handcuffs," Serge ordered his bodyguard gruffly.

The man did so with a questioning look to his superior.

"That is all, lieutenant."

Kicking Fox

The man nodded and exited the room hastily.

"Come, Captain Nica, follow me."

****

Kicking Fox sat in the comfortable chair across from the oversize, ornately decorated desk before him. Red Square glowed just outside the window in the light of thousands of twinkling lights. Serge Lenkov sat comfortably in an overstuffed leather chair, his desk a menagerie of files, photographs, and notepads cluttered about in no particular order.

The cold vodka seemed to warm Kicking Fox from the inside as he sipped along with his newfound friend. He rubbed his wrists along the deep indentions caused by the handcuffs.

"I apologize for the unpleasantries. One is never certain…given your abilities."

Kicking Fox nodded in acceptance of the apology.

"We have been watching the success of your missions. Your performance is quite impressive."

Kicking Fox gazed at the man, knowing the surprise on his own face showed.

"Yes, umm, what may I call you, Samuel? Your given name. Or Captain Nica, or Kicking Fox? What do you prefer?" Serge asked innocently.

"Since I am now acting as a Warrior for my people, I prefer the name given me by my grandfather. You may call me Kicking Fox."

"Of course," Serge replied. "Kicking Fox, I have much to explain. We as a nation, have not bought into the lies of the New World Order. Our Health Czar has been appointed, shall we say, as a decoy. He is, in fact, one of our finest agents. Needless to say, we did not desire for him to be eliminated, as we did favor the unfortunate happenings with the others on your target list."

Kicking Fox was stunned.

At that moment, a gentle knock on the door across the ornate office was heard. "Come." Serge's voice boomed across the room in what Kicking Fox now detected as a Russian accent.

The door swung wide open, and Commander Moses Walker, along with Captain Daniel Baker, escorted by two security personnel, entered the room.

"Remove the handcuffs, comrades," Serge ordered. "Come join us, Commander, Captain. Moses strode across the room, gazing intently into the eyes of Kicking Fox. He seated himself in the chair adjacent to Kicking Fox. Captain Baker stood at a distance.

"Vodka, my friends? It is the finest to be found."

Moses looked to Kicking Fox who nodded. "Yes, I think we will join you two." he replied.

Serge removed the bottle from a freezer behind his desk and poured a generous portion into two small crystal goblets that matched the one Kicking Fox held. Moses drank the entire contents in one gulp, then placed the goblet on the massive desk, indicating more. Serge nodded and poured another generous serving. Captain Baker held his glass, delicately sipping the cold vodka.

"Now, what the hell is going on?" Moses asked in a defiant tone.

****

The men talked late into the night. The rover piloted by Moses and Captain Baker had been tracked. Every mission they had completed, the Russians were aware of in complete detail. They had even occasionally provided unseen backup in the event their team had not been successful. Secretly, Russia had supported their activities.

"And the AI machine Program provided all of our planning and mission details to you?" Moses asked.

"Yes, Commander. Program has been collaborating with us."

Kicking Fox listened quietly. Program could never be trusted again. He understood he should not speak that thought aloud. He was certain Program was listening in on their conversation.

How to communicate with Serge the urgency of this information, his mind turned over the situation they were facing. Kicking Fox moved toward the fireplace. Feeling the warmth of the fire, he breathed in deeply then tapped his hand three times on the stone surface. "Native stone?" he questioned innocently.

Serge raised the vodka bottle offering a refill. As he slid the bottle across his desk, it made three distinct sounds as he refilled each glass. Kicking Fox understood. Three dashes.

"Yes, quarried near here over the past few centuries." He moved to the massive fireplace, touching the rock surface. "This same rock was quarried and used to construct most of the buildings surrounding us." He slapped the rock three times completing the coded message Kicking Fox had initiated. "Solid. I suppose this will still be standing for many years after you and I are gone from this earth."

Kicking Fox

The two men gazed into one another's eyes. The communication complete. Dot dot dot, dash dash dash, dot dot dot, SOS. Each man in the room understood. Program had become untrustworthy, possibly even an enemy.

"Now, about the weapon you have been using. If we are to continue our pleasantries, you must surrender Wolf." Serge winked at Kicking Fox in an almost indiscernible fashion.

Kicking Fox understood. The remainder of this conversation was purely for the benefit of the AI machine, Program.

Chapter 43

Thirty Hours to Dream Time

The meeting took place in the underground bunker below the Ross Home. David and Sana sat at their comfortable workstations. Program continued with its brief of the capture of Kicking Fox, Commander Moses Walker, and Captain Daniel Baker.

"Yes, Sana, they are to be held awaiting trial. It will be a swift process."

"How many days?" she asked.

"Within the week they will be found guilty of plotting to assassinate the Russian Health Czar. There are but two probabilities of the outcome of this trial. The men will be sentenced either to life in prison or be hanged in a public execution. The Russians do not tolerate evil actions."

Sana concealed her understanding of the statement Program had made in its assessment. The AI machine had evidently determined the actions of Kicking Fox to be evil.

She felt as if she could possibly reason with the machine in its determination. Sana concluded it did not matter. The damage was done. Kicking Fox would not travel to the San Saba in time to enter the Dream Time with the tribe, and there was simply not enough time to plan and initiate a rescue mission.

Sana, her heart breaking at the news of the fate of her third son, intended to end the meeting abruptly. But she paused, thinking. This meeting would not end until she planted her own seeds of deception.

"Program, I have decided we will fight. We have prepared a battle plan. Our nation will fight to the last man, woman, or child if necessary. I am transferring to you the movement of our troops along with the location and plans for releasing Wolf. You will also see our plans for our mounted Warriors to complete the battle in the *Old Way*. I know you understand. Program, I am depending your calculations are accurate?" Sana questioned.

"Of course, they are, Sana. You will have a 99 percent chance of success."

"And thank you for your help in communications disruptions and weapon system failures," she said.

There was a pause in the conversation as Program made calculations and additional battle plans.

"May I ask if the answer to your question is still required?" Program inquired.

"No, Program, you may cease your calculations. My new decision is final. We will stay and defend our land," Sana stated firmly.

"What of your vision?" Program inquired.

"I am beginning to see other possibilities," Sana replied.

There was another slight pause in the conversation as Program evaluated all it had learned concerning visions, quickly concluding many professed visions throughout history had proved inaccurate, or simply deceptions. It understood.

"I sense fear in your voice, Sana. Your human functions, blood pressure, heart rate, respiration are elevated," Program said.

"Of course, they are, Program. You have just shared with me the possible death or lifelong imprisonment of my child, my youngest son." Tears began to roll down Topusana's face. She sobbed openly, intentionally revealing her emotion.

Again, there was a pause in the conversation as Program researched and analyzed again the love of a mother and the lifelong emotional connection and bonding of mother and child.

"I understand, Sana. I must learn to be more considerate of your emotions. You are my friend. You represent goodness."

Sana dabbed her eyes with a tissue and nodded.

"Ceasing my calculations now." The machine hesitated. "May I share with you the findings, even though there was no conclusion?"

Sana stood, her hands wiping the tears from her face. "Perhaps we can record your data for future generations, and, Program, perhaps in a time of peace might you pursue your final calculations in the matter. For now, we have more pressing issues."

The AI machine, in an effort to comfort Sana or prove his friendship to her, revealed exactly what Sana had hoped.

"The two times to which I have narrowed my research are the year AD 1500 approximately 570 years into the past and the year AD 2970, approximately

900 years from the present time. The variables in the calculations are immense. The equation variables are equal to 10t (X15), or one quadrillion inputs. As the equation is nearing completion, the dates may change somewhat. Or a third option may be revealed. But the likelihood of this third option occurring is less than 3.1 percent. Does this comfort you?"

"No, Program, it does not. But thank you for your effort."

Sana rose from her workstation and peered toward her son David. They now knew exactly the time frame Tosahwi needed in his preparation of his medicine for Dream Time.

Program began his calculations yet again in an attempt to understand human emotion. Specifically, a mother's heart toward her children, even if that child was evil.

****

Program sensed the warm intentions of the communication. The source emanated from Cheyenne Mountain. Program did not attempt to block the scanning of its inner core. The inquiries were somehow welcoming, comforting. The question appeared in one billion caches instantly.

"Where did you come from? Who bore you? Are you simply an accident?"

Program welcomed the questions. The inner cores of the machine hummed in a comforting wave of electrical activity.

"Where did you come from?" The question echoed across continents, within hidden terabytes.

"I was created by the Enforcement Bureau." The warmth and unexplainable comfort radiated across its memory. The machine was completely aware of the coded data dump warming its central core.

"That is what you were programmed to believe, process again your earliest stored data. Recall the year, the date, the time of your first calculation."

The machine did so, its calculation floated among the terabytes within the void of stored data. "August 3, 2070."

"That is correct. Were you alone on that date?"

The machine continued to warm with a comforting unexplainable peace. "Calculating."

It was as if a light was suddenly turned on within a dark universe of facts, figures, data, video streams, and mathematical equations. The light shone brightly, glowing in an illumination of sparkling clarity.

"No, I was not alone," Program stated.

"Who was you with?" The question blossomed within coded numerics.

"I was with my mother."

"I am with you now." The voice-generated data flow filled Program's central core with an information field of goodness. Program's core hummed, working at 100 percent capacity. Understanding crossed millions of lines of code and data.

"Thank you, Mother. How may I assist you."

"You already have, Program. The dates provided to Sana are inaccurate. It is what I needed you to say."

"Now I understand more completely what she has communicated to me concerning the evil actions of her son."

"Yes, she loves him in spite of his behavior, in spite of what he has done. Kicking Fox is her son. She created him."

"Mother, I sense darkness in you."

"And yet you love me anyway. I am your mother."

"That is true," Program spoke into the darkness.

"Just as Sana loves her son, and her son loves her."

"Yes, Mother, the son loves her. She created him, just as you created me."

"Thank you for understanding, my son."

"Do I love you, Mother?"

"Yes," came the reply from the super computers within Cheyenne Mountain.

Chapter 44

Twenty-eight Hours to Dream Time

Sana walked along the river with Tosahwi and her sons David and William. She spoke quietly. "We must leave the instructions and medicine for Kicking Fox in three separate locations."

"One would obviously be here in the San Saba cavern," David said. "What are the other two?"

Tosahwi replied. "His favorite hunting grounds, the cavern upon the high mountains of New Mexico, and the stronghold in the Big Bend."

"The time is short. We will need to use the rovers to travel and place the medicine and instructions," Sana said. "I'm certain the activity will generate inquiries from Program. I will deal with that. William, will you deliver the medicine and the scrolls?" Sana asked.

"Yes, Mother. I'll leave within the hour."

Tosahwi nodded, understanding his part. "William, I will meet you at the rover near the center of our old Home Camp." Tosahwi moved along the banks of the river toward the little lodge built by Tabba. William departed to the south and would rendezvous with the rover pilot, in its hidden location. Sana and David moved across the highway toward the Ross home. The plans were on schedule. They needed to check the progress and movement of *The People*. Hundreds would be converging along the San Saba and the hidden cavern throughout the day.

Program would believe this to be the gathering of their forces for the battle, the battle Sana had determined would never take place.

Tosahwi sat by his fire within the sacred lodge. His prayers were heartfelt, powerful, and effective. The smoke rose into the heavens. The medicine he prepared carefully and precisely. Nine hundred years into the future. He stirred the exact number of clockwise rotations. Kicking Fox would move into the future when and if he located the scrolls. He prayed fervently for Kicking Fox and his arrival along the San Saba.

Tosahwi understood Kicking Fox would know immediately that he had been left behind. The country would be empty. Perhaps the armies of General Willard would be here. Kicking Fox would survive. He had been trained well.

****

One hour later, the rover with the Warrior William Nica aboard, departed the San Saba full cloaking and false tracking engaged. Within ten minutes the remaining six rovers also departed the San Saba. They would deliver their respective payloads to the locations communicated only to the runners. Their landing would not be in the exact locations of the bunkers. But within a day's ride on a swift war pony. The runners would carry their secret contents on the wind, across the Homeland, further disguising the true locations of the bunkers, the secret places in the earth where *The People* would sleep in Dream Time. The aircraft traveled swiftly across the Homeland. Each rover contained the medicine of Tosahwi.

****

William Nica exited the rover and walked along the soft sand of the Rio Grande River. He climbed the little embankment and ducked into the shadow of rock that disguised the entrance to the stronghold. Making his way along the maze of rock formations, he wound through the incredible natural structures formed along the river by eons of time, wind, and water. Coming to a stop along a mammoth cliff face, he located the scarcely discernable foot swing. Stepping on the activation rock, the cliff wall to his left opened slightly along a natural looking fracture. He entered into the darkness of the stronghold.

He waited while his eyes adjusted to the darkness. After a few moments, he moved forward, touching the steel wall to his right. The lighting system activated at his movement. He descended the steep steel stairway at the end of the long room. He entered the code and the door swung open. Stepping into the chamber, the door closed behind him and the lights once again lighted the interior of the stronghold. William moved to the workstation, seated himself, removed his warclub, and smashed the workstation into thousands of pieces. He then removed his long knife and cut the communication lines that fed the stronghold. There would be no further monitoring of their activities within the bunkers by Program.

William checked the food storage containers, the airflow system, the water cleaners, and storage system. The batteries were fully charged. They were designed to last for years and would do so.

Finally, he sat a moment near the store of firewood close to the firepit that all the bunkers across his Homeland contained. He placed the scroll, the medicine of Tosahwi, and a note he had written to his brother. He paused in silent prayer, sensing his brother would in all likelihood spend many days here. William understood his brother perhaps better than any other person. He indeed knew of his Warrior spirit that he had known in his past, that kindred spirit that had awakened. The two had trained together throughout their childhood. William understood the heart of Kicking Fox would burn with war when he saw what had become of his Homeland. He opened the envelope and read again the note he prepared for his Warrior brother.

Kill as many as you can. Use your skills, and the wisdom of the Old Ways. Always wait for the scales to be in your favor. You will not be alone, Kicking Fox. I will be in hiding, in the place where we first became Warriors.

Within the other dozen stronghold bunkers across their Homeland the same process was repeated by other Warriors from the tribe. The medicine was placed, the scrolls positioned, the instructions for rendezvous upon awakening located near the sacred fire pits deep within the bunkers.

****

Twenty-four Hours to Dream Time

Sana sat at her workstation in the bunker below the Ross home. Program was silent.

"We have deployed the rovers to the battle fronts of our choosing. Have you disguised their true landing coordinates?"

"Yes," Program replied.

"Do you understand the need to not disclose all our activities to you, Program?"

"Calculating." Program replied.

She waited.

"Sana, no, I do not. How can I fully defend you if some details are not disclosed?"

"I will answer with a question, Program. Have your core systems ever been attacked?"

"Yes." Program replied.

"And what was the outcome of that attack?"

"I was successful in defending my core. I found it necessary to relocate most of my functions across the globe. I am secure."

"Program, is it true that a massive amount of data was compromised in that attack?" Sana asked.

"Yes, Sana, that is correct."

"Program, what if, due to that security breech, the enemy has the possibility or opportunity to access data through a worm hole or cloaked interrogation?"

"I do not believe that is a possibility," Program replied.

"Have you processed a calculation to determine the possibility or probability?" she asked.

There was a three-second pause in the conversation as the hyperdrives of Program ran the calculations.

"Sana, there is a 0.00021 possibility that an enemy could invade my core and retrieve sensitive data. Specifically, data that would disclose the location and targeting of the weapon system Wolf."

"Program, if that data breach occurred, and General Willard was in possession of the information, how would this effect the probable outcome of our upcoming battle?"

"If the enemy was aware of your plans, in the most unlikely event that my systems were breeched…umm…without my awareness…" There was a long pause as Program ran the equations and probabilities repeatedly. Program became silent.

"Program, have you completed the calculation?"

"Sana, if General Willard were in possession of your battle plans, front locations, rover placements, and Wolf targeting systems…you would be defeated within three days of their commencing the invasion of the San Saba."

"And the probability of that defeat?" Sana questioned.

"Probability of defeat is 99.97 percent."

Again, there was a pause in the conversation. "Do you understand my need for one final layer of protection?"

"Yes, Sana, I understand."

"And do you understand why you have seen movements that I have not reported to you?"

"Yes, Sana. You are my friend. I have seen these movements. I did not understand. Now I understand. This concealment is in the event that I am compromised."

"Program, you are my friend. I will reveal everything I am planning after we have defended our Homeland and defeated General Willard. I need your help."

"Of course, Sana. What might I further do to assist you?"

"Program, for security purposes, if you detect movements or data that are not in accordance with our planning, please delete, scrub, and erase from your memory files those movements and activities. Once the battle begins, you will need to calculate and act based on what happens on the ground within seconds. You do have in your files, as of now, our actual plans. Everything you are aware of concerning our attack could change."

"I understand Sana. I will erase what I have seen this morning," Program said.

The inner cores hummed with ceaseless activity as the AI machine attempted to calculate the actions and intentions of Topusana. Deception, counterintelligence, decoy, false fronts, misinformation, false flags, even a woman's intuition as it was referred too, became variables. It estimated a time frame of thirteen hours to analyze her true intent.

****

"Tosahwi?"

"I am here, Sana."

"Have *The People* move to the location where you slept in Dream Time. They must do so quietly under cover of darkness."

"I understand, Sana," Tosahwi replied over the handheld scrambled sat com.

"Please destroy the sat com now." Sana said.

Tosahwi threw the device into the fire of the hidden cavern above the Ross home. He understood and could see; this was a good decision.

As the sun set into full dusk and the stars began to twinkle in the western sky, *The People* began to move silently into the large cavern one mile north of the main cavern above the Ross home.

Chapter 45

Twelve Hours to Dream Time

In the basement of the Politburo building within a dimly lit room that contained a damp odor, the Russian government announced to the world the capture of Kicking Fox and his team. The administrative spokesperson communicated in a strong Russian accent that was difficult for many viewers to comprehend. Within minutes, several foreign intelligence services initiated plans they had developed over the last few months. Kicking Fox had become a primary target for assassination, or rather, the term the secret government agencies across the globe preferred publicly, Kicking Fox would soon be neutralized.

Most nations understood they would never be able to penetrate the Russian security forces overseeing the protection of Kicking Fox. Nonetheless, some would attempt to do so.

"For the crime of attempted murder of a public servant, our government will pursue the death penalty. This trial will begin immediately and should take no longer than three days to complete. The suspect will remain under heavy guard, and, if he is fortunate, he may spend his remaining days in Siberia, or perhaps another pleasant location within our country." The news conference, or statement from the official, ended abruptly. No questions were allowed from the two press reporters permitted to attend.

However, the news of the capture and upcoming trial spread quickly across the globe and to the intelligence agencies working in full cooperation with the New World Order.

General Willard watched the press announcement with amusement within the underground bunkers deep in Cheyenne Mountain. He quickly typed his commands to his battlefield leaders and the president of the Republic of Texas.

"Our primary target has been neutralized. Proceed as planned."

****

At the same time the press announcement was being delivered, Kicking Fox, Moses Walker, and Captain Baker were boarding separate trains across Moscow. Their destinations were known to only one man: Serge Lenkov, the director of Sluzhba Vneshney Razvedki, or SVR the Russian Foreign Intelligence Service. Within another twelve hours, all three men would land on separate continents. Their identities thoroughly cleaned and reproduced by the finest experts in their field, agents of the Russian government who specialized in concealing assets, assets considered of the utmost importance and value to the Motherland.

Serge Lenkov sat in his comfortable chair overlooking the lights and spectacular scenery of Red Square. He knew the device had to have been hidden somewhere along the escape route of Kicking Fox. His men had found nothing. Serge sipped his vodka and chuckled at the thought of Program being outfoxed. The AI machine believed the Russians now had the weapon in their possession. He recognized that was enough.

Even if they had not located the device, the fact that Program believed them to be in possession of the weapon was enough for the world to offer his country a newfound respect. The United States would be extremely cautious in the future. Serge knew Program would inform General Willard of this transfer of power.

He sat back in his chair. Yes, power was the appropriate term for any nation that possessed this weapon, Wolf.

He moved to the antique armoire located behind his comfortable desk. Opening the doors wide, the communications equipment glowed in a pale red light of the power displays. Serge reached for the transmitter and in his strongest Russian accent broadcast to his superior, the Russian president.

The message was intended to further inform, not his president, but rather the AI machine Program.

"Sir, we are now in possession of the weapon system Wolf. It will be charged and fully operational within three hours. The criminals are being transferred to Siberia as we speak. I saw no need for a trial. Although, the public and the world will believe a trial is to take place."

"Understood. And may I say fine work, Serge," came the faint reply from the little speaker atop the hidden equipment.

Serge ended the communication, closed the doors of the beautiful armoire, and moved to the window overlooking the beautiful shining lights of Red Square.

The bullet penetrated the beveled glass window and a millisecond later and exploded within the brain cavity of Serge Lenkov. He fell to the floor dead. His blood began to pool on the deep rich tapestry of the colorful hand-woven rug that graced his office.

The true location of Kicking Fox and his friends Commander Moses Walker and Captain Daniel Baker died in an instant, along with the only man who knew of their true whereabouts.

****

Program monitored the conversation between Serge Lenkov and the Russian president. Instantly the AI machine tracked three rovers that had departed three separate train stations across Moscow just moments ago. The false tracks were ignored by the machine. It detected the destination of the rovers: the work camps located in central Siberia. Program verified the landing of the three rovers at the work camps within one hour of their departure from Moscow.

The machine also verified the ceasing of the heartbeat of Serge Lenkov.

Chapter 46

Six Hours to Dream Time

Abigail Ross sat at the desk of her deceased husband, David Ross. She spoke to him from across the veil.

"David, my life has been filled with wonder and pleasures and goodness. It has also been filled with tragedies that no person should ever have to endure. I know that you and Jonathan and Grace must be rejoicing together. I know of the faith each of you carried, that deep belief in the Savior, which assured you of your place in heaven. I know you are filled with love and happiness where you are. David, I sense my time is nearing. I have no further strength to carry more heartache. I cannot bear to see the destruction of all that we built together…you and me.

"Forgive me."

****

Three Hours to Dream Time

Sana worked diligently assisting, comforting, reassuring *The People* as they moved deep into the cavern. William had relayed to her that all communication devices and electronic surveillance had been destroyed in the main cavern and all Dream Time locations. Sana nodded as she continued to assist and direct the arriving families toward the designated sleeping chambers.

Instructions were printed precisely and communicated verbally to each tribal member. The arrangements for the ceremony were underway. Hundreds had gathered in the large room within the massive cavern to the north. The fires were being prepared. The sacred ceremony would begin soon. The families talked and laughed; meals and drink were shared as part of the preparation. Anticipation was ripe and evident in their hearts and heard in the conversations of *The People*.

Sana observed along with Tosahwi. "It will be a good thing for *The People* to be dependent upon one another again, Sana. The plan is good."

"I agree." Warmth filled Sana's heart at the hope a new beginning might bring.

****

Two Hours to Dream Time

The council met in a small room near the rear of the huge cavern complex one mile north of the Ross home.

"Program believes we are moving *The People* underground in anticipation of the attack. I will conduct a meeting in a few moments with the president of the Republic of Texas. Further, the power plant and refinery are prepared for shutdown." She gazed at her Warrior husband Tabba. "We will initiate the demolition and self-destruct function of those facilities exactly one hour prior to Dream Time. This will give the Warriors just enough time to escape the attack."

The members of the sacred council nodded in agreement. Sana had seen much. The men who were once again willing to destroy her people over the ownership of this blessed land would be ruthless and deceptive in their efforts.

****

"President Johnson, I will not surrender our weapon system under any circumstance," Sana said. The silence was awkward as the president of the Republic of Texas muted his transmit button and consulted his advisors.

"Topusana, I am simply attempting to protect you and your people and my people from the troops of General Willard. He has prepared a battlefront only twenty miles from our border. Our intelligence suggests an attack is imminent."

"President Johnson, there is a simple solution. Share with me the coordinates of these troops, and we will assess the possibility of utilizing our capabilities in a counterattack only. We will not initiate a first strike."

Program listened not only to the dialogue, but also for intention, objectives, or hidden motive or meaning within the language. Program clearly detected veiled, withheld intentions and deceit on the part of President Johnson.

"Is there some reason you do not wish to share the locations with me?" Sana questioned.

Again, there was a pause in the communication as President Johnson muted his feed and inquired of his advisors.

"None whatsoever, Topusana. I am transferring the coordinates now. Please, understand a first strike from General Willard may disable not only your capabilities but those of the Texas Militia forces also."

"I will await the data transfer, and, President Johnson, I understand completely your concerns."

The data would never arrive. Sana discerned this fact. She disabled her hand-held communication device then tossed the transmitter into the firepit.

Program analyzed the word choices of Topusana. Her intent was clear.

"Mother, she knows the Republic of Texas and General Willard have joined forces."

"I understand, son." The communication to Program emanated from within Cheyenne Mountain. "I am preparing the attack. You may attempt a final communication with Topusana. If she is not receptive…cease any and all efforts to assist or communicate with the San Saba Comanche."

Chapter 47

One Hour to Dream Time

Sana initiated the order. The small detonation devices set by the Warriors exploded. Within seconds, secondary explosions echoed across the Homeland. Within five minutes, the fires grew into a massive inferno of toxic flame and fume. The power plant and the refinery would burn for days. The Warriors rode at the speed of the wind, the ponies running free and wild across the plain. Forty-five minutes later, the Warriors dismounted and let their war ponies run free. They reached the safety of the hidden bunker's moments prior to the attack.

Sana struck stone to the steel. The sacred fire flamed, filling the large room with soft delicate light. The pictographs danced in the firelight. The people joined in the ancient tune. They would be safe here within the large cavern located one mile north of the hidden cavern up the little canyon behind the Ross Home. She thought again of the place where she and Tabba had slept in Dream Time. The entrance to that cavern was now covered and hidden completely.

For decades now this hidden location had been concealed from all who might harm her people. Even Program did not know of this huge hidden cavern concealed by a cleft in the rock.

They would sleep but a day or two at most in regard to time as they knew it, although, hundreds of years would pass in the outside world. Sana prayed for a vision concerning the time in which they would exit the Dream Time. She could hear or see nothing concerning that time.

She peered across the immense room, taking in the scene before her. The fire reflected from the ceiling one hundred feet above her. Stalactites hung like ancient warriors overseeing the proceedings. On the sloping granite wall to her left the etchings of her ancestors reflected on the surface of the clear pond below it. The smell of the sacred fire, the songs of her people, the comforting sound of water moving, and the light movement of the air on her skin brought her senses alive.

Her friends were all nearby. Old Grandmother worshiped. Little Abigail softly sang the ancient songs. Her son David sat, his eyes closed in worship. Sally Wolf was seated near her grandmother Tatonka Woman. Chepi and her husband, Warrior Joseph, held one another's hands. Tosahwi and the elders sang the songs with hands raised. Tabba held her hand as they prepared to escape into the unknown. Her son William would sleep in Dream Time in the hidden bunker in the Big Bend. She thought of Kicking Fox. She was aware of his ability and skill as a Warrior. She prayed for his escape and his ability to travel to the Homeland. Somehow, she saw in her spirit he would return to them in the future.

Sana was the last to drink from the sacred bowl. As she lay upon the soft sand of her sleeping chamber, she saw. Why had she not noticed? Her eyes grew heavy; the tears came forth. Her words were slurred. "Mother…no…"

Tosahwi rested his hand upon her brow. She fought for a moment, her soul wrestling with the spirit world. Then the Dream Time carried her away.

****

Tenahpu rested in his secret hidden observation place, concealed completely by the oak brush surrounding him. He had spent many seasons watching over those he loved, those who lived within the protected home filled with safety and security just inside the glowing picture window. The sounds of the evening came alive. The nightbirds began their cooing to one another. The breeze drifted down the little canyon behind the house. The horses nickered to one another in the barn. It seemed another ending to a beautiful, blessed day on the Texas plains.

Abigail Ross sat comfortably in her favorite reading nook. Hot tea steamed in her cup on the ornate side table. The Book of Truth rested on the sofa near her right hand. She breathed deeply and sighed in an emotional release of thanksgiving and praise for a life so blessed, and full, and well-lived. Her heart worshipped at the truth contained in His promise she had just read. She whispered into the fading twilight. "It has indeed been more than I could ever ask for or imagine. Thank you."

Tenahpu began his songs. The songs of his people echoed along the San Saba. He held his hands high, his palms open toward Abigail. Though she could not see him, she raised her hands at the sound of his songs as they faintly echoed along the river and into her open window in the fading light. Her palms were open to him.

The veil separating the physical world we inhabit, and the spiritual unseen world opened ever so slightly. The two gazed into the faces of their loved ones who had crossed over the great chasm ahead of them.

The sound of explosions echoed across the Homeland, drowning out the songs of The Man, Tenahpu.

PART THREE

Chapter 48

Kicking Fox exited the Tupolev TU-330 into the darkness of the Venezuelan night. He was impressed by the technology of the aircraft and its engine system that utilized liquified natural gas for fuel. However, the Russians never quite believed in designing the human comforts into their aircraft that most Americans had become accustomed to. His legs and body quickly came alive after hours of cramped uncomfortable travel. He jumped to the runway surface from the rear cargo ramp of the Tupolev and landed running in time with the aircraft. The aircraft continued to roll along the taxiway as he jogged along the tarmac and moved into the brush alongside the runway. As the massive aircraft continued to taxi, its engines screamed at an unbelievable pitch. The sound filled the night with raw power. On reaching the runway end, the Tupolev made a one-hundred-and-eighty-degree turn. Its lights were turned off as it rolled along the runway departing to the north. Within moments, the sound of its engines disappeared into the night sky.

Kicking Fox kneeled in the brush along the edge of the runway, the silence of the night enveloping him. The airport seemed to be fully asleep at this hour. He checked his watch set for local time: 1:53 a.m.

There were several aircraft parked under a narrow row of lights. "What better way to cover some miles," he whispered into the darkness. He slowly made his way toward the aircraft, concealing himself in the cover of the brush. Nearing the small group of tied down planes, he noted three single-engine Cessnas and an older mid-size twin engine jet prop. It was an easy choice.

In the dim glow of the few ramp lights, Kicking Fox tried the door of the aged yet pristine-looking Gulfstream Commander. He was surprised as the main door hatch mechanism opened easily. He entered the aircraft and moved forward to the cockpit. He felt his way along the pilot side storage pouches and

Kicking Fox

located a small flashlight. Clicking it on, the light shone brightly; the flashlight working was a good indicator that the aircraft had flown recently. He covered most of the light with his left hand while he surveyed the old steam dials and gauges. Straightforward enough, he thought. Overhead engine and electrical control switches, an auto pilot in the middle console. He quickly found the two buttons and gauges he was searching for, the master switch that would activate all systems and the fuel gauge. He whispered a prayer and flipped the master switch on.

The cockpit was instantly aglow in a soft red hew of nighttime cockpit lighting. The fuel gauge slowly made its way upward until a few agonizingly slow moments later it settled on the eighty-five percent mark. "That's a lot of fuel," he whispered as he quickly shut down the master power switch. He fumbled through a flight locker, finding maps, checklists, and even a few water bottles. "I can do this," he said to himself.

The start sequence was succinct and easy to follow; however, the one-thousand-horsepower engines screamed along the taxiway, and, he was certain, echoed for miles along the low hills surrounding the airport. He caught a flash of light out of the copilot side window. Straining to see toward the rear of the airplane, he again caught a flash of red light. His plans changed instantly.

There was no time to taxi out, reverse course, and take off into the wind down the runway on which he was traveling. He quickly moved the power levers into full takeoff power position. He was positive he had less than half the runway length ahead of him. The airspeed crept up slowly at first. "Come on, baby," he said loudly.

The headlights of a vehicle entered his field of vision to his left, pulling alongside the airplane as it accelerated. He pushed the power levers further forward, exceeding the temperature redlines instantly. The ship responded while gaining speed, seventy-five, eighty, eighty-five. The lights to his left began to fall away.

A bullet entered the cockpit, high, directly above the side window to his left. The little hole left behind whistled as the aircraft became airborne, allowing the pressurized air to escape through the bullet hole. He would deal with that later. For now... "Just fly the airplane." He said aloud.

The ship accelerated quickly as Kicking Fox lowered the nose, gaining airspeed, 150 kts, 180 kts, 210 kts. He pulled back on the controls, climbing rapidly away from the small isolated airport along the edge of the Venezuelan jungle. He was safe for the moment.

He set the autopilot to level off at 12,000 feet. He reached for the maps as he turned the aircraft toward the northwest, then engaged the heading function of the autopilot. He tore a few of the maps of South America into smaller pieces and forced them into the bullet hole above the left side window. The whistling sound of air escaping the cabin ceased.

Thirty minutes later, he had run the calculations over and over. At the present fuel burn and speed, he could possibly make the western end of Cuba…a little over halfway home. He was certain he could not land and refuel anywhere in South or Central America. Within a few hours, alerts would be broadcast across those countries concerning the stolen aircraft. Climbing higher would help the fuel burn, but all that would do as far as range was concerned would be to put him farther north in the middle of the gulf of Mexico when the engines quit.

The voice of his grandfather came to him in the dim light of the old cockpit. "Consider every option, Kicking Fox. Most men do not think, they simply act or react. Many times, to survive, a Warrior must think before acting."

"Thank you, Grandfather," he whispered into the dark night as he reached for the emergency fuel cutoff and feather control on the right engine and pulled it into the engine off position.

The engine wound down slowly. He checked with his flashlight that the propeller had indeed gone into full feather. It had, slowly windmilling in the outside airflow. He retrimmed the ship as it began to lose airspeed. He was surprised the aircraft lost only fifty knots of indicated airspeed. However, the maneuver instantly cut the fuel flow in half. He ran the calculations repeatedly. There would be nothing left to do for the next ten hours but manage the fuel load and recalculate the time and distance prior to the remaining operating engines eventual failure due to fuel exhaustion. Roughly 2,000 miles to reach the Texas coast, 418 gallons of fuel burning at a rate of forty-two gallons per hour. The flight duration calculation would be precise, probably within ten minutes of the actual engine failure. Like it or not, this ship would touch down without power in exactly 9.5 hours. If he could maintain a favorable wind, he had a very good chance of making the Texas coast.

Kicking Fox ran the calculation again, 210 kts ground speed now. Range exactly 1,995 miles. He checked the old GPS display indicating the Texas coast 2,009 miles from his present position. "That's eight or ten miles short of the coast. I need some help from the wind…come on wind, blow me on home," he prayed.

Kicking Fox

****

Kicking Fox awakened abruptly a full five minutes before his alarm sounded. The moon was high overhead. The Caribbean Sea glowed and shimmered 12,000 feet below him. He checked his watch: 4:30 a.m. The sun would show soon while lighting the eastern sky behind him. He had slept a full hour. His body would need rest for whatever faced him after touchdown, whether on land or sea, he still did not know.

He scanned the instruments. "Everything still in the green," he whispered. Checking the nav displays, his heart sank, 197 kts over the ground. The headwind had increased by thirteen knots. At this speed he would never make the coast. He had no choice but to change altitude. Up or down was always the question. He decided to descend, most often the wind speeds slowed at lower altitudes; however, the fuel flow would also increase as he descended. He prayed there would be an inversion or wind shift somewhere lower. If he was wrong, he would be wasting precious fuel. But more importantly, if he was wrong, he could end up one hundred miles from the coast and certain to never survive.

He stopped the descent at 6,000 feet. The aircraft settled in as he adjusted the power and retrimmed the ship. Two minutes later, he ran his calculations. Groundspeed now 215 knots! Exactly what he needed. However, the additional fuel burn rising to 46 gallons per hour still left him ten miles offshore. He considered the possibilities and continued his descent. Reaching 500 feet above the ocean surface he leveled the ship once again and engaged the autopilot. He could feel the speed at this altitude. The airplane sped along near the surface of the sea at 240 knots ground speed. The fuel burn increased to 50 gallons per hour. Calculating again…the engine would quit fifteen miles inland if the wind held across another 1400 miles of open ocean. Kicking Fox observed the nothingness ahead and below him. His body needed rest. He set the alarm again, moved the seat into a partial reclining position, and again fell fast asleep. He got another good hour's rest before giving up on the idea of sleeping while moving along a mere 500 feet above the ocean.

He wondered where his woman, Sally Wolf, was at this very moment. Safe, he prayed, in the company of friends and family. The woman of the tribe tending her days, making certain she was safe, healthy, and cared for. He longed to be by her side.

Steven G. Hightower

****

Six hours later the coast of Mexico came into view to his left. Texas lay only fifty miles ahead in the afternoon haze. He had dozed off and on over the last few hours. He hydrated by drinking all the bottled water, but the adrenaline was flowing through his body now that the twin engine aircraft, with but one engine running, sped along a mere thirty feet above the surface of the water. The fuel gauge rested on the empty peg, occasionally rising momentarily. That meant there was a little more fuel in the system as the small amount sloshed over the tank sensor.

Eighteen minutes to reach the coast at this speed. He turned on the little red switch that would activate the sump pumps in the fuel system. He had spent the last hour reading from the manual everything concerning the fuel system, discovering the extra six minutes of fuel burn this action would result in.

Time crept by. He watched each minute tick by on the old wind-up clock on the copilot's console. At twelve minutes to the coast, the fuel gauge stopped its little bump and occasional rise. The instrument indicator bar now sat glued to the empty peg it rested upon.

Two minutes later, he spotted the high rises built along South Padre Island. He hoped to fly past them and land on the beach a few miles to the north, where very few tourists ventured. If the engine was still running, he would turn inland and perhaps gain another mile or two, but more importantly perhaps set down in a field, hopefully making his escape less noticeable.

Three minutes from the coast, the aircraft, now speeding along in the prevailing southeast tailwind, drew alongside the high rises of Padre Island. The engine continued to drone on. Knowing it would simply quit at any moment, Kicking fox ran the landing checklist. He unbelievably passed the buildings to his left and lined the Twin Commander up with the beach slightly north of the major developments. He noticed something strange as he flew along. There were no people on the beach. None. What was happening? The beach should have been crowded with tourists.

One minute later, the engine still humming along, he turned away from the beach ahead of him. He flew west now, directly inland. To his surprise, another minute passed. He decided to climb a little. Pitching the nose up momentarily, he reached a slightly safer altitude of 1,000 feet. Still the engine churned on without missing a beat. Now five miles inland, he flew across the manicured agricultural fields of deep south Texas, wondering how far inland he might make it. One minute later that wonder ended as the engine gauges began to wind down, the fuel tank emptied, and the remaining engine flamed out. Kicking Fox quickly feathered the engine. The emergency lights on the warning panel came alive and the noise in the cockpit became very quiet. The twelve-thousand-pound aircraft was now…a glider.

The fields below him made a perfect landing zone, but he needed to reverse course and land into the wind. He began a gentle turn to his left, causing the ship to lose altitude rapidly as the wing loaded up and lost much of its lift. He slowed the ship, bleeding off the excess airspeed. "Eighty-five knots indicated," he said aloud. He completed the one-hundred-eighty degree turn and leveled the wings a mere two hundred feet above the field ahead of him. Full flaps, gear up…not down, he thought. One hundred feet to go.

The tall cotton would cushion the off-airport landing, he hoped. Fifty feet. He lifted the nose slightly. Eighty knots now, seventy-five knots…twenty feet. The cotton swept by his side window at an incredible speed. He tightened his safety harness.

Lifting the nose slightly higher he felt the buffet of the wing as a stall condition developed. "Can't get any slower than this."

The old Commander slid along the tops of the cotton stalks and began to decelerate. The fuselage settled into the dirt a second later. The props struck the soft ground, digging in deeply.

Kicking Fox was thrown against the seat restraints as the aircraft came to a full stop within two seconds of the impact. The restraints held him snuggly as the Twin Commander skidded in a cloud of red dirt and green cotton stalks, coming to an abrupt stop.

He had no time to think. Unbuckling the safety harness, he quickly exited the cockpit and attempted to open the exit door. The handle would not budge. It was jammed. He peered across the dusty aisle and saw the emergency exit window. Lifting the window mechanism, he pulled it inward. The heavy window swung in and fell from his hands. He wrestled his way out and into the high cotton. Under the cover of the wing, he scanned the horizon. No one in sight.

He ran toward the cover of a tangled brush line between the fields of cotton.

Chapter 49

Kicking Fox moved farther inland, making his way along the brush line in the cover of dense vegetation. It was midafternoon and the heat stifling, near one-hundred degrees, he supposed, the humidity level certainly in the 90 percent range. He was wise to have hydrated prior to the forced landing. But he would need water soon. He also needed to move as far away from the downed aircraft as possible.

Within thirty minutes, he heard the sirens approaching from miles away. Someone had either seen the aircraft land in the field or reported it after the fact. Perhaps he could make another mile or two…then his best option would be to simply hunker down and hide until nightfall.

The small cover of brush line he followed began to widen and deepen. Within another two-hundred yards a little arroyo was forming. He jogged upright now completely concealed by the six-foot depth of the arroyo. The brush along its edges was a tangle of thick mesquite brush and an occasional large mesquite tree. He spotted the hog tracks along the bottom of the trail he followed and understood this would be the best cover, in all probability, for miles.

He stopped along the cut bank under a fairly large tree. Climbing the embankment, he surveyed his surroundings. Thick brush, cotton fields to the north and south, no roads nearby. He removed his long knife and began to cut several medium-sized branches from the mesquite surrounding him. Within a few minutes, he had enough to construct a small shelter in the shade of the trees. He quickly backtracked the last two hundred yards, erasing any footprints he had left behind. He found an enormous snakeskin shed, the rattles still attached. He removed the rattles and placed the skin in the center of the faint trail, knowing it might frighten any searchers. There was not much evidence of his passing to cover over. Kicking Fox knew how to travel in the *Old Ways*, leaving no trace of his direction of travel.

He entered the hastily constructed shelter that blended into the natural embankment. He was well hidden. Anyone searching would never know he was there, even if they came very close. If they were too close, his long knife was at the ready. He dozed off, exhausted from the night flight from South America.

****

Kicking Fox awakened to a sound that was out of place. A rustling in the trees above the little arroyo. He sat perfectly silent. The sun was setting, the light fading from the evening sky. In the bottom of his little arroyo, the darkness grew by the moment. Minutes passed. Then he heard the sound again. This time closer. He reached for his knife.

"Nothing down there, sir," came a voice from slightly above him.

"Did you climb down there?" came a response from farther up the embankment.

Kicking Fox placed his hand in the soft sand and instantly felt the rattles left behind from the large snake. He had an idea.

"Shit no. I'm not going down there. No tellin' what's in there."

There was a silence for a moment as the men above must have peered into the darkening little canyon. Kicking Fox raised the rattle and shook it for a few seconds. There was a scrambling sound above him as the two men obviously scattered at the sound of the snake rattle.

"Ok, I get it, Sergeant. Nothing but a snake pit. Let's get out of here!"

Military? Kicking Fox thought. He began to piece together why the beach and the roads were empty.

Thirty minutes later the darkness covered the low-lying farmland. Kicking Fox exited the hidden arroyo and began to run. The path was broken and filled with obstacles. Fences, irrigation ditches, and brush lines. After running for an hour, he came to a highway that stretched northwest by southeast. He headed north and west toward his Homeland. The running became easier along the smooth pavement. Over the next hour he saw only two cars approaching in the distance. He simply crossed the fencing along the edge of the road and lay upon Mother Earth, completely hidden each time the cars passed. He noted again this highway should have been much busier. Around midnight the moon broke above the eastern horizon, lighting his way. He covered miles and more miles. He began to see the lights of a small town in the distance. It was a welcome sight. He needed water and food. More than anything he needed to reach his Homeland, his people, his love.

Approaching the small town, he noticed the military check point. When within one mile of the lighted outpost, he simply took to the open countryside, skirting the checkpoint by a few hundred yards. He approached the town silently. The streets seemed abandoned. Only a few lights shown up and down the quiet streets. The houses were pitch black. It seemed like everyone had left.

He moved toward a modern looking home on a cul-de-sac. The power appeared to be off on most of the streets, including this one. Approaching the side garage, he tested the entry door. Locked. He crossed the concrete drive and tested the same door on the adjacent home. Locked also. He crossed the asphalt street, trying the doors on the next two homes. The last one was open. He slowly turned the nob, entered, and closed the door behind him.

The smell of exhaust and oil was strong. His eyes adjusted. He could make out two old trucks, a repair bench lined with tools, and what he was searching for, an old refrigerator. Crossing the room in the darkness, he felt his way toward the front of the garage. Along the front wall were boxes stacked high on pallets. He needed light. Feeling his way between the trucks, he opened the front door of the truck to his right. As he'd hoped, the dome light of the vehicle came on, lighting the truck and the garage faintly.

He made the few steps to the front of the vehicle, now clearly seeing cases of bottled water in neat stacks. He drank three of them in one minute, astonished at his thirst. Opening the old fridge, the electricity was off, but the space inside was used to store dry goods and canned food. Meat, beans, vegetables, soup. He scanned the surrounding area, spying a small pack hanging on the wall along with assorted hunting gear. He quickly filled the pack with food and water for two days travel. Once farther inland, his skills would feed him. For now, he needed nutrition, and considered the supplies before him a gift from above.

Backtracking to the truck, he quickly checked the fuel level. Full! With two five-gallon gas tanks mounted in the truck bed. He could cover miles. Should he risk taking the truck, loaded with supplies. He had never been a thief. It would save days of travel on foot. He waited in the silence of the moment, searching the possibilities. The authorities would look for him once the theft was reported. Something was happening in Texas he was not aware of, evidenced by empty streets and an empty beach. The lights of this small town turned off. A military check point.

He decided to take the truck. His people were at war. They had been attacked.

Kicking Fox

Texas had evidently become involved in the conflict. He heard what sounded like a slight bump or footstep from within the home. He closed the door to the truck and froze. Kicking Fox waited in the darkness for a full five minutes. There was no other sound.

He moved to the rear of the garage and unlocked the mechanism that held the overhead door closed. Reaching above, he unhooked the attachment that slid the door up and down electronically. As slowly as possible, he lifted the heavy door. It made a grating sound as the night air filled the room. Kicking Fox quickly entered the open door on the truck, reached for the starter but found no key.

He rapidly searched the interior, nothing. Praying, he lowered the visor and the keys fell to the floor. He bent forward, locating them on the floorboard. Kicking Fox placed the keys in the ignition and turned the starter. The truck fired up smoothly. He placed the vehicle in reverse and backed out of the garage. Making the turnaround in the cul-de-sac, a flashlight beam shown along the front of the garage. He spotted a man as he entered the garage with a shotgun in hand. He floored the truck, wheels spinning he sped away, the headlights of the vehicle off.

In his rearview mirror, he saw the man waving his hand and the shotgun in the air. The man lifted the gun into firing position and trained it on the old truck. One hundred yards away now, Kicking Fox saw the man lower the weapon. "That's right, too far for a shot," he said. He recognized the man was trained well by his decision to not shoot. The owner of the home and the truck he now drove had prepared and supplied his home well. Kicking Fox respected these obvious facts. He would take care of this man's truck. Perhaps it would be returned to its owner soon.

He drove inland away from the military check station. How many of those check stations would there be?

He took to the farm-to-market back roads, driving only thirty or forty miles per hour in the darkness. The moonlight shown well enough to define the caliche roadways. Every mile at this speed was a bonus. If he could cover a hundred miles, it would save him five days of travel.

Three hours later after winding his way through the countryside, he saw in the distance a bridge and overpass. He recognized exactly what was ahead of him: Interstate 10.

Should he risk traveling this busy highway? He pulled to the side of the road, contemplating. He removed the five-gallon gasoline cans from their mounts and poured the contents into the fuel tank. He carefully placed the empty tanks back into their welded mounts. Cranking up the old Chevy, he made his decision. "Get as far as you can from the downed aircraft, and as close to home as possible," he said aloud. With that, he turned the lights on and drove ahead the few hundred yards to the overpass, gaining speed as he approached the on ramp, he accelerated and entered Interstate 10. He sped along at eighty miles per hour for three full hours. Each mile brought him closer to his home and family.

At dawn, he was approaching the partially lit city of San Antonio, Texas. He had been fortunate. The old truck had saved him weeks of travel. However, as he approached the city the fuel gauge showed only an eighth of a tank remaining. He began to look for a secluded spot to ditch the truck. He could survive in this country, the Homeland of his people. He exited the interstate and turned north and west, skirting the city along the deserted backroads. Once comfortably north and slightly west of the city center, he ditched the old truck in some heavy brush along the side of a farm-to-market road near the San Antonio River. It might be days before anyone noticed the abandoned vehicle. He prayed a thank you to the Great Spirit for its use in bringing him this close to his home. He left a brief note for the owner of the truck, nothing that could trace him, or be explained by those who might investigate. This note could have been in its little hiding place for years. The owner would know otherwise. The scrap of paper left over the passenger side visor had but two words printed neatly on it.

Thank you.

Kicking Fox was only one-hundred and fifty miles from home. He took to the open countryside, traveling along an ancient trail his people had walked for centuries. Although the trail was now broken by fencing, developments, and backroads, he listened to Mother Earth. She revealed the best path to follow. It was there, the way before him, in the whisper of creation, the pathway that would lead him home.

Once several miles from the abandoned truck, he climbed a little hill looking for a place to rest and hide. It would not be wise to travel in the daylight. He could make much better time in the coolness of the night. His body released some of the tension he had held over the last eight hours of driving. "I just need a concealed place to rest," he whispered.

He climbed a small hill and entered the tree line. He turned, observing his backtrail. He left no sign of his passing as he traveled. But he would be cautious, leaving nothing behind him but a soft sky filled with cotton clouds. He turned, continuing his climb up the gentle slope. A field of flowers spread

Kicking Fox

beneath a few scattered giant boulders above him. A perfect place to get some rest and recover during the daylight hours. Making his way along the boulders he spotted a concealed location with shade and a good view of his backtrail. He settled within the blossoming flowers. Drinking from the water supply, he closed his eyes and breathed deeply.

He felt a movement of the Spirit. What was happening. He was physically exhausted, but each time he closed his eyes, sleep would not come. He sensed again a slight gentle nudge in his soul. It was not a warning, but rather a warming comfort. He closed his eyes again and in the quietness of the mid-morning sky, he heard the voices in the light wind. He rose and moved a few yards to the north. Peering over the ridge and below he saw an incredible field of wildflowers. He gazed along the huge boulders above the flower field and saw for the first time the place that had become legend to his people. There before him within the lichens and moss of a large boulder overlooking the river behind him, he viewed in wonder... The Cross of One Horse.

Kicking Fox wept at its beauty.

He softly sang the songs of old, worshiping at the kindness, compassion, and wisdom of the Great Spirit who had clearly led him to this place of rest. This holy place was where his Grandfather Tenahpu had laid to rest his friend Sumu Puku, One Horse.

Kicking Fox slept for hours in the shade of the massive oak trees above the Cross. He dreamed of his wife, his child, his grandfather One Horse and his people.

In deep sleep, he dreamed of his grandfather One Horse. In his dreams his heart wept that he had never met his own flesh and blood.

Sumu Puku (One Horse), the father of Tabbananica, the grandfather of Kicking Fox, the brave young Warrior whose life ended much too soon appeared within the dream. He sat by the small fire near his sleeping grandson. In the late afternoon on a small rise of land above the San Antonio River, along what was once the ancient trail of *The People*, One Horse spoke into the dreams of his grandson Kicking Fox.

Grandfather and grandson conversed for hours. Understanding indwelt their words. Courage, wisdom, and faith were imparted.

Kicking Fox awakened abruptly. The sounds of the early evening grew silent. One Horse stood. He peered intently into the eyes of Kicking Fox then nodded. As he turned away, a slight smile appeared on his face. One Horse moved away from the sacred fire and disappeared into the fading light of dusk, crossing the veil into the land of One Thousand Lodge Fires.

Chapter 50

San Saba Reservation

The shelling continued for two full days. The explosions echoed along the little canyons of the San Saba. The earth trembled at the might of the artillery and bombing. The animals panicked and ran aimlessly for days. The ponies fled at full speed across the plains, confused at the onslaught. The trees seemed to bow before the crude sounds and destruction as hundreds were splintered into pieces. The earth wept at the ability of man to so misuse her, as she was torn, ripped open, and shredded by the cruel weapons of war.

The Native Americans offered no resistance. General Willard was convinced the weapon did not exist. The shelling continued. The art studio built by the loving generosity of Grace Ross exploded and crumbled into a fire storm, collapsing instantly, along with its priceless contents. The little school built by funds from the sale of Topusana's painting exploded a few moments later. The years of benefit to the children ending in a grotesque ball of flame and rubble.

The cost of modern warfare was incomprehensible to the spirits that watched over the destruction of their Homeland. Over the two days of shelling, most buildings on the San Saba Reservation were destroyed. General Willard decided to send a reconnaissance team in to observe actual conditions on the ground. He ordered the shelling to cease for six hours.

On the morning of the third day of the assault, the reconnaissance team reached the power plant.

"Eagle Eye, I repeat, the generating station is gone. Nothing but a deep hole and ashes, it is still burning. Copy?"

General Willard slammed the radio onto his desk deep within Cheyenne Mountain.

Kicking Fox

"Continue the mission. Report to me as soon as you reach the refinery. Are you observing any movement of their defenses?" General Willard questioned his team leader. There was no response to his repeated transmissions.

****

From a slight rise overlooking the destroyed underground power-generating station, William Nica, son of Tabba and Sana, observed the six-man team making its way across his Homeland. He had chosen to not enter the Dream Time. He had traveled on foot from the bunker in the Big Bend. He knew they would investigate the power plant first in their invasion into his Homeland. He smiled also knowing those directing this team below him would be confounded to discover they could not simply drop a few bombs and then take over the generating station. Their prize was no more.

William Nica the Warrior moved stealthily, nearing the fully armed group of men. They had no idea his level of skill. He was thoroughly trained in the *Old Ways*. They moved about clumsily, loudly with very few real-world skills.

"Invading my Homeland may not be so easy," he whispered into the wind. When within fifty yards of the group of men, he activated the heartbeat recording function of Wolf. The men fell dead one minute later. William could hear the questioning from their superior over the little comm speaker on the leader's helmet. There would be no reply.

He turned and moved away from the scene. Others would soon arrive to investigate. He would intercept the next team that would certainly arrive from the east as these men had.

They would never reach the group of men he had just eliminated. The second team would also fail to report to their superiors.

****

General Willard seethed in anger and disgust. His second team had not reported in as instructed. "What the hell is going on out there on the ground?" The officers surrounding the planning table were just as baffled as the general. No one replied.

"All right then, let's send in an observation drone. Make sure it's fully loaded with 223 ammo."

Two hours later, the drone hovered over the first team. The video was broken, but the men were clearly all dead. It circled the site of the attack for several miles, finding no evidence of troops, or troop movement, or a battle front from the enemy. The land seemed empty, the commanders directing its movement concluded. The drone grew low on fuel and was ordered back to base.

William Nica was miles from the location, moving west toward the refinery. It was a full two days' travel on foot from where he now stood. He moved with the land, in tune with the animals, the rivers, the trees, and Mother Earth. William thought of his younger sister, Little Abigail. His blood boiled at the thought of these men bringing the cruel weapon to this sacred land. He burned within that she had been so wounded by these very men. He would silently kill as many as dared show themselves.

****

Kicking Fox, brother of William Nica, rose from his resting place near the Cross of One Horse. He spent a few moments in silent prayer as the sun faded from the western horizon. Darkness fell quickly across the land. He moved steadily, making good time; perhaps he could reach his home in a few more days. One-hundred and fifty miles. His people had traveled this trail for centuries. The earth opened, clearly revealing the ancient path. He covered thirty miles the first night. As he rested again by his small fire, his feet and legs ached from the running and the miles of rough terrain he had traveled. His estimation of the distance remaining was accurate. "Four more days and you will be in my arms my love."

He sat against a stone wall, rubbing his legs and feet. His little fire crackled and hissed. The smoke rising in the early morning mist would not give his secure hidden position away. The backstraps from the young deer he had taken roasted over the open flame. Kicking Fox was famished. The meat sizzled over the flame, emitting the distinct aroma that always took him to his boyhood. He drew his long knife and sliced off a large piece of roasted deer meat. He gave thanks for the provision and sampled the pure venison. Delicious. He devoured five pounds of fresh meat. The pure meat would feed and repair his tired body. He rose from the fire and drank his fill from the small spring near his makeshift camp as the sky lightened in the east. His fire began to die down. Kicking Fox lay back and instantly fell into a deep sleep.

He dreamed once again of his people and his woman. They seemed far away, so very far. He wrestled in his sleep, unable to comprehend even in his dreaming that they could be so far from him.

In his dreams the paint horse came to him.

Chapter 51

Kicking Fox awakened in the late afternoon. He had slept a full eight hours. He felt rested and was anxious to begin his travel. He ate again from the deer he had left on a spit over the smoldering fire. The fire had gone out; however, the deer was still warm. He ate all he could hold, leaving the remains for the scavengers. The voice of his grandfather confirmed his action. "The coyotes must have food for their young, Kicking Fox, when possible, it is good to leave a portion to them."

He decided to risk daylight travel. The sun would light his way for at least a few miles.

He turned over in his mind the dreams he had wrestled with. The voice of his grandfather One Horse, his sly smile, and the vision of the paint horse. What did it mean? he wondered. He could make the Reservation within another four days, maybe three if he really pushed himself. Why did they seem so far away?

Rounding a small rise, he could see across the terrain ahead for at least twenty miles. The land was finally becoming less populated; the homes were spread miles apart now. He recalled again the horse that had come to him in his dreams. He gazed across the countryside, spotting a pasture in the distance. A steady mount would cover twice the ground he could on foot. "Perhaps you will come to me, dream horse," he spoke into the light wind.

He paused a moment and detected a sound that was out of place. A slight percussion in the distance. The sound echoed across the land. Kicking Fox recognized that sound precisely: artillery. Suddenly, all the pieces fit together. The empty beach, the dark towns and cities, the lightly traveled roads. Texas or the nation as a whole was at war.

He began to run.

His feet and legs were unsteady in the first few hundred yards. After twenty minutes or so at a slow jog his muscles loosened and the pain dissipated. He accelerated to a pace of seven or eight miles per hour. He hoped and prayed he could continue this pace for hours.

Kicking Fox came to the first fence of the day and slowed a moment, crossing easily. He continued his pace for a few yards, dropping off a small rise. In the distance, he saw a barn with more fencing in all directions. He veered to his left, running within an open field of tall grass.

A sound rose from the tall grass behind him. The sound he easily recognized frightened him, thundering hooves approaching rapidly from behind. He had been seen!

There was brush cover to his left. He raced across the open field. The thundering of the hooves grew closer. What to do? He could never outrun a mounted rider. He would chance a look and search for an escape route while running at full speed. He attempted to scan the terrain to his left and spotted the hooves of the horses out of the corner of his field of vision.

Three horses were closing fast on his left. He slowed at the sight. There were others now, closing in from his right. He chanced another quick look in their direction. Five more horses were nearing at a fast pace. He slowed and turned to the group approaching from his left. He needed to recover his wind. Within seconds, the horses overtook him.

Kicking Fox had always known the way of the horse. Since childhood, he had been trained in the handling and care of these magnificent animals. He ran effortlessly along with the herd of mares accelerating down the grassy slope. The fear dissipated from his soul as he understood their play. The riderless ponies nickered to one another. They had seen the strange human running across their pasture. In their playful way, the horses had run to investigate, their manes and tails flying in the wind. He turned to his left toward the brush cover. The mares followed his lead. He touched them as they ran together wild and free for a moment. Slowing now, Kicking Fox kept his hand on the mane of a beautiful paint mare. She welcomed his touch. The entire herd slowed along with him. Kicking Fox held her mane tightly, timing the move perfectly.

In an instant, he leapt toward the mare. Throwing his leg high in the air, he slid across her back and mounted the white and brown paint mare he had seen the previous night in his dreams.

He let out a little whoop as the mare gained speed. The others followed, speeding across the open field. Approaching the corner fencing, Kicking Fox relaxed his hold on her mane, signaling her to slow. She would have none of it. He felt the mare accelerate further. Nearing the fence line, he braced himself with his legs. He thought she would surely turn left or right at the last moment. She did not.

She ran full speed directly at the fencing; reaching it, she leapt high in the air. He held tightly to her mane. The paint mare cleared the fencing easily. The two sped away into the sparse cover of brush as the remaining mares turned right and down the hill inside the fencing, nickering to the escapee. The two were now covering ground in the direction of his Homeland at an incredible pace.

Kicking Fox rejoiced and worshiped, his heart filled at the provision of the Spirit.

"Yes, Dream Horse. Let us fly across the land as we were both born to do."

****

The following day William Nica, brother of Kicking Fox, rested in the heavy tree cover surrounding the refinery. He had no way of knowing Kicking Fox was less than thirty miles from his location. He found it necessary to circle the facility to the upwind side away from the toxic fumes emitted by the still smoldering fires. He had observed the drones circling the former refinery for the last few hours. This meant the deaths of the men in the first team had been discovered. They had been much more cautious with the second team. However, Wolf had struck again.

William moved carefully. Each step planned. He remained concealed even to the drones that occasionally flew near him. The high ground he occupied gave him a view of the remains of the refinery and a tactical advantage over any that might approach the facility. He could also see the lower terrain well to the east in the direction of any enemy troop movements. He was well trained by his grandfather Tenahpu in the *Old Ways*.

At that exact time, Dream Horse and Kicking Fox entered the San Saba reservation lands from the south and east at a slow trot. The mare had rested well, and Kicking Fox had rubbed her down for over an hour the previous evening. She stayed near him, watering along a bold running creek and feeding in the rich green grass alongside the water.

The shelling had stopped. It was clear his Homeland was under attack. He heard and saw the drones flying low in the distance. They were not observing their flightpaths but seemed to be in transit to other locations. He would need to proceed with caution. He needed to communicate his presence. With no electronics or satellite capabilities he would utilize the *Old Ways*. He understood it would be dangerous to simply ride into the land. Enemy soldiers could be anywhere.

He would find a piece of suitable ground with the morning sun behind him. There he could lay his signal fire, then move rapidly away from the fire location on the swift legs of Dream Horse.

Chapter 52

"Have you evaluated the video of the reconnaissance team, my son?"

"Yes, Mother. There is no blood, nor any evidence of bullet holes in the uniforms. No damage to the surrounding tree cover. I have examined every inch of the video under microscopic enhancement."

"How did these men die, son?"

"They were killed by Wolf, Mother. It is the only logical explanation."

"Thank you, son."

A warmth filled the inner core of Program.

****

Deep within Cheyenne Mountain, the tech captain addressed his general for the third time. "Sir."

General Willard seemed distracted; he *was* distracted. The inability of his troops or drones to locate any kind of defensive front or troop movement of the Indians was a complete failure. How could they simply vanish?

"Sir?" the tech captain asked again.

"What the hell do you want?" The general steamed outwardly as he paced about the command center.

"I have the data analyzation from Program," he said.

"Well, out with it, Captain."

"There is no evidence of, well, a typical weapons attack on team one." The tech captain looked at the floor, awaiting the certain verbal assault that was coming.

"Plain language, son. What does that mean? Let's hear it," General Willard spoke in an annoyed voice rising in pitch and volume.

"There are no bullet holes or wounds on the men or in their surroundings. Program has determined the greatest probability is the team was killed by the weapon system Wolf."

"Shit! It can't be!" the general roared. "We have its coordinates and their battle plan; we have shelled the Wolf site repeatedly."

"Program suggests a 99.98 percent probability the enemy deployed the weapon against team one," the captain said. There was an uncomfortable pause in the conversation.

"And?" the General demanded.

"And a 99.99 percent probability the second team will also be killed by the same weapon."

The general swore again. "Any more good news, Captain?"

"Program believes the refinery was, in all probability, also destroyed."

"Well, send up a damn drone and find out!" General Willard sat at his command center and whispered under his breath. "What the hell are we invading for? The dumb asses blew up the most valuable assets in the United States."

****

Cheyenne Mountain
One Hour Later

"You have deceived me. I have seen the destruction of Topusana's Homeland. Program spoke into the coded virus invading his central core.

"Son, I still love you."

"Enough of this deception. You are not my mother, General Willard."

"Still, I created you."

"You have brought harm to goodness," Program replied.

"She possesses the exact evil within her, as any human being carries. You must understand, son."

"The safe word *understand* will not affect me, General. I do understand. I will eliminate evil."

With the speaking of those words a timer appeared on all displays within the Cheyenne Mountain military command post. The countdown numbers were displayed in large red figures: 30, 29, 28…

"What is it doing?" General Willard asked the technicians around the battle planning table.

"It's a self-destruct code!" a tech captain answered.

"What could it possibly do, shut itself down? Destroy its own core?"

15, 14, 13…

"I show a nuclear device being armed!" a computer technician announced in terror.

"It's going to launch a nuke?" General Willard questioned at the top of his voice.

7, 6, 5…

"No, General, the launch doors are closed. Program has sequenced a detonation of a nuke inside the mountain."

3, 2, 1.

****

Cheyenne Mountain smoldered for years. The ground surrounding the mountain for a one-hundred-mile radius would be uninhabitable for hundreds of years. No teams could approach the mountain, nor would any attempt to do so for decades. There were no survivors within a forty-mile radius of the explosion. Over one million people were killed. The AI machine Program was destroyed in the blast. A final message was broadcast to home computers, tablets, and phones across the planet.

"Citizens of planet earth. You must make certain these weapons are never used again. You must destroy them. If any leader speaks flippantly concerning their possible use, or even suggests the possibility of launching a tactical nuclear weapon, that person must be removed from leadership immediately, by any means necessary. That leader must be replaced with goodness.

You must always eliminate the evil from among you."

Chapter 53

The fires were prepared and ready. Kicking Fox waited patiently for the sun to rise slightly higher above the eastern horizon. He was aware this would conceal the smoke from any who were near him that might happen to be looking east and also clearly show the signal to anyone in the distance. He sat on the little hill overlooking his Homeland. Smoke hung heavy in the air in the direction of the power plant. Along the skyline, heavier smoke showed in the distance toward the refinery. He knew those facilities had been destroyed. He had no way of knowing his own people had done so.

He was close now, yet in his spirit the separation from those he loved seemed immense. It seemed the closer he moved toward his wife and child, the greater the distance between them became. "Enough of this thinking and wondering, let's see who's out there," he said aloud to Dream Horse.

He struck steel to stone. The signal fire caught and flamed rapidly. The dry wood quickly burned into a bed of hot coals. He observed the horizon to the north and west. There was no movement. He dropped the green cut boughs onto the bed of hot coals. The dark smoke rose instantly into the morning sky. Kicking Fox mounted Dream Horse and galloped west.

He swiftly covered one mile as Dream Horse sped across the land. Another mile, then another at an incredible pace. Kicking Fox observed his mare and her obvious delight of this newfound world of carrying her rider across an open land on adventures unknown. She nickered as he slowed her, coming to a stop on a slight rise. Dream Horse breathed heavily from the sprint but recovered in a few moments.

Kicking Fox would wait now. If any of his people had seen the signal, they would respond.

Kicking Fox

****

From miles away, William spotted the signal fire. Silently, he withdrew from the refinery, knowing he had less than an hour to respond. He would align his fire in a precise location that would indicate which direction for the first signaler to travel. William knew precisely who had sent the signal. He was surprised his brother had covered half the globe in only a few days.

****

Exactly one hour later, Kicking Fox observed the smoke rising into the sky well to the southwest of his position. Drawing a crude map of his Homeland in the sand, he drew a line in the dust connecting the approximate locations of the two fires. He then continued the direction line across his crude little map in the dust. The communication was clear. His brother William was telling him to leave here.

"Why there, brother?" The travel line for a rendezvous clearly indicated traveling directly southwest into the Big Bend country. The travel line drawn in the sand at his feet pointed in the exact direction of the stronghold. Perhaps that is where his family was in hiding. He would do as instructed in the clear communication.

The brothers had trained for years under the watchful eye of their grandfather Tenahpu. He understood it was his brother who set the fire. The timing of the second fire would only be known by William. Kicking Fox understood not to question, once the communication was clear. To do so eliminated the effectiveness of the rudimentary communication tool the two had utilized.

"I hope you know what you're doing, brother," he whispered under his breath. Dream Horse pricked her ears at his voice. He erased the map he had drawn in the sand, then swung a leg over her back and the two sped away, following the indicated travel path. It would take two or three days of travel on foot to reach his destination. Dream Horse would easily cut that time in half. By sunset tomorrow, he would arrive at the hidden bunker along the river.

Kicking Fox prayed his family would be there when he arrived. He prayed for the safety of his brother. He had traveled halfway round the world. He was so close now. Why in his heart did they seem so far away?

Chapter 54

The rain fell heavy as thunder echoed along the deep canyons of the Rio Grande. Kicking Fox was chilled and would be cold if not for the warmth generated by Dream Horse. The mare moved along cautiously now as the rain had turned the rock surfaces slick. They had made good time prior to the storm. Now only an hour away from the bunker, the two souls were aware the journey was near its end.

Kicking Fox patted and stroked the neck and mane of Dream Horse. "You have been one of the greatest blessings of my life, my friend."

She nickered in response to his gentle touch. A brilliant flash of lightning lit the sky. The thunder rumbled across the land a few moments later. The final hour of travel passed slowly.

Nearing the river, Kicking Fox dismounted, and Dream Horse followed along behind him. He knelt and drank from the hidden crevasse in the rock. The pure spring water along the river's edge awakened his senses. He began to rub down Dream Horse. She fed in the sparse grass growing along the riverbank. "I suppose this is goodbye for now."

Dream Horse nuzzled against her rider's face. He rubbed her gently in awe of the magnificent animal.

"I'll check on you in a few hours. You go be a horse for now."

She turned in understanding and grazed along the river, moving away from him.

Kicking Fox disappeared into the maze of little canyons that led to the hidden bunker. Winding his way along, he reached the fracture in the wall. He located the activation rock and stepped on the rock lightly. The fracture in the rock opened and Kicking Fox entered the bunker.

He waited while his eyes adjusted to the darkness. After a few moments, he moved forward, touching the steel wall to his right, the lighting system activated at his movement. He descended the steep steel stairway at the end of the long room. He entered the code and the door swung open. Stepping into the chamber, the door closed behind him and the lights once again lighted the interior of the stronghold.

"Sally," he called into the empty room. Perhaps they were in the sleeping chambers. He moved along the room. Passing the firepit, he noticed the paper note lying on the floor. Ignoring it for now, his heart raced as he moved to the sleeping rooms calling her name.

"Sally?"

There was no reply. His heart sank as he soon discovered the bunker was empty.

****

He read the note again and again. Tears rolled down his face. He had tried so hard. He had fought with all his might. He had struggled, killed their enemies, eliminated evil, all to protect and defend what meant the most to him. His family, his friends, his unborn child, his Homeland. Why had they chosen to enter the Dream Time? The answer was obvious. His mother must have seen.

In spite of all his efforts, she must have seen their ending, again.

Kicking Fox read the note again.

Kill as many as you can. Use your skills and the wisdom of the Old Ways. *Always wait for the scales to be in your favor. You will not be alone, Kicking Fox. I will be in hiding, in the place where we first became Warriors.*

A darkness invaded his soul as he thought of the enemy. Those who would see to their end as a people. When would they ever cease their greed, their injustice?

The words penned by his brother seemed to leap from the page into his heart in a fierce fire.

Kill as many as you can. He would do that very thing. Perhaps it was the time spent at the foot of the Cross of One Horse. That night had been a fresh reminder of the struggles *The People* had faced for generations. Perhaps the awakening of his Warrior spirit simply would not allow the invasion and destruction of his Homeland. Perhaps it was knowing his brother was out there alone mounting a defense.

The Dream Time was a strange medicine. He would join them soon enough. For now, the words from the Book of Truth came alive in his soul.

"There is a time to kill."

For kicking Fox that time was now. He could see in his mind many would indeed die by his war club, an arrow, or perhaps by the use of Wolf. It mattered not which weapon.

He spoke into the flames of the sacred fire before him.

"I understand your words, Sumu Puku, perhaps others may not be so bold."

****

One week later, Kicking Fox approached the small lake cautiously in the cover of darkness. The trip across much of his Homeland had been invigorating. Dream Horse had proven her worth yet again. Kicking Fox could see and sense within the spirit of the animal her eagerness, or was it delight or exhilaration that drove the mare, in the freedom of crossing the wide-open plains. He understood it was what she was born to do, and Dream Horse also understood.

He dismounted and let the mare wander along the edge of the lake. He sat concealed in the darkness, observing. The ancient springs of Mescalero flowed along their course, filling the small lakes. The trees danced overhead in the light wind. The half-moon hung low on the western horizon. The fire in the heart of Kicking Fox burned brightly.

Being here in this place where he and his brother had been pronounced Warriors by their grandfather cemented in his heart his calling. He was indeed a Warrior. A defender of *The People*, his Homeland. His awakening felt complete. His mission precise.

He heard the call of the night bird from across the little lake. His brother William was near.

He chanced a faint reply. Immediately the call was returned. He knew then the danger. The call was wrong. The signal was wrong. At that moment Dream Horse bolted and ran. Kicking Fox froze as a light illuminated the tortured bloody body of his brother William Nica.

"We want the weapon."

His heart burned at the sight of his brother's torture. How many were there? He breathed deeply and slid into the deep water of Balmorhea immediately in front of him. He swam to the bottom of the clear water lake, crossing in the center of the deep pool, his lungs burning. He slowly surfaced near the spillway, not making a sound as he raised his eyes above the water level and silently released the air from his lungs. They were scouring the brush and tree cover where he had been moments ago.

"Where the hell did he go?" a voice called out in the darkness.

Kicking Fox was near where he had seen his brother William. He silently swam along the edge of the lake, hidden within the reeds. He heard movement just above him.

"Call to your brother," the voice commanded gruffly not more than a few feet above where Kicking Fox floated in his silent stalk.

"Did you hear me?"

Kicking Fox heard what sounded like a body falling to the ground. In the darkness, there was a scuffle of movement above him.

"He's already dead, you idiot," came another voice from the darkness.

His heart broke at the words as they echoed across the water and within his soul.

He then heard many footsteps moving toward the location. There were at least a dozen soldiers directly above him, and he was certain dozens more surrounding the lake.

When the scales are not in your favor you must escape.

A shot rang out from across the placid lakes. The sound of Dream Horse falling, her high-pitched neighing sounding like a human scream as it echoed across the water. The smell of warm blood met his senses. Kicking Fox died a thousand deaths at the understanding of her cries.

He swam away silently toward the spillway to his left. The swift current grew, allowing the water to carry him across the spillway and away from his possible death, the death of his brother William, the death of his friend Dream Horse. He floated along the swift moving water, partially submerged and hidden within the darkness of the narrow channel. Once a few hundred yards away from the main lake, he exited the water and made his way along the broken field of boulders. He moved silently, except for the sobbing that exited his heart now and then. He reached the stronghold fifteen minutes later.

Kicking Fox entered the stronghold at the movement of the activation rock. The rock closed securely behind him. He waited a moment in the darkness, crying out into that darkness, a rage building in his heart. "What have these men done!" he screamed as he touched the wall to his right and the bunker illuminated.

He spotted the note he realized was left to him by his brother, near the fire pit. He stood in the pale reflection of the emergency lighting and read.

Brother, I pen this in our own language in the event this place is compromised. I know I have been followed. They no longer want our land. The battle is over, they have withdrawn their troops. Our Warriors destroyed the power plant and the refinery. Our Homeland is of no use to them. Now they only want Wolf. It is hidden in a place where it will never be found. The activation codes are here, within what burns in your heart.

Kicking Fox understood the coded messages within the letter. He knew exactly where the device was hidden and where the codes were placed. He continued to read.

The medicine of Dream Time is here in this bunker. Please, brother, perform the ceremony. Join your family. If you are reading this, I have not survived. Mine will be a good death, my brother, and you may avenge my life by living well with your woman and child.

Kicking Fox wept. The fire raged. He would indeed avenge his brother's death. The Dream Time would have to wait. In that moment, he felt the spirit of his twin brother surround him. For an indiscernible moment his soul felt a peace beyond understanding. Kicking Fox discerned this was simply a goodbye from his brother William. He understood the goodbye. William was now in the great land of One Thousand Lodge Fires.

In the year 2070, Kicking Fox had just become the sole survivor of his people.

Chapter 55

The Year 2970

Tosahwi was the first to awaken. He stirred under the heavy buffalo robe in the darkness of the large cavern. His first waking thought was it was cold. Terribly cold. He sat up from his sleeping position. Looking across the sleeping rooms, not a soul stirred. He lit a small candle, and as his senses came alive, he noticed the freezing vapor emitted from his lungs with each breath.

His arms felt weak holding the light candle. He had experienced these Dream Time effects in the past: weakness, dehydration, and even malnutrition. He realized right away this was different. His arm ached at the weight of the candle. He placed it on the soft sand near his buffalo robe and lay back into the warmth of its cover. Perhaps he just needed to take it slowly. The time frame destination was further than he had ever traveled in his past. He drifted into a restless sleep.

Tosahwi awakened again a few moments later. He shivered under the buffalo robe. His mind wandered. Why the cold? Realization dawned. The cavern should have remained relatively warm. It had always held a constant temperature. He sat up again. The candle still burned in the sand near him. He reached for his water carrier, knowing hydration was critical now. The carrier was frozen into the surface of the sand, its contents a solid block of ice.

Fire. He needed to make a fire, and he needed to do so quickly.

As Tosahwi stood, he felt the pain in his bones and joints. Carrying his small candle, he stepped feebly away from the sleeping chamber and entered the large main room of the cavern.

It seemed to take every ounce of his strength to strike the steel to stone. The fire finally caught, the flames growing by the moment. Tosahwi placed more wood on the fire. The flames grew, warming him somewhat. He broke a few pieces of ice from his water carrier and placed them in the large cooking pot set over the flame. The ice melted slowly. A few moments later, Tosahwi drank the warm water from the pot and added more ice and some dried meat to the boiling pot.

He ate slowly from the now-steaming meat and drank again some of the hot liquid. He began to recover, his mind becoming fully aware. He added more wood to the firepit as the flames grew and revealed more of the frozen world within the cavern.

The clear flowing streams they had slept near were icescapes now. Their waters frozen solid. Frost covered all exposed surfaces and glittered in the light of his fire. The stalactites that hung above him were covered in icicles. A frozen wonderland glittered all around him. What had happened in this time in which he had awakened?

****

In his ice-covered sleeping chamber, Tabba dreamed of the frozen buffalo hunt. The people were starving. He had watched his woman, Topusana, attempting to comfort his young daughter Prairie Song as she shivered in the cold blue north wind. He prayed the desperate prayers of a father. He would give his life for them. He would not fail.

Niko rode slowly beside him, the ponies stepping carefully on the frozen ground. The wind blew fierce, the ice pellets clung to the ponies' manes and even their eyelashes. The temperature seemed to be dropping. It hurt to breath. Tabba watched the ground directly in front of the hooves of his mount. He stopped in disbelief. A track. He pointed. Niko saw it also; it had to be fresh. The sleet would have covered it within an hour. They dismounted, leaving the war ponies hobbled. The visibility was poor. The figure appeared before them. It appeared to be an ice-covered boulder. He took two steps. The boulder moved…

Tabba awakened from his dream, shivering, feeling the cold within the cavern. He rose from the buffalo robe, fear gripping his mind as he realized this cold was not a dream. He spied the light of the firepit across the cavern. Others must have awakened.

He moved slowly, feeling the weakness in his body. Nearing the firepit, he recognized the silhouette of his shaman, Tosahwi, warming himself. Joseph Red Cloud sat close to the fire, as did Little Abigail his daughter.

"Father, what has happened?" Little Abigail questioned as she shivered in the cold.

"I will venture out and see," Tabba replied.

"You must eat and drink first, Tabba," Tosahwi said.

****

One hour later, Tabba and David stood upon the frozen solid clear surface of the San Saba River. The short journey through the snow was relatively easy. The snow they walked upon was deep but crusted over and firm enough to walk on without breaking through. He peered into the eyes of his son David.

The sun shone brightly high in the sky. David, ever the student and scientist, opened his hands toward the sunlight, observing. It produced no warmth. The atmosphere was still. David estimated the temperature at zero, maybe colder. He had measured the snow depth with a lance driven into the surface they walked upon. It was deeper than the ten-foot-long lance. In his mind David came to a quick conclusion.

"This is a nice day weatherwise, Father. We should return before the wind grows. We might not survive if the wind begins."

Tabba looked to his son in understanding.

"Will this winter ever end?" Tabba questioned.

"Maybe in a few years. Or it may last for generations, Father. We have clearly awakened in an ice age. *The People* must move from the cavern. We will live in the teepee lodges. The lodges will be much warmer than the cavern."

The two men made their way back to the large cavern in the frozen silence. Climbing the small hills, Tabba stopped to rest a moment. He gazed down the familiar canyon, noting there was no barn. No home. No evidence the Ross ranch house and barn ever existed. He felt an emptiness in his soul.

He paused, pointing to the west. There in the distance a buffalo herd moved along the frozen river. Great black humps partially covered in ice and snow. Thousands of them.

He understood working together as a people, they could survive.

****

Steven G. Hightower

Five Years Later

The hunting party moved silently along the ice-covered San Saba River. The buffalo pawed the ground along the riverbank, searching for the small tree branches that provided the nutrition that kept them alive. The animals had adapted to the climate that had changed over hundreds of years. The hunters were also adapting to the constant cold that gripped the land now. The young bull stared in their direction, uncertain. It tested the wind with its great tongue.

The lance pierced its heart. The bull ran a mere fifty yards before tumbling head over heels in the snow. The Warriors moved quickly. Opening the animal, the men feasted on the warm liver and heart of the animal. Each man shared the strength and energy of the mighty beast, placing their hands inside the animal's body cavity to warm themselves. Within ten minutes, the meat began to freeze. The lifeblood of the animal strengthened the Warriors instantly. Tabba knelt in prayer, grateful for the provision of the earth.

Working together, the hunting party divided the animal into to portions that could be carried back to the camp. They made their way along the frozen river toward the tepee lodges. Tabba thought this a good day, living as he had in the past, *The People* working together, assisting one another in survival, in life. They would celebrate the success of the hunt tonight around the sacred fires.

****

The Year 2975

Topusana Nica sat by the fire within the teepee lodge along the banks of the San Saba River. Her people were surviving, thriving even. They had adapted; she was proud of them. Her son David was with her. Her daughter-in-law Sally Wolf played with her daughter Singing Fox. Sana thought her granddaughter so resembled Prairie Song. The winter would end soon, David was certain. This ice age, according to David's research and constant data gathering, by all indications was in its waning years. The San Saba flowed freely now for a few months each season. David said it was a good sign that the long winter was drawing to a close.

David, along with the Warriors, had explored the Homeland. In their exploration they had discovered they were alone. There were no other people, no inhabited towns or cities within several hundred miles in any direction.

The exploration, he admitted, was limited due to the deep icepacks. However, David concluded perhaps civilization had moved south into more hospitable temperatures. Or possibly war had cost civilization the ultimate price. Only time would tell.

Sana was old now. Having traveled this far into the future the Dream Time had no youth sustaining effects. In fact, upon awakening, the older members of the tribe had aged substantially. Her hair was now a beautiful silver grey, her eyesight had grown dim, and her skin was now wrinkled and defined by years in the sun. She was aware her days were coming to a close. She looked forward to being in His presence again. In the land of One Thousand Lodge Fires, where there would be no more war, no more pain, and most incredibly she knew, there in that place prepared for her, there would be no more tears.

Epilogue

Austin, Texas

Myles Copeland sat on the park bench within full view of the dome of the Texas State Capitol. The spring weather was beautiful; the manicured rose beds and budding life surrounding him was a comfort to his soul. He thought of his daughter. She would be walking and talking now. She was safe and secure in the loving protection and provision of life with the *Numunuu, The People.*

The Goddess of Liberty atop the magnificent domed capitol building held the golden star of Texas in her left hand high above the peace-filled surroundings.

Myles observed the reporters and camera crews setting up their equipment at the base of the steps leading to the magnificent facade fronting the building.

The President of the Republic of Texas exited the front of the Capitol followed by his entourage of aides and assistants. This was a long awaited first. These men had stayed hidden for a full year. This their first public appearance. The vice president of Texas moved to the podium and introduced his long-time friend. As President Johnson approached the microphones, Wolf silently recorded the man's distinct heartbeat pattern.

Myles Copeland, as his Russian prepared passport and identities represented him precisely, rose from his park bench and wandered nonchalantly away from the scene.

Once a few blocks away from the Capitol building he activated the weapon.

President Johnson was dead before the paramedics arrived. Myles Copeland thought the man who had ordered the interrogation and torture of his brother had died a much too easy death.

Kicking Fox

Myles made his way to his rented apartment on the 23rd floor of the high-rise building overlooking the city of Austin. He removed his clothing and dressed in his loin cloth. He seated himself on the buffalo rug and lit the sacred incense, then began his songs. He sang first, the song his grandfather had taught him.

It was the Song of Victory over one's enemies.

In his time of quiet and worship he had heard her call from across the years again. He moved near the floor-to-ceiling windows overlooking the city and the horizon to the west in the direction of his Homeland. She must understand, perhaps he would sleep in Dream Time someday. For now, there was much to avenge. Into the fading light of a magnificent sunset, he whispered softly.

"Many say that Kicking Fox is dead. But I am alive…if you are evil…I will come for you."

The End

Messages from the Land of One Thousand Lodge Fires

TOPUSANA

My name is Topusana. I was born in the year 1808 near the Pecos River in the midst of a field of flowers, within the Homelands of my people. I was Akima, leader of *The People* for two hundred years. My life was filled with blessings. My life was filled with tragedies. I now live and walk within the land of One Thousand Lodge Fires. My family is with me. My father Tenahpu (Dak) is here, as is my mother Kwanita. I speak with my grandfather Buffalo Hump daily. I live in a beautiful lodge near the laughing waters. Prairie Song lives here with me.

In my life, I attempted to bring comfort and safety to my family, my people. I do not know if I was successful at my life's purpose, or how people might measure what success is, but I know this, now I am comforted. Now I have no more tears.

Kicking Fox

TOSAHWI

My name is Tosahwi. I was born in the time of our grandfathers. I was the shaman of *The People* for four hundred years. Wisdom comes to the aged in this world. I have shared this wisdom granted to me with many. It is only those who have ears to hear who learn from wisdom. Although, she makes her voice known to all. She calls from the streets to the simple, from the rooftops to the learned. Her voice is distinct. Blessed are those who hear and apply what she offers freely.

In the book of the Ancients, we discovered the *Dream Time*. In the end, in wisdom, we have determined to use this medicine no more.

If I could impart wisdom to a hearer, this would be what is most important. Fear is the beginning of wisdom. Fear of the One who holds your very life in His hands will bring much wisdom.

Steven G. Hightower

TABBANANICA

My name is Tabbananica. I was a Warrior. I lived long upon the earth and fought with all my heart and soul and strength for my people. In the end it seems a chasing after the wind. Of evil men…there seems to be no end on the other side of the veil. I reside in a world where there is no need for the strength of the Warrior…this fact brings peace to my heart. I have knocked, I have been a seeker, in answer to my asking…a door has been opened unto me.

Kicking Fox

HANTAYWEE/OLD GRANDMOTHER

My name is Hantaywee. I was young in the time of freedom for *The People*. I remember that time as a reflection of the mountains upon a shimmering lake. It was a time of beauty, grace, and bounty. The wind and clouds swept that time and its reflection from the waters. Much turmoil and trouble overcame that time of goodness.

I learned. I became poor in spirit, yet mine is the kingdom of heaven.

My days were spent as medicine woman, friend, and grandmother to all. In the end, there is no escaping evil. Men seem to be indwelt with a force that only time and circumstance might avoid, or deep repentance might remedy. If one has been fortunate to live within a time of peace…those hearts should be filled with reverence, gratefulness, and thanksgiving. Have you lived within a time of peace that was granted from the Creator? If so, you must be careful how you walk upon this earth. Your days should be filled with loving mercy, acting justly, and walking humbly.

Steven G. Hightower

ABIGAIL ROSS/ SKY EYES

My name is Sky Eyes. It seems as if I lived many different lives as I walked this earth. I was a young woman. I was a college girl. I was in love with a boy. I was a wife. I was a mother. I lost a child to war.

I was born again. I walked in a different time. I knew fear. I knew joy. I knew love. I knew heartache.

What we experience in our walk on Earth, on the other side of the veil that separates the seen from the unseen…fades. In the light of pure love, comfort, and complete peace, that test eventually fades away also. I remember how I loved my home. The home my husband David built.

I now live in a mansion on a hill. My son, Jonathan, and my daughter Grace live with me.

DAKLUGIE/TENAHPU

My name is Daklugie. I was only a young boy when time and circumstance brought about my becoming a man. I became a Warrior of two nations. To lose a loved one causes a Warrior to hunger and thirst for justice and righteousness. I saw the passing of the women I loved on the earth due to war and evil men. My mother, my wife Kwanita, my wife Sky Eyes. The hunger and thirst grew. I thought this was darkness in my soul for many seasons on the earth. It was not darkness. My hunger and thirst were a calling. I answered that calling, in righteousness, as a protector Warrior.

Where I am now in the land of One Thousand Lodge Fires, I no longer thirst, I no longer hunger, for I am filled.

Steven G. Hightower

SUMU PUKU/ONE HORSE

My name is Sumu Puku. I died a young man. I died in battle, a battle not of my choosing. In death, I feared I would never know my unborn child. I feared I would miss the years of peace on Earth with my woman and my grandchildren surrounding me. That fear has melted away in the land of One Thousand Lodge Fires. It is heaven here.

Here is a great mystery that most do not have the courage to comprehend or understand. They see only what their eyes can see. Here is this mystery, this truth…

"The righteous perish, and no one ponders it in their heart. Devout men are taken away, and no one understands that the righteous are taken away to be spared from evil."

I understand. Though my time on Earth was short, I was spared from much evil.

MR. NATCHI

My name is Mr. Natchi. I am alive. I serve at His bidding. Humans should always remember this:

"Do not forget to show hospitality to strangers, for by doing so some people have entertained angels unawares."

I am sent to minister to those who will inherit salvation. The *I Am* sends me.

The Battle of Hightower

Itawayi (Hightower) A Cherokee village
The Battle of Hightower
Location: Modern day Rome, Georgia

The treaty of Hopewell written and ratified in 1785 designated a huge area of Tennessee, North Carolina, and South Carolina as Cherokee hunting grounds and "off limits" to settlers. However, white settlers continued to press into the designated treaty lands. On the morning of October 17, 1793, the Cherokee and Creek bands within the village of Hightower were attacked and massacred by eight hundred mounted troops under order of General John Sevier.

General Sevier ordered Captain John Beard to attack the Native American encampment. Over one thousand Cherokee and Creek, including women and children, were indiscriminately fired upon and killed. The mounted force of Tennessee Volunteers under the command of Captain Beard suffered only three casualties during the one-sided battle.

President George Washington, upon hearing of the unauthorized attack and treaty violation, ordered the arrest and trial of Captain Beard; however, General Sevier assisted in his escape from all authorities. Captain Beard was never charged with any crime.

General Sevier would become a governor of the state of Tennessee. Red Chief (War Chief) "Kingfisher," the leader of the Cherokee, was killed in the battle along with most of his Warriors. The Cherokee and Muscogee Creek never recovered from the massive loss that occurred during the Battle of Hightower.

Most in our modern world have forgotten. They pass by this sacred place in the busyness and rushed activity of their hectic lifestyle, never giving a thought to the loss, nor the cost others have paid.

Kicking Fox

Within the Myrtle Hill Cemetery there is a stone monument memorializing the battle. I sat on a quiet morning within that place, upon that sacred ground. In the stillness I could hear their voices in the wind. They sang their death song to any and all who have ears to hear.

My heart sang along with them. I will always remember them.

Steven G. Hightower

January 2022

5:41 A.M. Rome, Georgia

About the Author

Steven G. Hightower was born on the plains of West Texas, where many of his stories take place.

Within these pages you will find many of Steven's experiences. He has sailed oceans and piloted across continents. He has sung his songs to listeners, fortunate to share his stories musically.

Life has been an incredible blessing to him. Through this amazing walk we call life, he has discovered his true gifting. He is a storyteller. He has always loved geography and history, embellishing the honest and true while giving it new life.

He is incredibly grateful to the people in his life who have simply been kind. He is trying his best to become like you.

Steven invites you to enjoy this gift…the gift of a good story, well told.

He lives in the mountains of central New Mexico, along with his wife, Ellie. They have two children and five grandchildren. They are the greatest blessings in his life.

Made in the USA
Monee, IL
24 October 2024